D0864821

PRAISE FOR *THE WRITER'S FIELD GUIDE TO THE CRAFT OF FICTION*

"There comes a time in every writer's education when they realize they don't know what the hell they're doing. At this point, a writer can throw in the towel, take out student loans for another round of schooling, or discover a brilliant book like Michael Noll's *The Writer's Field Guide*. With patience, good humor, and fortitude, Noll provides a field manual for taking fiction apart and putting it back together again, gaining technical know-how and inspiration along the way. An indispensable book that belongs on every serious writer's desk."

—AMANDA EYRE WARD, author of *The Nearness of You*

"These exercises are a true inspiration for both novice and experienced writers. *The Writer's Field Guide* is an invaluable book that will energize any writer's imagination and help overcome any writer's block."

—HEIDI W. DURROW, author of the *New York Times* bestseller *The Girl Who Fell from the Sky*

"Michael Noll, having grown up a curious, pragmatic Midwestern farm boy, now passes along some of his hard-earned fiction writing wisdom, freeing us from the 'Behold! Genius-at-work' writing myths in the process. As a writer you'll still find yourself in awe of what Nabokov, Morrison, or Chekhov do on the page, but Noll shines some new light on how fiction writers might reexamine story form, character, and language through an old but nearly forgotten method—close reading and imitation—and build their own entirely original works. Because there's less theory and more practice, we all benefit. 'Tell me a story,' he quotes one of his former instructors urging, which seems simplistic until you look at how often we avoid doing just that. A terrific, truly curious book about the humbling practice of writing fiction."

—SCOTT BLACKWOOD, author of *See How Small*, winner of the 2016 PEN USA Award

"For years, Michael Noll's *Read to Write Stories* blog has been one of my favorite resources, period. Now, at last, along comes his *Writer's Field Guide*, in which reading and writing are rightly treated as inextricable, such that every sharp insight and lively provocation is rooted in the terra firma of great writing. Indeed, its primary text excerpts are impeccable, but it is also Noll's own intuition, reading acumen, and willingness to push beyond the obvious that ultimately make these exercises so worthwhile, and the book a gem."

—TIM HORVATH, author of *Understories*

THE WRITER'S FIELD GUIDE TO THE CRAFT OF FICTION

THE WRITER'S

FIELD GUIDE

TO THE

CRAFT OF

FICTION

BY MICHAEL NOLL

DEEP VELLUM
Dallas, Texas

A STRANGE OBJECT
Austin, Texas

Published by A Strange Object
An imprint of Deep Vellum Publishing
3000 Commerce Street
Dallas, Texas 75226
astrangeobject.com | deepvellum.org

© 2018 Michael Noll. All rights reserved.
Printed in the United States of America.

No part of this book may be used or reproduced in any manner without written permission from the publisher, except in context of reviews.

ISBN 978-0-9985184-1-1
ISBN 978-0-9985184-2-8 (electronic)

Cover design by Lisa Laratta
Book design by Amber Morena

For Stephanie

CONTENTS

INTRODUCTION: A GRAND THEORY OF
NOT KNOWING WHAT YOU'RE DOING   **1**

HOW TO USE THIS BOOK
(OR, HOW TO BE TAUGHT TO WRITE FICTION)   **8**

PART 1. TOOLS OF THE TRADE

HOW TO START AND KEEP WRITING

DROP AN ELEPHANT INTO THE ROOM:
"The Heart" by Amelia Gray   **20**

GIVE YOUR CHARACTERS WHAT THEY WISH FOR:
"Lazarus Dying" by Owen Egerton   **25**

LET A CHARACTER RESPOND TO AN EXPECTED SCENE:
Jam on the Vine by LaShonda Katrice Barnett   **30**

TURN A PREMISE INTO DRAMA:
Percival Everett by Virgil Russell by Percival Everett   **35**

HOW TO MAKE SETTING DRAMATIC

TAKE A TOUR:
"Pomp and Circumstances"
by Nina McConigley   **42**

BREAK SETTING INTO NEIGHBORHOODS:
"It Will Be Awesome Before Spring"
by Antonio Ruiz-Camacho   47

GIVE SETTING A HUMAN GEOGRAPHY:
Gone Girl by Gillian Flynn   53

MANIPULATE CHARACTERS WITH SETTING:
"Waiting for Takeoff" by Lydia Davis   58

HOW TO CREATE COMPELLING CHARACTERS

CREATE CHARACTERS WITH A SINGLE, DEFINITIVE TRAIT:
The Regional Office Is Under Attack! by Manuel Gonzales   66

MAKE YOUR CHARACTERS INTO SOMETHING NEW:
Half-Resurrection Blues by Daniel José Older   72

DEFINE YOUR CHARACTER'S EMOTIONAL RESPONSE TO
CONFLICT: "My Views on the Darkness" by Ben Marcus   77

GENERATE TENSION BY GIVING CHARACTERS
UNEQUAL ACCESS TO AN OBJECT OF DESIRE:
"Proving Up" by Karen Russell   82

HOW TO WRITE SCENES

GIVE YOUR CHARACTERS SPACE TO BE THEMSELVES:
Honky Tonk Samurai by Joe R. Lansdale   90

USE REPETITION TO INCREASE TENSION
TO AN UNSUSTAINABLE LEVEL:
"Encounters with Unexpected Animals"
by Bret Anthony Johnston   96

WRITE ACTION SEQUENCES WITH MINIMAL CHOREOGRAPHY:
The Flamethrowers by Rachel Kushner   101

MAKE INTERIORITY THE FOCUS IN ACTION SCENES:
Open City by Teju Cole   106

HOW TO MAKE DIALOGUE SNAP

CREATE A POWER IMBALANCE:
NW by Zadie Smith   112

TURN DIALOGUE INTO NARRATION:
Pull Me Under by Kelly Luce 118

CRITIQUE HOW A CHARACTER TALKS:
Cartwheel by Jennifer duBois 124

RESIST CONCLUSION:
The Peripheral by William Gibson 130

HOW TO MOVE THROUGH TIME AND SPACE

SLIDE BETWEEN THE PARTICULAR AND GENERAL:
"Nobody You Know" by Elizabeth Tallent 136

CREATE SPACE FOR ALL OF YOUR NARRATIVE TOOLS:
"The Night of the Satellite" by T. C. Boyle 143

MIX ACTION AND INTERIORITY:
A Brief History of Seven Killings by Marlon James 148

CREATE SIMULTANEITY:
Salvage the Bones by Jesmyn Ward 153

PART 2. LENSES FOR THE ARTIST'S VISION

HOW TO CREATE STRUCTURE

INTERVIEW YOUR CHARACTER:
"Boys Town" by Jim Shepard 166

JUXTAPOSE EMOTIONAL STATES:
Who Do You Love by Jennifer Weiner 171

REPEAT YOURSELF:
"The Lost & Found Department of Greater Boston"
by Elizabeth McCracken 177

USE STORYTELLING TO EXPAND YOUR STORY'S WORLD:
The Moor's Account by Laila Lalami 183

HOW TO DRIVE PLOT FORWARD

ADD PLOT ELEMENTS THAT CHANGE THE COURSE OF THE
STORY: *Station Eleven* by Emily St. John Mandel 190

PREDICT THE FUTURE:
The Queen of the Night by Alexander Chee 197

TURN A CHARACTER'S DESIRE INTO KNUCKLE-BITING
SUSPENSE: *Aristotle and Dante Discover the Secrets of the Universe*
by Benjamin Alire Sáenz   202

USE THE POSSIBILITY OF ESCAPE TO RAISE THE STAKES:
An Untamed State by Roxane Gay   207

DEVELOP YOUR PROSE STYLE

RIFF OFF A SINGLE DETAIL:
"The Semplica-Girl Diaries" by George Saunders   214

USE LANGUAGE AND STYLE TO SURPRISE THE READER:
"Summer Boys" by Ethan Rutherford   219

LEAP BETWEEN LINGUISTIC FRAMES:
Mr. Splitfoot by Samantha Hunt   225

REFRESH OLD STORIES WITH NEW PROSE:
The Radiant Road by Katherine Catmull   231

PART 3. PUTTING IT TOGETHER ON PAGE ONE

MIGRATORY ANIMALS BY MARY HELEN SPECHT   241

Introduce setting with a few strong details—
or one detail viewed many ways.   242

Get the reader's attention with a statement that needs
explaining—then, explain it in an intriguing way.   244

Use figurative language, but be quick about it.   247

Show readers the kind of story they're reading.   249

LONG DIVISION BY KIESE LAYMON   252

Give the voice something to comment on that isn't itself.   253

Introduce something interesting that will happen,
but don't tell us yet how it happened.   255

Introduce and then break a rule.   257

THE FRIENDSHIP OF CRIMINALS BY ROBERT GLINSKI   260

    Start with a shared experience and make it unfamiliar.   261

    Make one type of character seem like another type
    of character.   263

    Add an element of danger.   265

EVERYTHING I NEVER TOLD YOU BY CELESTE NG   268

    Begin with incompatible ideas.   269

    Introduce character personalities in a single line.   271

    Use short sentences.   273

CONCLUSION: NOW WHAT?   277

APPENDIX: FICTION BY NARRATIVE TROPE   281

THE WRITER'S FIELD GUIDE
TO THE CRAFT OF FICTION

INTRODUCTION: A GRAND THEORY OF NOT KNOWING WHAT YOU'RE DOING

When I was sixteen, I was accepted into a monthlong camp for smart kids, the Kansas Honors Regents Academy, an honor that verified what I'd long suspected: I was brilliant and bound for greatness. I packed my bag, and my father drove me from our farm to a city I had never visited. The academy was held at Wichita State University, where the bunch of us budding scholars took two classes for college credit. I signed up for a course on Plato's *Republic*, having never read Plato, any piece of philosophy, or even a single text older than Shakespeare's plays. But I was smart and curious, and I figured that I'd catch on fast. Then I began reading.

I couldn't make heads or tails of the book, and the lectures weren't much easier to understand. In *The Republic*, Plato introduces the concept of ideal forms, which the professor explained by pointing at a table. When you see a table, he said, you *know* it's a table. Why? There are many different kinds of tables—some with four legs, some with six, some with leaves, some that fold, some made from wood, others made of metal. How can you look at such varied objects and instinctively identify them as tables? The answer had to do with *tableness*, the ideal form that all worldly tables aim for but never quite reach. Some students nodded, ah yes, we understand. Mostly, these were the students from the big high schools in major cities. A few well-read rural kids intuitively seemed to grasp the concept as well. But not me. I kept looking at tables, peering under them, trying to puzzle out what *form* meant.

A few days after the academy ended, I spent the morning working with my dad and brothers. Who knows what job we were up to: vaccinating or castrating pigs, grinding feed, shoveling the last couple hundred bushels of corn out of a grain bin, or fixing some broken machine. Farm life revolves around manual labor, not just knowing how to do something—like stack hay bales so they won't fall over—but also how to do it efficiently so that you can throw and stack hay for eight hours on a muggy summer day. On this day, my brothers and dad and I came home for lunch, grabbed the mail, and shed our manure-crusted shoes and jeans, our piggy shirts and dusty hats. My dad handed me an envelope from the Academy. It was my final paper on Plato. Everyone wanted a look, but I shielded them and read the professor's comments. The only part I remember was this line: "You are not excessively intelligent." I was dumbstruck but tried to play it off like I wasn't surprised. My brothers and dad thought this was hilarious, and when I tried to explain to them that the professor really meant that I wasn't *too* smart, *overly* smart, they quickly agreed with him.

After living with the description for a couple of decades, I think the professor meant that I was not an egghead. It may have seemed unlikely to him that I would become an academic. I was more suited for engineering or medicine, some profession that values the practical application of knowledge rather than grasping after answers to abstract, rather than concrete, questions (What is a table, really? What is justice?).

It's satisfying to say that he was wrong. I taught writing at a university for twelve years. I've even taught students to write about Plato's *Republic*. But my professor was right about my intellectual temperament. Though I worked in an English department, I'm not a philosopher or even a literary critic. My mind works with the material of the world, not the abstract universe of forms, and that is why I became a writer.

I TOOK SEVERAL WRITING WORKSHOPS as an undergrad, and in the final one, the teacher mentioned story structure. It had never occurred to me that such a thing existed, yet once I knew that it did, I could feel the absence of it in my work. I didn't know how to begin, where to end, and what to put in the middle. Nonetheless, I was somehow accepted into a MFA program, and one of my first questions once I arrived was "What is story structure?" The instructors gave various examples, some based on the claims of famous writing instructors (like Frank Conroy's triangle, which I much later learned was the same as Freytag's pyramid but stamped with an Iowa Workshop brand) and others based on the writings of philosophers and classical literary critics like Aristotle and Longinus. I even took a class called "Form and Theory," and unlike my encounter with Plato, it made sense. The professor even told me once, in her office, "I can tell you're really smart," which was exactly what I wanted to hear. Yet, when I tried to apply the knowledge from the course to my work, I failed miserably. My stories still had no structure. The characters were thin and the plots nonexistent or implausible. Form felt like something that existed on a plane I couldn't access. After three years in the program, I was a much more skilled writer, but I still didn't know what a story was—which is, basically, what we're really asking when we ask, "What is story structure?"

On some level, of course, I was beginning to intuit an answer. I wrote a story that was published by a well-regarded journal, *American Short Fiction*. An agent saw the story and contacted me. Someone even wrote a piece of fan fiction based on the story. I felt like a "real" writer. But when I tried to follow up this success with another, I failed. My one published story had appeared to me as I wrote it, and trying to replicate the experience was like waiting for lightning to strike or the muses to whisper in my ear. They never did—or, they gave me plenty of ideas but no sense for how to bring those ideas to fruition. I'd written a good story once but didn't know how to do it again.

Despite this ignorance, I was teaching writing workshops, giving advice about how to write stories, saying things like, "This is what you need to do." I knew what *not* to do, of course: Don't start with an alarm clock. When writing dialogue, don't write the boring stuff ("Hi. How are you?"). And I had a general sense for how to proceed: Introduce conflict. Raise the stakes of the story to create tension and suspense. Anyone who has taken a workshop has heard these statements. But when students asked *how* to do these things—write tight dialogue or raise the stakes—I bumped against that hole in my knowledge. I didn't know.

So I began cheating. I'd pass around a few pages of a published story by a great writer—Julian Barnes, Anne Enright, Dagoberto Gilb—and say, "Let's look at what this person does." Thus began my second education in the craft of fiction. I'd invent exercises to tinker with our own work using those writers' words. If Anne Enright could move through time effortlessly, in and out of moments at will, then I'd isolate a passage in her story, find the entry and exit points for a scene, and say to the class and myself, "Let's do what she did." If Dagoberto Gilb could create an electric narrative voice, I'd find a few of his great sentences and puzzle out what made them tick. It was a nuts-and-bolts approach to craft. It made sense to me. I still couldn't wrap my head around structure and form, but I was beginning to figure out how sentences and passages worked.

THE MOST COMMON QUESTION posed to writers is, no doubt, "Where do your ideas come from?" The person asking doesn't really expect an answer. The question is basically a way of saying, "Wow, your books are great. I don't know how you do it." When stories are working, they feel like magic. You can't imagine them existing in any form other than the breathtaking final draft in your hands. This is especially true of experimental writing or writing with a distinctive prose style. Only a dope reads *Lolita* or *Beloved* and thinks, "I could have written *that*." Great books dazzle us, especially great books by young writers. When we learn that Philip Roth won the National Book Award for *Goodbye, Columbus* at age twenty-six or that Jonathan Safran Foer's first novel, the bestselling *Everything Is Illuminated*, began as his undergrad thesis or that Bobbie Ann Mason's first story *ever* was published in the *New Yorker*, it's tempting to throw up our hands. Writing requires talent, we think, and you either have it or you don't. It's easy to become jealous: for example, we might think to ourselves, Karen Russell only published her MFA thesis to great acclaim because she went to Columbia, the Hogwarts of MFA programs. But this ignores both her incredible talent and skill and the fact that most writers who pass through even the most prestigious MFA programs never publish a word. The odds against success as a writer are so high that it's natural to despair. This is why some writer, somewhere, is asking right this minute whether writing can be taught. After all, who could *learn* to write *Jesus' Son* or *The Brief Wondrous Life of Oscar Wao*?

But if you want to become a writer, you've got to overcome this overwhelming awe and despair. You must believe, against all odds, that you can be as good as anyone. Writing classes don't always support such belief. They're often divided into beginning, intermediate, and advanced categories, but those distinctions are mostly inventions, not connected to any actual differences between writers. Junot Diaz, Denis Johnson, Vladimir Nabokov, and Toni Morrison started their novels the same as every writer: with a blank page. If there is any difference between those masters and "beginning" writers, it's that they've accumulated a larger set of tools to try out, tinkering with story and prose until something comes together. How did they do that? Likely by reading books with a trained eye.

I once heard an editor for a literary journal remark that when she reads queries that mention how the submitters' favorite writers are James Joyce and Ernest Hemingway, she knows the manuscripts won't make the cut. Writing good contemporary fiction means engaging with the contemporary world. That means reading books published today, not fifty or two hundred or even twenty years ago. The classics are wonderful, yes, and they shouldn't be ignored, but they're not fresh. When I was a kid, one year for my grandfather's birthday, we bought him a set of tapes of Bob and Ray, an old radio comedy duo he'd enjoyed listening to as a young man. A few months later, I asked him if he liked the tapes. He said, "It's funny how things aren't as funny as you remember." Bob and Ray may have been hilarious at the time, but in the years since they'd retired their show, comedy had moved on. Anyone who pitched a show today in the vein of Bob and Ray would get nowhere. This is the conundrum at the heart of the Jorge Luis Borges story "Pierre Menard, Author of the Quixote." In it, a man rewrites Miguel Cervantes's *Don Quixote* word for word, but when it's read through a contemporary lens, the novel has an entirely different meaning. If you're lucky, you'll write like a dead author and reinvent a style or form or discover fresh meaning in old ideas. But it's also possible that you'll simply create something stale. Writers over the last one hundred years have picked up where Joyce and Hemingway left off. If you want to know what stories editors, agents, and readers have in mind when they pick up your work, you need to read *to-day's* writers, the people your age, inhabiting the same world as you.

To read them, you may need to get over your jealousy at their success and awe at their talent. And besides, who says you can't do what they've done?

THIS ENTIRE BOOK IS BASED on the premise that anyone can become a better writer by carefully reading novels and stories and borrowing strategies used within them. To demonstrate how this works, I've chosen one-page excerpts from forty different novels and short stories, discussed some of the craft contained within them, and developed writing exercises aimed at putting that craft to work in your own writing.

But let's be honest. Many writers feel about exercises the same as NBA great Allen Iverson when asked about his lack of effort at practice: "We talking about practice. Not a game. Not the game that I go out there and die for and play every game like it's my last. Not the game, but we're talking about practice, man. I mean, how silly is that?" As a rule, writers dislike writing exercises—and for good reason. We're driven to write the way that preachers are called to the ministry or birds are called to fly. This goes for genre writers as well as literary ones. Our heads are buzzing with stories, images, and questions, and writing those things down calms us. Exercises often don't feel like flying—but these are not those kinds of exercises. This book's basic approach is this: choose a great piece of writing, figure out how it works, and try out that technique in your own work. You're not trying to write *Gone Girl* or *The Flamethrowers*. You're using those novels' tools to hone your own craft and write your own story. This is how you learn: by building and tinkering. By *reading* and *doing*. To that end, this book offers ten basic skills needed to write stories and one-page excerpts from great books that demonstrate strategies for practicing those skills.

Of course, some writers don't need any help. They are, in the words of my former professor, excessively intelligent, succeeding early and often. It's not always clear why. Perhaps they're geniuses. Perhaps they were exposed to great, contemporary books and writing instruction at an early age. Perhaps they have an intuitive sense for how to tell a story.

Maybe they're just lucky. If you're one of those writers, you are fortunate and blessed. May your every effort lead to magic. But if you should become stumped and stuck, or if you're like me and need to take a story apart, examine its pieces, put it together again in your own way, repeating the process over and over until you learn something, then this book may help guide you in your education.

Even then, a grand theory of structure may always elude you. Plato's student, Aristotle, kept it simple. He said a story has a beginning, a middle, and an end. That's structure. The trick is to figure out what to do in each part. Let's begin by studying how other writers have solved those same problems and putting their solutions to work.

HOW TO USE THIS BOOK
(OR, HOW TO BE TAUGHT
TO WRITE FICTION)

A BRIEF HISTORY OF HOW WRITERS
LEARNED THEIR CRAFT

In 1936, the Iowa Writers' Workshop was founded, the first time any university asked a question people are still asking today: How should fiction and poetry be taught? Because it was an academic institution asking this question, as opposed to, say, friends at a bar, the answer involved a pedagogical format that could be repeated in class after class, year after year. It didn't depend on some genius touching budding writers on the shoulders and transforming them into National Book Award winners. That is why if you have taken any writing workshop (at a university or community organization or at some writer's house), it has almost certainly operated like this: a dozen or so students take turns submitting creative work and an instructor leads a critical discussion of that work.

What did people do before 1936? They formed their own workshops. In 1920s Paris, Modernism's most famous writers (Eliot, Fitzgerald, Hemingway, Stein) read and critiqued each other's work, laying the groundwork for the modern MFA program in more ways than one. They supported one another and then, behind each other's backs, ripped one another to shreds, the way that modern students often wait until after class to tell their friends what they *really* think of so-and-so's work. Workshop isn't for the faint of heart. It was true then, and it's true now.

It's natural to ask if there isn't some *other* way to learn how to write, one that doesn't involve students baring their tender fictions and souls (among other things) for the study and critique of smart jerks like Hemingway.

The answer, of course, is yes, sure. Of course there is. But it's also important to remember that workshop and its successes and evils exist because it's how we *think* we learn.

WORKSHOP STARTS YOUNG

I spent countless evenings during my childhood playing board games and cards: pitch, hearts, spades, pinochle, cribbage, poker, king on the corner, and—when no one would play along—solitaire. I can't recall ever being taught the rules of these games. If we switched between ten- and thirteen-point pitch, someone might say, "Wait, what are the points again?" and someone would list them. That was our instruction. We learned by making mistakes and playing cards that made our partners groan in disgust. My sister once threw a Risk board across the room because she felt that the rest of us had ganged up on her—she was in college and I'd brought my girlfriend home for perhaps the second time ever. In stunned horror, she told us (mostly me) that we were being jerks and that we should apologize to my sister. My brothers and I protested, "But that's how you play the game!"

And it was—in our house. You developed a thick skin, a killer instinct, and threw yourself back into the game. I thought everyone learned this same way. Then I tried to teach my girlfriend to play pitch. My siblings couldn't believe she didn't know how to play. Didn't everyone? "It's easy," they said, and explained about points and bidding, but when you've never played cards, these things make no sense. So I said, "Just play. You'll figure it out."

As it turned out, what was fine for siblings wasn't so great for girlfriends trying to make a good impression. Stephanie eventually stalked off and told me in no uncertain terms that I was never to teach her how to play cards again. It's a wonder she ever married me. (It's *not* a wonder that I haven't tried to teacher her pitch again.)

We often teach and learn writing the same way. Someone introduces the basics (setting, character, plot, conflict), we jump into the game, write a story, and then submit it to workshop where people groan and tear our work apart. If you've got a thick skin and no pressure, this system works fine. But if you're nervous about your writing, if the work is personal, if you've spent hundreds or thousands of dollars that you don't really have on the workshop, then perhaps you'll react like my wife did to our pitch instruction and walk away, never to try again. Workshops and all writing classes should do the opposite: get students excited to get back to their work.

WORKSHOP ISN'T THE ONLY TEACHING METHOD

One of my high school teachers organized an annual trip to San Salvador Island in the Bahamas so that two dozen rural Kansas kids could snorkel among tropical fish and coral reefs. To go, we had to take a marine biology class. I was used to catfish, bass, and blue gill, and I remember watching a film about tropical fish and coral and being overwhelmed by the amount of color on screen. They all looked different, but the differences were theoretical. To my untrained eye, they were just a bunch of fish.

Yet, for one semester we studied photos of those fish, learned about their habitats and behavior, and then we flew to the island and jumped in the water. At first, I forgot everything I'd learned. It's one thing to look at a photo of a fish and another to be immersed in fish. I'd never snorkeled before, and like most first-timers, my brain was convinced I was drowning, and so, reasonably, it instructed my arms and legs to thrash around and my head to come up gasping for breath. I finally calmed down, swam among the fish, and soon began to distinguish among them. The learning came back to me—and I wasn't the only one. By the end of one morning in the water, a bunch of Kansas kids were talking about fish and coral like they knew what they were talking about. Nobody was going to mistake us for locals or marine biologists, but we reliably could identify an angelfish, butterfly fish, parrotfish, and damselfish. It was a baby step that counted for a lot.

Of course, stories and novels aren't fish, but there are some similarities in how we learn to write and identify marine biology. Just as a reef's ecosystem isn't a singular entity, so a block of prose is made up of smaller parts. Learning to write means learning to see a passage or page as more than just a lot of colorful words. The problem is that successful writers can't necessarily describe what they do. Ask them, "How do you write?" and they're likely to say, "I just do it." When I was in grad school, one professor was famous for exclaiming in the middle of workshop, "Just tell me a *story!*"

I wasn't in the class, but I felt frustrated for my fellow students. What did he think they were trying to do? Yet his demand actually makes a lot of sense. In workshop, we talk about setting, character, plot, and conflict as if they're parceled out distinctly in a story or novel—as if you can point at them and say, as I did in the Caribbean, "That, right there, is a damselfish." But you can't. Writers write *stories*, and when they're written well, we read them as singular entities. Try to write *setting* without thinking about *story*, and you'll get a well-crafted passage that readers will skim over—because readers aren't interested in setting, only story. This is why it's important to trust your basic reader's gut when critiquing your own work or someone else's. If you're reading a manuscript and begin skimming, something is wrong with the prose. It's stopped telling a story and is doing something else—like describing setting, character, plot, or conflict.

And yet, like those Kansas kids floating above the reef, if you're trying to learn how to write, it's important to know what to look for when you read. Don't look for setting; look for the parts where *place* drives the story forward—where *character* and *plot* and *conflict* and *dialogue* draw you from one sentence to the next. You can't take a picture of *character* and then find that same thing in a story or novel. Every story and every character is different. But read enough fiction, and you'll begin to see certain strategies over and over again. That's what this book offers: strategies for pushing a story or novel forward that involve the classic story elements that we all know.

WHAT THIS BOOK DOESN'T OFFER

This book is focused on craft, on how to write. It won't tell you what to write about or how to figure that out. In part, it's because other books have covered that territory pretty thoroughly. More importantly, though, I'm a big believer that developing your skill set as a writer will help unlock your creativity and imagination. I can't help it. As a kid, I was surrounded by television commercials telling me, "The more you know. . ." But I also believe this because it has been my experience.

When I first entered my MFA program, I had no idea what to write about beyond a vague notion that I wanted to write about Kansas. So that's what I wrote: vague stories set in my home state. Early drafts would have titles like "Tornado Story" or "Wizard of Oz Story." In all fairness, there *are* writers who seem to know right away the story they want to write. For them, the trick is getting their craft to catch up to the story they've been telling themselves in their heads for years. I don't think most writers are this way. We love reading and have some anecdotes we love to tell but nothing that can fill even a four-thousand-word short story. We often discover what we want to write about as we write it. I've seen this happen. For years, I taught workshops in Austin, using exercises an awful lot like the ones in this book, and when I gave my students specific instructions about a strategy I wanted them to try, their imaginations populated that strategy with characters, setting, and conflict. I wrote with them, and the same thing happened to me.

This book doesn't discuss where ideas come from because it's been my experience that our minds are stuffed to the brim with memories and ragged inventions spawned by those memories. If we build a vessel to hold them, our minds will pour them out. Do the work, and the creativity will follow. Sit around, wondering what to write, and you'll never write a word.

HOW TO USE THIS BOOK

STEP ONE: READ THE EXCERPT. Each chapter contains a one-page excerpt from a story or novel. The excerpt might come from the beginning, the middle, or end. You likely won't know what's going on in the story, but you'll find that the sentences draw you forward anyway. These one-page excerpts demonstrate craft elements working together to create a piece of story in action.

STEP TWO: READ THE DISCUSSION OF THE EXCERPT IN ORDER TO IDENTIFY A STRATEGY FOR STORYTELLING. After each excerpt, I'll say something about it, along the lines of "See that? This thing right here? This sentence, this phrase? See what it's doing?" There's nothing academic or theoretical about this process. It's the equivalent of jumping into the Caribbean and watching someone swim up to an angelfish and saying, "See this? It's an angelfish."

STEP THREE: TRY OUT THE EXERCISE. Each chapter ends with an exercise, the equivalent of me saying, "That thing you just saw? Now you do it." At first, trying to emulate these great writers might feel like watching Miguel Cabrera hit a 100-miles-per-hour fastball and being told, "See that? Now you do it." The good news is, writing a sentence isn't like hitting major league pitching. Nobody's trying to get you out. It's just you, the page, the same twenty-six letters available to all writers, and clear instructions for how to assemble them into something that resembles the brilliant writing in the excerpt. The goal is not to make you write someone else's story but *your own story, using your own sentences that just happen to resemble someone else's.*

This isn't copying. Everything that these writers are doing—each strategy they use—can almost certainly be found in some other passage in some other book. Each story might be unique, but the ways that writers tell those stories have been around since people first sat down around a fire to tell a story. There are no *rules* for writing fiction, but there are strategies that you find over and over in fiction from every time and place and culture (at least the ones I've read). Somewhere, right now, a writer is trying to get a reader to stop breathing for just a split second, and that writer will stumble upon a strategy that some other writer has used too.

As Francine Prose claims in her great book *Reading Like a Writer,* finding those strategies is a lot easier if you know what you're looking at when you read. It's not just a bunch of colorful fish, not if you pay attention in the right way.

Also, if you mess up, no one will yell at you. It's just you, this book, and your story.

TOOLS

OF THE

TRADE

IN COLLEGE, I MAJORED IN ENGLISH AND JOURNALISM because I thought that newspapers were like hospitals or schools: we'd always need them, and so working for one was a financial sure thing. Beyond the flawed economics of my plan, I realized that studying literature meant taking on assignments such as reading like all of Lord Alfred Tennyson's *In Memoriam* and writing scholarly essays that were even more boring than the dead white guys they were about. On the other hand, I often loved working as the sports editor at the *Collegian*, Kansas State University's student newspaper, where I experienced the thrill of being screamed at by two Division One head coaches and covering the Cotton Bowl, with its press buffet of grits and fried pork chops in the shadow of Big Tex, the 52-foot-tall talking cowboy.

I haven't worked a day as a real journalist, but it has influenced my approach to the craft of writing—though not in the way you might expect. Ernest Hemingway also loved journalism and often quoted the *Kansas City Star* style guide's advice to "Use short sentences. Use short first paragraphs. Use vigorous English. Be positive, not negative." This advice was taped to the wall of the *Collegian* newsroom and enforced by editors and professors. Yet I came to value something else even more: the incredible, soul-crushing tedium of everyday newsroom work. One class assigned us to write obituaries, police reports, city council meeting reports, and other articles that require no imagination or creativity whatsoever. I hated it, griping to anyone who would listen that this kind of writing was the literary equivalent of flipping burgers or pumping gas, nothing but a set of mechanical tasks that could be accomplished with your eyes closed. Which was the point, I came to realize. Journalism was a trade. Like welding or fixing diesel engines or wiring a house, there were certain skills necessary to do the job. A carpenter might be an intuitive genius when it comes to designing beautiful cabinets, but if he can't use a measuring tape, what good is he?

The same is true for fiction writers. Everyone's ideas for stories are stupendously brilliant. Then, they sit down to describe setting or character, move a character into a room, or let those characters speak and quickly realize that these are mechanical skills. Different writers handle them in their own ways, but most of the basics are the same whether you're reading Stephen King or Toni Morrison.

In this first section of the book, we'll examine some of these skills and how great writers put them to work. They might not seem glamorous at first, but they're the basic building blocks of the artistic vision we'll develop later, in Part 3. Without them, a writer is like a journalist who can't write an obituary: just a dilettante in a *Newsies* cap. Learn these skills, and you'll always have them at your fingertips, even when your artistic vision feels lost or dimmed.

HOW TO

START AND

KEEP WRITING

"THE HEART" *Amelia Gray*

I think it's a whale's heart. I saw one in science class on a video, and I asked Miss Prichard if there was any kind of animal bigger than a whale and she said there was nothing bigger than a blue whale, so I figure that's what it is, a blue whale's heart, here in the living room, as wide as a car. One of the kids at school says You would be cool if you weren't so stupid, and I think like Yeah, this heart is the same way. We came downstairs one morning and there it was, and Dad said whatever kind of heart it was, we needed to get rid of it.

Reprinted from Amelia Gray, "The Heart," *Gutshot* (New York: Farrar, Straus & Giroux, 2015), 119.

DROP AN ELEPHANT INTO THE ROOM

THE STRATEGY

When I was a child, I didn't know where babies came from, and so I imagined them floating in a kind of cloud soup until one day they were placed inside of their mothers. These spirit babies were a source of infinite interest: what did they think about; what did they experience and know? These were the same questions I asked about the souls who'd gone to heaven or hell after dying, and I couldn't figure out answers for either group. Because heaven is an unimaginable and featureless place, its inhabitants lose all sense of identity and personality. How can you be someone in a place where you can be anything?

This is the challenge that writers face when sitting before a blank page. You can write anything: any story, plot, character, and setting. As a result, we often start with an impossibly vague phrase: "There was a man who . . . " or "In a world where . . ." And since we're talking about spirits and heaven and hell, it's worth pointing out that the Bible starts in basically this same way: "There was a void that . . . and a Being who . . ." and "There was a baby who . . . and it was born in a place where . . ."

Beginning a story always requires creating something from nothing. How do we do it? What will the first detail be? The answer can be this easy: pick something, anything, and go with it, even if it doesn't, at first, make any sense at all.

This is what Amelia Gray does in her story "The Heart." The title reveals the first detail, and that detail shapes the story that is born from it like an elephant in a room. No matter what else is in the room or who shows up, everyone and everything must deal with the elephant—which is, in this case, a whale's heart.

Like the elephant, the heart demands that every addition to the story acknowledge it, and so it appears in every sentence, no matter the context:

- During science class: is there "any kind of animal bigger than a whale"?
- In the room: "as wide as a car."
- At school: a bully says, "You'd be cool if you weren't so stupid," and the narrator thinks that the heart is the same way.
- At home: the characters wake up, and there's the heart.
- With the dad: "We've got to get rid of it," he says.

What must the characters do (the only thing they must do, at this point in the story)? Get rid of the heart.

When I read stories, I sometimes imagine the writer creating it: Gray starts with a heart and an "I". She taps her finger lightly against the keys on her laptop. What comes next? It depends on who the "I" is. Where did "I" see the heart? Let's try . . . science class. Turns out, "I" is a kid in school and not, for example, a retiree in Boca Raton. Now that she knows the narrator, she can introduce a conflict that makes sense: school bully. But the heart isn't at school; it's at home, and so she must ask herself, "What's it doing there?" We don't know yet. All we know is that "I" saw a whale's heart on a video at school, and now there's one in the living room. How did that happen? What will happen next? What does it mean? Those are questions the story will attempt to answer, and the search for those answers *is* the story.

THE EXERCISE

Let's create a story by dropping an elephant in the room, so to speak, using "The Heart" by Amelia Gray as a model:

1. FIND YOUR ELEPHANT. Because there are infinite possibilities for a story's elephant, there are likely infinite ways to find them. Let's try two. First, dig into obsessions. Here's a good way to identify them: imagine . . . you're a guest on your favorite podcast. What are you talking about? If it's *Fresh Air* by Terry Gross (not really a podcast, I know, but it's where I fantasize myself being interviewed), then you're probably talking about your life and childhood and where you come from. But the podcast could center on some aspect of pop culture—like *Back to the Future Minute*, the daily podcast that discusses the film *Back to the Future* one minute at a time. (Yes, such a podcast really exists.) Almost all stories follow the writer's interests or sensibilities. What are yours? Make a list. Brainstorm. Then pick one and search within it for some object (specific, tangible) to use as your elephant.

   But what if you don't have any obsessions? In that case, forget your subconscious and unconscious. Instead, look outside yourself. Is there a filing cabinet in the place where you write? Use it. Make it your elephant. Or, is there a closet, an envelope, or a pair of scissors? Is there a pot or a stained couch cushion or a dog bed? Is there a pile of bed sheets on the floor? Any of these things can be the elephant in the room. All you have to do is write something like, "I can't think about anything except this envelope." Or, "Dave kept the envelope close at hand at all times." Why? That's what your story will figure out.

2. BEGIN TO DEFINE YOUR CHARACTER. It doesn't matter if you're writing in third person or first (she or I). Inevitably, you're starting out the same as babies on the day they are born: with personhood, existence, identity. Fiction is even more wide open than real life because your characters can be any age. Gray narrows her character's age down to school age. You need to begin narrowing down as well. If you know or sense something about the character, write it down. If you don't know or sense *anything*, write down the first thing that comes to mind. And the second thing. And third thing. Keep going until something strikes your fancy. It might take a list of a hundred things, which is fine. You'll end up with ninety-nine more ideas for another story later on. Once you have your detail, connect it to the elephant in the room. Or demand that it acknowledge the elephant. (After all, the elephant commands attention.) Gray does this by introducing

science class and a video about whales. In short, force your character to talk about the elephant. No matter what you write, in every sentence, address the elephant. Deal with the elephant.

3. LOCATE THE ROOM. Gray's room is an actual room in an actual house. *Room* can also be translated more broadly as *place*. Put your elephant in a building, neighborhood, city, state, or country—real or imagined.

4. CREATE AN IMPERATIVE. Once you have a defined character with a defined elephant in a defined room, figure out what must be done with the elephant. Or, decide what must be done *because* of the elephant. If there's a pile of bed sheets on the floor, what must be done with them? Do they need to be cleaned? Thrown out? Put on the bed? Burned? You may not know why this action needs to be taken, and that's fine. Once your character takes action, you automatically have a story and a plot to follow, wherever it leads.

The goal is to immediately focus a story on a specific detail that is compelling because the characters cannot think of anything else. Treat the exercise—and the writing that you do—as play. Don't take it too seriously. If something weird pops into your head, write it down. If everything you write is boring, write it down anyway and then ask a radical question about it: What if it were taken away? What if it wouldn't go away?

"LAZARUS DYING" *Owen Egerton*

I stepped through the curtain. She looked up. Her face stretched in fear.

"Mary," I said. She stood quickly, dropping the needle.

"Martha is at the market. She'll be home soon," she said. I moved forward. She stepped back into a wall. "She'll be home soon."

When I was dying Mary sat with me through the night. She dipped a cloth in water and cooled my forehead. I was sick with fever, often asleep, but each time I opened my eyes, Mary was there. "Shhh, brother. Peace," she had said. How I wish she would say this now. Cool my head now. But I was no longer her brother. I could see that in her fear. I looked down at my hands, my blue skin. I hated it. I wanted to be dead. I wanted to be mourned, not feared.

I waited without moving. She didn't move either. Then I screamed. She fell to her knees and covered her face. She didn't see me leave.

That night I tried to die. I tied a rope around my neck and hung myself from a tree. I choked and spat, but I did not die. Thieves came and stole my sandals. I kicked at them and tried to yell, but the rope only allowed me to croak. They laughed and pushed me. They left me swinging. At dawn the rope snapped and I dropped to the dust. I wept because I could not die. The dying part of me had died the first time. So I went for Jesus. I wanted him to undo what he had done. He would grant me that.

I asked wherever I went, but people were afraid. Of me and my mold. Of the Romans and the priests.

Owen Egerton, excerpt from "Lazarus Dying" from *How Best to Avoid Dying*. Copyright © 2014 by Owen Egerton. Reprinted with the permission of Soft Skull Press.

GIVE YOUR CHARACTERS WHAT THEY WISH FOR

THE STRATEGY

The most boring story in the world goes like this: He dearly loved her, and so he asked her out, and the date was wonderful; then they got married, and that was wonderful, too; and when they had children, the babies were so beautiful and wonderful that everyone who saw them felt joyful and said, "What a wonderful family this is! Look how much they love each other!"

There's a darker version of this same boring story: She hated him because of the terrible things he did, so she vowed to get revenge; one night she reached under her pillow while he slept and pulled out a gun . . . and took her vengeance; every day afterward, when she went to bed, she patted the cool pillow beside her and felt glad and peaceful.

Neither example feels like a complete story. We're intuitively waiting for the moment when something goes wrong. It might be unexpected that the woman kills her husband, but because it happens quickly and easily, with no repercussions, there's no story. This is often the case in our early drafts: everything goes according to plan. We sense that something's wrong but aren't sure what. Sometimes we try to add that missing piece by amping up the weirdness of the details. But novelty cannot hide weak storytelling. Even if we replaced the characters in both stories with velociraptors and set them on Mars, the result would be the same, which reveals something crucial about what is required to develop a story beyond its premise.

In "Lazarus Dying," Owen Egerton starts with a premise that is familiar to anyone who's read or heard stories from the Bible: a man named Lazarus falls sick, so his sisters send out a call for Jesus to come and heal him, but Lazarus dies and Jesus doesn't arrive until four days later. The sisters are sad, and so Jesus opens the tomb, calls for Lazarus, and Lazarus walks out. In its storytelling, the Bible's version does the same thing as the two invented examples: the characters get what they want and feel great about it. This works in the Bible because the writer was trying to make a theological point: Jesus is more powerful than death. (Egerton uses that point to set up a great comic line: After seeing the condition of Lazarus' body, Jesus says, "I wanted to see what four days would do . . . I think I'll keep it to three.") But a modern story can't rely on theological lessons to carry the reader forward. It needs drama, and Egerton supplies it. Something goes wrong.

In his version, Lazarus is living with the apostle John two thousand years later, in New York City. They're still alive but for different reasons. Lazarus *can't* die; he already did. John has been granted everlasting life because, in an argument with Peter, he claimed that *living* for Christ was more difficult than *dying* for him. So, here are John and Lazarus, not dead and struggling with theological disillusionment (where is Jesus, anyway?) and the exhaustion of immortality. They don't need to eat or sleep because only mortals rely on food and sleep to survive. As a result, all of the pleasure in life has been taken from them. What's the point of living forever if you can't eat or sleep? It's a fresh take on the old question, "Be careful what you wish for." The story version is this: "What happens when characters get what they want?"

On this page, Lazarus flashes back to the days and months shortly after his resurrection. Like Frankenstein's monster, he's a grisly sight that people respond to with fear and loathing. In the final full paragraph, we see Lazarus become overwhelmed with despair at his situation and try to kill himself. He fails and seeks a solution: "I went for Jesus. I wanted him to undo what he had done." This is the moment when the story takes off. Lazarus has gotten what he wanted, but it doesn't feel the way he hoped.

This is the difference between "Lazarus Dying" and my earlier examples. Something must go wrong. Either the situation must turn out different than anticipated or the character must feel differently about the result than he expected. The story will naturally jump into gear: characters that can't bear their situation will act. As readers, we keep turning the page to see how they act and what happens when they do.

THE EXERCISE

Let's give characters what they want but not the results they expect, using "Lazarus Dying" by Owen Egerton as a model:

1. IDENTIFY WHAT THE CHARACTER WANTS. This should always be one of the first steps to writing a story. The only thing more boring than a character getting what she wants is a character sitting in a chair, not wanting anything. Most stories revolve around desires for common things: love, vengeance, money, possessions, security, certainty, self-validation (the ability to say, "I told you so"), or the resolution to some unresolved matter. Lazarus and his sisters desire life— and, more broadly, an escape from death and suffering. What does your character want? What keeps your character up at night?

2. LOCATE THAT DESIRE IN A SPECIFIC OBJECT OR CHARACTER. We love someone or seek vengeance against someone *in particular*. But it's worthwhile to find other ways to make desire tangible. For example, in most love stories, the love causes a character to desire to give something to the beloved. Pursuit of the right gift becomes a secondary desire. In stories of vengeance, there is usually the pursuit of the tool required to accomplish the act of vengeance. So, think beyond your character's initial desire. What smaller desire goes along with it? You can also think about who has the power to grant the desire. For Lazarus, the desire is for life, yes, but that life (theologically and practically) is located in Jesus. Is there a character in your story that can grant or deny desires?

3. GIVE THE CHARACTER WHAT IS DESIRED. In almost every story, this happens far before the end arrives. In "Lazarus Dying," this happens before the story begins—Lazarus comes back from the dead— which is possible because Egerton assumes that his readers already know who Lazarus is. Another example of this is Emma Donoghue's novel *Room*. A man traps a woman—and then her son—in a backyard shed. The woman wants freedom more than anything else, and the

first half of the novel is spent establishing that want and the obstacles to achieving it. The second half focuses on (spoiler alert) what happens when she gets what she wants.

4. SHOW THE CHARACTER'S *INITIAL* REACTION. Let the character be pleased, at least momentarily. Don't jump immediately to the unexpected. Lazarus is happy and his sisters are happy—until they aren't. In *Room*, the moment of escape is one of the most exciting, satisfying moments I've ever read in a novel—and then things go south.

5. ADD A NEW ELEMENT OR HIGHLIGHT A DETAIL THAT CHANGES THAT REACTION. Once the character has savored the moment, now you can complicate it. Egerton does this by extending the timeframe of the story. Rather than ending immediately after Lazarus has been brought to life, it goes on for days and months and, eventually for two thousand years. In this extension, we learn two key details: 1) Lazarus's resurrection hasn't erased four days of bodily decomposition and 2) he can't die. Both of these facts have consequences for his daily life, and those consequences change his perspective on the thing he previously desired. With your character, ask yourself what details would change his/her perspective on the object of desire? Or, in other words, the desired object is great until your character realizes _____.

6. TRY TO MAKE THE CHARACTER REGRET GETTING THE OBJECT OF DESIRE. Too often, writers (especially literary writers) end stories on a kind of wah-wah, sad-trombone note. Things don't work out for the character—but things aren't *so* bad, not bad enough to cause the character to take drastic and immediate action, only enough to bum the character out. Sometimes this works, but it's often a cop-out, an unwillingness on the writer's part to up the ante for the character. So, press hard on those details that change the character's perspective on the desired thing. Can you get the character to do a 180, as Egerton does: "I went for Jesus. I wanted him to undo what he had done"?

The goal is to create conflict and drama (and, ultimately, a complete story) by giving a character what he desires and then making him wish he'd never gotten it. Don't be afraid to work with extremes: the character wants/fears something *so* badly, is *so* happy/devastated when it happens, and then is *so* miserable/surprised when things turn out differently than expected.

JAM ON THE VINE

LaShonda Katrice Barnett

The man must've been blind to miss a boulder that big. Must've been driving the horse too hard and fast 'cause when Ennis came up on the cart it was a pile of lumber and the man was crumpled up against the tree. Looked like his arm and leg were broken. "Take my horse, go into town, and get help," the man said. Horse was hurting but it would be all right. Ennis thought about ripping the shirt off the man's back to plug the hole bleeding from his head when he saw a small black case on the ground near a wheel still spinning on its axle. In fits and starts, the man explained that he had been on his way to Caldwell to play at a circus.

Ennis screwed the three wooden pieces together, but blowing into it didn't sound like much of nothing. "This a clarinet—ain't it?"

Ennis wondered if anyone had seen him leave his shed that evening. Wasn't nothing for a Negro to up and disappear, but sooner or later they'd come looking for this man.

"See, you can't all the time do what you got a mind to do, even if you thinking with your right mind. You laying there thinking I'm studying on you with my wrong mind. It ain't that. Can't take you to May-Belle's. She liable not to be home and ain't gonna do me a bit of good to get caught with a ailin' white man. I could tell it just like what you and me know to be true and they still gonna find some wrong in it. Can't help you, sir."

He couldn't end the man's life or leave him there to rot. It took a few hours for the bleeding to kill him. Ennis used a rock to hew out a grave, took the clarinet, and started for home.

LaShonda Katrice Barnett, excerpt from *Jam on the Vine: A Novel*. Copyright © 2015 by LaShonda Katrice Barnett. Reprinted by permission of Grove/Atlantic, Inc.

LET A CHARACTER RESPOND
TO AN EXPECTED SCENE

THE STRATEGY

When readers pick up a book, they read the back cover, and as soon as they find out what the book is about—the *kind* of book it is—they read it expecting certain things. Detective fiction, for example, will have snappy dialogue. High fantasy will have swords. Erotica will have, well, you know. Those expectations extend to particular scenes. Detective novels with male detectives will probably have some version of the scene where a woman walks in the door looking for help. In a spy novel, the spy will need to return a secret document to its place without getting caught. As a writer, it's tempting to avoid these scenes because they loom so large. Surprise the reader, right? Do something different. But these scenes pop up again and again for good reason. They're tense. Or they're an intrinsic part of the world of the novel.

LaShonda Katrice Barnett's novel, *Jam on the Vine*, is a historical novel, and as the tag on the shelf where I found my version indicates, it's been categorized as African-American fiction. The novel starts in East Texas in 1897, the post–Civil War, Jim Crow American South. As such, the world has defined rules about the roles and behavior of its white and black characters. It was a world defined by injustice, and so readers expect a scene that hammers home that injustice, a scene in which a white character does something very bad to a black character. It's an unavoidable scene, and so it arrives as it must.

The scene: Ennis has taken his daughter Irabelle to town to run errands, and afterward, they're strolling past some shops when they hear music. They follow it to a store and to a phonograph (record player). Ennis and Irabelle are find themselves drawn to one particular sound in the music, a clarinet, and so Ennis buys the record and the phonograph, which leads to trouble. The shop owner suspects that Ennis is a thief and that his money is ill gotten, so he calls the sheriff. The scene that follows is exactly what you expect, as is often the case with expected scenes: the detective will resist taking the woman's case but then relent, and the spy will narrowly escape undetected. In *Jam on the Vine*, the white police are racist, mean, and brutal, and Ennis and his daughter are humiliated and lucky to get out alive.

The question is, now what? The answer matters. For example, if a detective novel contains a scene with a mysterious, beautiful woman asking a male detective for help, it had better change up or develop that premise in an interesting way; otherwise, it risks playing to outdated stereotypes. One of the pleasures of Sue Grafton's Alphabet series is that the detective is a woman, and the person asking for help is often a man. It's a simple twist that changes everything. But you can also write a scene exactly as expected and still change things up and avoid stereotypes. In *Jam on the Vine*, Ennis is at risk of becoming entirely a victim, definitely completely by his situation. Certainly, Jim Crow was larger than any individual, but if black characters who suffer under it are *only* shown as suffering victims, they lose part of their humanity. So, the question becomes, what does Ennis do in response to the expected scene?

The answer comes one page later:

He discovers a white man lying severely injured on the road after a horse-and-cart accident. The man asks him to go for help, but Ennis doesn't do it. First, he notices that the man has a clarinet. Then, he thinks through his options:

"Can't take you to May-Belle's" [a local black doctor]. "She liable not to be home and ain't gonna do me a bit of good to get caught with a ailin' white man. I could tell it just like what you and me know to be true and they still gonna find some wrong in it."

The expected scene has reminded Ennis and the reader how the white power establishment (the police) treats black men. So, he makes a logical decision. He waits for the man to die, buries him, and takes the clarinet home. It's the last part (taking the clarinet) that makes this scene so good. Ennis doesn't *just* make the logical choice. He makes it in a way that is personal, in a way that has meaning to him.

This scene has a powerful effect. After the expected scene, we thought we know how things stood. But now we're not sure. After Ennis watches a man die and takes his clarinet, more is possible in the novel than before the scene arrived—when all we knew was what we expected to know.

THE EXERCISE

Let's let a character respond to an expected scene, using *Jam on the Vine* by LaShonda Katrice Barnett as a guide.

1. FIGURE OUT YOUR STORY'S EXPECTED SCENE. To do this, think about the premise of your story. If it involves ghosts, there will be an encounter with a ghost, right? If it's a war story, someone's going to kill or get killed. In a coming-of-age story, a character will be humiliated or embarrassed. Immigrant stories and American-abroad stories usually involve a moment of cultural difference, ignorance, or miscommunication. What is a scene that is promised by your premise? These scenes are usually the reason people want to read your type of story. Readers *want* to see encounters with ghosts. What do they *want* to see happen in your story?

2. KNOW YOUR CHARACTER'S EXPECTED RESPONSE/REACTION. Just as readers expect certain scenes, they also expect characters to react in a particular way. In *Jam on the Vine*, Ennis is angry—because of course he is. He's angry because any human would be angry if treated so unfairly. That universality is key to how the scene works; making the character feel something *other than* anger probably wouldn't work. With expected scenes, it's not necessary to run counter to expectation. Instead, it's often better to give readers exactly what they expect— and in spades. Aristotle believed in the idea of catharsis—the emotional toll that drama has on the audience. We rejoice and weep with the characters we're watching. (This is, oddly enough, the trait that made Plato want to ban Homer from his ideal city. Homer was such a good storyteller that he kept getting the populace riled up, and Plato

wasn't in favor of riling.) I'm with Aristotle on this one. Make your reader experience emotion along with the character. The reader knows it's coming, so make it good.

3. CREATE AN OPPORTUNITY FOR THE CHARACTER TO ACT ON THIS REACTION. This is where your story can veer off course in unexpected ways. In *Jam on the Vine*, Ennis's anger has consequences. In good fiction, characters don't suffer passively. They act. So, give your character an opportunity to act. After the expected scene, the character is angry, sad, joyful, giddy—whatever. Let that emotion persist, even as the character leaves the scene and enters another. This is what James Joyce does in his story "Counterparts," when a man gets drunk and angry at the unfairness of the world, comes home, encounters his son, and beats him. The kid had nothing to do with the man's emotional state. He just happened to be on the receiving end of it. The same is true of the musician that Ennis encounters. So, create an encounter. Who can your character meet while still experiencing the emotion from the expected scene? Make it someone the character has power over (power = permission/ability to act). What happens when the character acts?

4. GIVE THE REACTION A PERSONAL EDGE. Ennis sees the man's clarinet, and that detail is key. Without it, he's responding to the man based purely on race. But with the clarinet, he's now a man who wants to give music—and a particular sound—to his daughter, and the man in the road is a musician. The clarinet moves the scene beyond the bare bones of racial conflict. So, in the encounter that you're writing in the previous step, add a detail that makes the encounter personal. Give one of the characters something that the other loves, detests, desires, or fears. Give one character a trait that the other is attracted to or repelled by. Think of your character's life as a hands-on exhibit in a museum: as a visitor, you're allowed to pick up objects from any point in the character's life. How can you drop one of those objects into this scene?

The goal is to give your character the opportunity to respond to a scene that is intrinsic to the story in which he or she plays a part. Almost every story is part of a genre of stories that have been written or told over and over again. The best writers are able to play to the genre's conventions while making the story seem fresh and unexpected.

PERCIVAL EVERETT BY
VIRGIL RUSSELL   *Percival Everett*

I'm bad with faces and names, Murphy said. When can I come by and look at your roof?

You can stop by anytime. I'm on my way out right now, but Donald will be around. Just tell him I talked to you. Blow your horn and wait in the yard though. Don't knock.

Okay. Why not?

Donald's kind of paranoid.

If you go back and read the first paragraph and even the first page you will note that there is no mention of the Eiffel Tower or the fact that it is on the Seine, and you will not find the fact that between the Saint Cloud Gate and the Louvre there are twelve bridges, but yet you know it now. Don't say I never told you anything.

Murphy wanted to tell the man to go fuck himself and his brother as well, but he needed the work and he didn't really know why he disliked them so much. In fact, Murphy really needed the work. He wouldn't shoot me, would he?

Yes.

How easily that yes comes and it makes you, me, wonder just why it would be so easy to not only say yes, but to shoot at a person. But I step outside myself here or at least outside the inside that I have established. There was apparently room here for little more than a monosyllable, circumscribed utterance.

I won't knock.

Yep, got yourself a nice view here. You got a nice big barn out back, too. Do you use it?

I keep my horse in it, Murphy said.

If you ever want to rent it out, Douglas or Donald said. Murphy had already forgotten which one he said he was. You know my memory. The funniest thing is I forget how bad my memory is.

I'll keep you in mind.

Percival Everett, excerpt from *Percival Everett by Virgil Russell: A Novel*. Copyright © 2013 by Percival Everett. Reprinted with the permission of The Permissions Company, Inc., on behalf of Graywolf Press, www.graywolfpress.org.

HOW TO TURN A PREMISE INTO DRAMA

THE STRATEGY

All writers can name a book that made them think, "Wow, maybe I could do that." For me, that inspiration came from Tim O'Brien's brilliant novel-in-stories *The Things They Carried*, which I discovered by accident in French lab as a college undergraduate. Bored with stumbling through *la plage* and *les hamburgers*, I flipped through a literature anthology I happened to be carrying in my backpack and discovered O'Brien's story, "How to Tell a True War Story," about American soldiers, tortured water buffaloes, and ghostly Viet Cong cocktail parties. To my surprise, according to his bio, O'Brien was *still alive*. Until that point (I'm not kidding) I had read exclusively dead writers, and so I thought, "How nice that Norton let this warm-bodied fellow into the canon." Then I read the story again. I was smitten. I sought out the novel, bought it, and read it in my childhood bedroom while on break—with the door closed because stories like "On the Rainy River" made me cry so much I couldn't make out the words on the page.

Since then, I've attended literary events where O'Brien read that story aloud, causing people in the audience, professors and veterans and college kids there only for extra credit, to wipe tears from their eyes. I've taught the book and watched students who swore they hated to read shake their heads in amazement and say, "This guy *gets* it."

Keep in mind: This is a book that begins with, literally, a list of stuff.

A book with a character named Tim O'Brien. A book that, two-thirds of the way through, pulls such a massive switcheroo that, upon reading it, many people have likely uttered words that you can't say on network TV. There's a scholarly word for this type of book: *metafiction*. If you know what it means, great. If not, don't worry. It really only matters to scholars, not writers.

One thing I want to stress in this book is that being a good writer doesn't require an advanced degree—or any degree at all. One writer featured in these pages never attended college. Furthermore, even the brainiest stories still succeed and fail on a gut level. As proof, there's no better writer to study than Percival Everett. His novel *Glyph* contains enough French philosophy to choke a horse. His most famous novel, *Erasure*, follows an obscure writer who gets frustrated at the success of so-called true life memoirs and invents one of his own. The resulting "memoir" is included *in its entirety* within the novel. The book basically says to readers, "You know that story you've been reading? Put it on hold because I want you to read this other story with totally new characters and a radically different style. Sound good? Okay. Cool." It's a book so smart that I can mention it in a group of writers and reliably expect someone to say, "Oh. My. God. That novel."

This page is from his novel *Percival Everett by Virgil Russell*, which is about a son visiting his ailing father in a nursing home, but it also contains a series of stories being written by either the father or son (it's not always clear), stories that start, stop, and change without an obvious logic. It's a mind-bending book, perfect for academic scrutiny. But it's also a gripping read, even if you've never heard the word *metafiction*, because Everett is ruthlessly efficient at hooking us with plot, even if we know it's all a charade.

Many of Everett's talents are at work on this page. He addresses the reader directly ("If you go back and read the first paragraph . . .") and muses about the nature of the story and characters he has created ("But I step outside myself here or at least outside the inside that I have established"). The story about Murphy is one of the "invented" stories that it juggles. In this version (there are several), Murphy gets an unexpected visit from his neighbor, who has a leaky roof and wants Murphy to fix it. The neighbor and his brother may or may not be cooking and selling meth, an interesting detail and promising premise, but here's a crucial secret about writing fiction: odd characters and premises aren't enough to keep a reader turning the page, especially not in a book structured like this one. The novel needs to turn the premise into story. Everett does that in three lines:

> Don't knock.
> Okay. Why not?
> Donald's kind of paranoid.

Of course, being a Percival Everett novel, the prose immediately jumps to meta-fiction, to Parisian bridges. But it's no accident that the next paragraph twists the story's tension a little tighter. "He wouldn't shoot me, would he?" Murphy asks and someone, perhaps Murphy or perhaps the author, answers, "Yes."

Finally, the neighbor asks Murphy about the barn behind his house and whether he'd ever rent it out—which is not a question you want to hear from a drug dealer.

By the end of the page, the novel has taken a premise (meth-cooking neighbors, leaky roof) and turned it into dramatic possibility: what will happen when Murphy goes to fix the leaky roof? What will happen when the paranoid drug dealer asks to use Murphy's barn? For readers, story and suspense are addictive, and the sooner you can move from premise to story (plot, suspense), the harder you'll hook your reader.

THE EXERCISE

Let's turn premise into story, using *Percival Everett by Virgil Russell* by Percival Everett a guide.

1. **IDENTIFY THE SOURCE OF DANGER IN THE PREMISE.** For many stories, this should be simple. If there's a villain, you've found your danger. If something can be broken (contract, relationship, trust), there's got to be a character who acts as the bull in the china shop. If someone doesn't play by the rules (whatever the rules are), that person is the agent of danger. In Everett's novel, the risk comes from the drug-dealing neighbor. He and his brother are the ones who will likely

do something bad. So, ask yourself, who in your story has the potential to behave badly?

2. FORCE SOMEONE NICE/GOOD/SYMPATHETIC INTO CLOSE CONTACT WITH THE DANGEROUS CHARACTER. There are subtle and not-subtle ways to do this. In Agatha Christie novels, characters are often invited to and then trapped in some isolated place. In *Star Wars*, Luke Skywalker is brought into contact with stormtroopers because a trapped princess sent a message via droid to a guy down the road from him and Luke happened to stumble upon it. In *Percival Everett by Virgil Russell*, Everett has the neighbor knock on Murphy's door. The reason? Leaky roof. It doesn't matter how you bring the characters together. The point is simply to put them into the same place at the same time.

3. PROMISE A SUBSEQUENT ENCOUNTER, MORE DANGEROUS THAN THE FIRST. This is the basic plot of all romance novels. Character 1 sees Character 2 and sparks fly, but Character 1 chickens out/gets dragged away/resists temptation. Then, however, they meet again, and this time there's alcohol/no one watching/characters in masks. The first encounter creates the risk, and the second (or third or whatever) meeting makes good on the promise made to the reader. So, consider what bad thing might happen if the characters meet again. In Everett's novel, Murphy might get shot. In other novels, the bad thing might be a broken marriage, ruined career, unsolved mystery, or failure to help someone who needs it. What is the appropriate bad thing for your story?

4. CREATE THE CONDITIONS FOR UNCERTAINTY. In Everett's novel, Murphy is told not to knock. But then how is he supposed to let the neighbor know he's there? In a romance novel, the character faces the uncertainty that we all face when attracted to someone: what should I say, how should I act? It's this uncertainty that draws the reader in, that makes the possibilities for the scene open-ended, not closed—*how* rather than *will she or won't she*?). How can you create some restriction (don't knock) that takes away your character's most obvious approach to the next encounter?

The goal is to turn your premise into a dramatic question. Suspense is often not wondering what will happen next but how an expected moment will play out. It's like when the Wicked Witch of the West tells Dorothy, "I'll get you, my pretty, *and* your little dog, too!" We know the witch will come after her, but we don't know how. We know that Murphy will encounter the drug-dealing neighbors again, but we don't know how that encounter will play out. The key is to develop your story like a road map. We know where the road is going and wonder what we'll see when we get there.

HOW TO

MAKE

SETTING

DRAMATIC

"POMP AND CIRCUMSTANCES"

Nina McConigley

"Chitra, I am going to show you something." He pronounces her name Chee-tra.

She follows him into the basement, past a pool table and more deer watching them in a solemn line. He takes her into a room with wood-paneled walls. The floor is concrete. In the room are several large safes—or what Chitra thinks are safes.

"This is where I keep my guns," he says, pointing to a safe. "Kids. I told the Senator if he takes up hunting, he needs to get something like this. You don't want Harry there getting into guns." Nancy and Richard have one other child besides Luke. A girl Gretchen Larson. She is in the army and stationed in Germany.

There is a narrow door with a lone padlock on it in the room. Richard Larson takes a ring of keys from his pocket and opens the lock. It is a small room, meant at one time as a kind of pantry. Inside is a little vanity with an oval mirror. A bench is tucked neatly in the middle. On the surface of the table is a wide array of makeup. Compacts, eye shadows that look like an artist's palette, brushes of all sizes, lipsticks lined up like bullets. There is a full-length mirror next to the vanity. It is also oval, and swivels on its wooden base. A stained-glass floor lamp stands in the other corner. Next to it is another plush chair. But unlike the cloud chairs from the living room, this one has a Victorian feel. It is an elegant chair. Light mauve with a kind of paisley pattern. It is not a Nancy Larson chair. There are framed paintings on the wall – and again they are different. They are of flowers, English cottages with thatched roofs.

But the thing in the room that delights her the most is a metal bookcase. Lined up are mannequin heads, all in a row. On each of the heads sits a blond wig in various hairstyles: a straight bob, a curly bob, long Rapunzel-like hair, and a cut with layers framing the face.

Nina McConigley, excerpt from "Pomp and Circumstances" from *Cowboys and East Indians: Stories*. Copyright © 2013 by Nina McConigley. Reprinted by permission of Curtis Brown Unlimited.

TAKE A TOUR

THE STRATEGY

It's easy to treat setting like a green screen in filmmaking: a background for the drama between the characters standing in front of it. When this happens in prose, setting is often introduced at the beginning of a passage and never mentioned again. Or, if it is, we skim over it, understanding that the writer has tossed it onto the page out of obligation or awe at a beautiful sentence or some other reason not connected to telling a good story. In fact, I'm willing to bet that nothing gets skipped more often in fiction than descriptions of setting. In good stories and novels, setting is essential to the story. Try to imagine, for example, *Moby Dick* without the ocean or *Beloved* without the horrible swamp the characters must crawl through, chained together, during their escape from slavery. Imagine *The Lord of the Rings* without Mordor. Probably the most quoted line from Tolkien is "One does not simply walk into Mordor."

Setting should be more than a backdrop. The best writers find ways to bring setting and drama together, forcing them to interact.

McConigley does exactly that in "Pomp and Circumstances." The entire scene on this page consists of one character taking another character on a tour of part of his house. When Richard Larson says, "Chitra, I am going to show you something," he is showing her the setting of the story. It's no longer a backdrop, but something the characters actively engage with. This tour is not random. Larson has a destination in mind and, ultimately, a request: he will ask Chitra if he can wear one of her saris. Because he has a purpose for the tour, the things that he points out are done so purposefully. For example, he stops to show her his gun safe. Maybe he would have done this for anyone, regardless of the reason for the tour. But it's no accident that the guns accentuate his masculinity, which he reinforces again by saying, "I told the Senator if he takes up hunting, he needs to get something like this." The dialogue gives him authority: "I told him," he says. Larson is using the setting to influence how Chitra sees him. In other words, the story turns setting into a tool to be manipulated by a character, the same as a gun or a screwdriver.

The story also uses place in a strategic way. This page happens in a basement, not in the living room or on the front porch. In this basement, there are various locked doors, and it's into one of these that Larson leads Chitra. This is important thematically (locked doors, hidden desires) but also dramatically. It's easy to walk away from a front porch or living room. A basement is much more difficult to escape. By taking Chitra into the basement, Larson has asserted control over her. Some people may read various meanings into that control, but we're interested in the dramatic meaning. Making characters uncomfortable is a good source of tension, and trapping a character is a great way to induce discomfort.

McConigley has also filled a page where she could have written, simply, "He took her into the basement." As a result, she has created a much longer scene that develops character, increases suspense, and creates plot. That is the work that setting can do when it's treated not as a backdrop but as an essential part of the story.

THE EXERCISE

Let's take a tour of setting, using "Pomp and Circumstances" by Nina McConigley as a guide.

1. IDENTIFY THE MOTIVE FOR THE TOUR. The character leading the tour may have a destination in mind. Or the tour might be a way to kill time until some scheduled or expected moment. In McConigley's case, the tour leads to both: a destination where Larson will make his request. This intention, or motive, is crucial. Without it, the characters are simply wandering around.

2. GIVE THE CHARACTER A PLAN. When Larson shows Chitra the gun safe, he may be doing it with the conscious intention to make himself appear more masculine, or he may be doing it unconsciously. It doesn't matter. The point is that it happens. For your tour, think about your character's desired conclusion for the scene. How can the character use the tour to set the stage for that conclusion? What effect, conscious or not, would the character like the tour to have on the others?

3. LET THE CHARACTER ENACT THAT PLAN. This will likely involve pointing out particular elements of the setting and talking about them: i.e., playing tour guide. What will the character single out for distinction? What will the character say about each thing, and *how* will the character say it? Think about tone: assertive or passive (or passive-aggressive), bold or shy, angry or joyful. If the tour is a kind of sales pitch for the hoped-for outcome, how is the character's commentary about the setting making that pitch? How does the character hope to be viewed during this tour? Larson needs to feel and be seen as manly, and so he speaks in a way that exudes that trait. How can your character do the same thing?

4. CREATE AN IMBALANCE OF POWER. Generally, if you're taking a tour, you're on the tour guide's turf. This power imbalance is literal. You give up control by confining yourself to a bus or boat or agreeing to walk and stand where told. The guide's control ends as soon as the other people realize they can walk away. So, in your setting, create a dynamic that prevents characters from walking away. McConigley uses a basement. Crime writers tend to set interrogations in abandoned houses in the woods or in urban areas where the person being interrogated knows no one. You can lock doors or create rules (nobody leaves the classroom until the bell rings). You can also invert the balance of power. What happens when the tour guide is in unfamiliar territory or in the company of someone who knows the setting better than her?

The goal is to charge setting with energy so that the lead-up to an expected moment becomes filled with tension. As a side effect, you may avoid the annoying problem of figuring out what to do with characters as they converse. Every writer has written some version of a character pausing during a bit of dialogue in order to pick up a coffee mug, tap fingers on a table, or look out a window. These are fillers that accomplish nothing. By forcing the characters to interact directly with the setting, each interaction becomes more meaningful because the characters are acting with intention. Larson doesn't idly tap his fingers on the gun case. He points it out and talks about it, turning it into a part of the story.

"IT WILL BE AWESOME BEFORE SPRING" *Antonio Ruiz-Camacho*

It is the year we take internships in museums across the city because we dream of becoming artists after college. Sash and Tammy land gigs at Centro de la Imagen, and Jen at Museo de Arte Moderno, and I get the best of all, at Antiguo Colegio de San Ildefonso, helping to curate the first-ever solo exhibit of David Hockney in Mexico, which is beyond amazing and makes my three stupendous friends rattle with jealousy. I boast about my job even though all I do for those ten hours a week is mail invitations for the opening reception, organize large boxes of leaflets into brick-thick stacks, fax documents overseas, drag superheavy crates to storage—tedious and exhausting chores I've never had to do before, the novelty of which feels exciting and paramount. I feel like I'm carrying Hockney's posterity on my shoulders, like his success in Mexico depends on me. I get a taste of what the real city feels like and I think it's not as bad as it looks from the outside.

It is the year I'm nineteen. It is the year life will change for us, but we don't know any of that yet.

It is the year we meet people that don't live in the same neighborhoods as us, Polanco, Lomas, San Angel, Tecamachalco. It is the year we get to know real artists who rent studios in dangerous districts on the other side of the city, and it is the year we socialize with historians and anthropologists and performance artists and book editors who live paycheck to paycheck and don't have cars; these are fascinating, glamorous people who ride the subway and take taxicabs. It is a new and unexplored world within the same city we were born and have always lived, and every time we venture into it we feel as if we're crossing an invisible fence, trespassing into a forbidden side of ourselves: messier, wilder, sexier.

Antonio Ruiz-Camacho, excerpt from "It Will Be Awesome Before Spring" from *Barefoot Dogs*. Copyright © 2016 by Antonio Ruiz-Camacho. Reprinted with the permission of Scribner, a division of Simon & Schuster, Inc. All rights reserved.

BREAK SETTING INTO NEIGHBORHOODS

THE STRATEGY

On the first day of my freshman composition classes at Texas State University, I always asked where everyone was from. Perhaps a third of the students would answer, "Houston," and I always responded the same way: "*Houston* Houston or the 100-mile radius that people call Houston?" Everyone thought this was funny because it was true. The students would smile and clarify: they were from Katy or Cypress or Sugarland. Once a kid said he was from Beaumont, which is literally almost one hundred miles from Houston. "That's not even close," I exclaimed, and he shrugged.

"No one ever knows where it's at."

It was a problem I understood. Even in a sparsely-populated state like Kansas, few people had ever heard of my hometown unless they'd been there. Texas is, as you may have heard, really big, with regions larger than many states, which is why students from the Rio Grande Valley always said they were from the Valley. They never, ever led with their hometown. Often, they wouldn't say it even after you asked. They just assumed you'd never heard of it—which was often true. Unless you're from the Valley, you probably never go there. But even if these introductory shortcuts make sense in a classroom, they're a terrible practice for fiction.

Neighborhoods matter. We understand this intuitively, of course, or at least our language does. Our clichés give us away: "the other side of the tracks" and "the wrong side of town." We give names to neighborhoods: downtown, the inner city, suburbs, exurbs, residential, industrial, the financial district, the warehouse district, the docks, the ghetto.

Some of these terms apply to any place where people live. Manhattan, of course, has many different districts, but the Manhattan where I went to college (Manhattan, Kansas) also had parts of town. I worked for a summer at Chili's Bar and Grill and once drove a server home to a house that she swore was in a bad part of town. It was by the tracks, near a gas station, near an industrial strip. Even my hometown of Hiawatha, with its three thousand residents, had neighborhoods. Some people lived on Miami Street, in old Victorian homes with columns; others lived in an area known as Teacher Row; and others lived, literally, on the wrong side of the tracks, in small houses with porches filled with old, broken toys and boxes of junk. A town isn't even required for neighborhoods. I grew up in the country, fifteen minutes outside of the city limits. In general, the farmers who owned land east of Highway 73 were wealthier than those west of it because the soil was better. (We lived west.)

When a person moves from one neighborhood to another, the effect can be jarring. Billy Joel sang about this in "Uptown Girl," Stephen Sondheim wrote about it for West Side Story, and it's strikingly present in "It Will Be Awesome Before Spring," the first story in Antonio Ruiz-Camacho's collection, Barefoot Dogs. In fact, the difference between neighborhoods is the basis for the plot, our understanding of the characters, and so, really, the entire story.

At its most basic level, the story is set in Mexico City. But it's also set in a particular part of the city: the part with famous, world-class art museums. Because no one lives in an art museum, the setting becomes a place where characters from different neighborhoods mix. Based on the narrator's description of "tedious and exhausting chores I've never had to do before, the novelty of which feels exciting and paramount," it's clear that she's from a relatively wealthy family, one where such manual labor is rare enough that it can give her "a taste of what the real city feels like."

She meets characters from different neighborhoods, "real artists who rent studios in dangerous districts on the other side of the city" and people "who live paycheck to paycheck and don't have cars." Those lives seem glamorous to the narrator, as do the mundane aspects of them like riding the subway and taking taxis. In short, the narrator is living a version of Billy Joel's "Uptown Girl," and this is her first introduction to neighborhoods that are different from her own. The result is plot:

> "It is a new and unexplored world within the same city we were born and have always lived, and every time we venture into it we feel as if we're crossing an invisible fence, trespassing into a forbidden side of ourselves: messier, wilder, sexier."

This passage is so wonderful because it so clearly lays out the possibility of action and drama. The reader knows that this young and naive girl will cross that invisible fence and get herself into trouble that will spiral into something greater than she is prepared to handle. But there's another implied possibility. Yes, she can cross that fence, but what happens when people from those dangerous parts of town travel into her neighborhood?

The answer is story and plot.

It's worth pointing out how much of this page is simply giving the reader information. Nothing actually happens. It's all setup, and if you've ever been in a writing workshop, you'll know that workshop critiques hate setup, preferring that the writer get the story moving. So, another reason this page is so great is because it turns information (which is, on its own, boring) and makes it a source of conflict. In fact, the conflict is inherent to the way the information is presented. If Ruiz-Camacho had left out the dangerous neighborhoods and the details about how the narrator feels about her job (or, you know, almost everything on the page), if he'd stuck only to the basics of the narrator's home and her job, the conflict would disappear completely.

THE EXERCISE

Let's create conflict by dividing setting into neighborhoods, using "It Will Be Awesome Before Spring" by Antonio Ruiz-Camacho as a model:

1. **GIVE YOUR CHARACTER A NEIGHBORHOOD TO INHABIT.** To start, choose a common term (downtown, suburbs, etc.) that broadly applies

to the neighborhood where your character lives, works, or spends time. Imagine that the character (or someone else) is explaining the location of this neighborhood. What phrase or term would be used? Not every character will necessarily use the same term. People who live downtown often view anything beyond their borders as the suburban hinterland, but people living outside of downtown will say things like, "I'm only 10 minutes from downtown," suggesting that the suburbs are farther out. What does your character (and others) call your character's neighborhood?

2. GIVE THE NEIGHBORHOOD CHARACTERISTICS. You'll sometimes hear people talk about some parts of town—suburbs, for example—as if they're the same everywhere. Suburbs, we're told, are generic. But, of course, that's not true. In Austin, Hyde Park was once the suburbs, but now its small, funky bungalows and cottages are pricey (when they're not being demolished for larger houses and complexes) because they're so close to the center of things. If you drive around Austin, you'll quickly learn that suburban homes vary drastically in size, quality, and appearance. So, treat your setting with an insider's perspective. Assume, for the moment, that you're writing for readers who live there, not readers who've never heard of it. What do the people who know it well say about it?

3. GIVE YOUR CHARACTER A NEIGHBORHOOD TO AVOID. A character can avoid a part of town for many reasons. Perhaps it's dangerous, like parts of Mexico City in "It Will Be Awesome Before Spring." Or maybe the character can't afford to live or shop in the neighborhood. Or the neighborhood is far away and hard to reach. Or the neighborhood has nothing (restaurants, stores, homes) the character finds desirable. As with all definitive statements in fiction, once you write, "so-and-so never went to X part of town," you've hinted to the reader that the character will almost certainly be forced to go there. Even if you hadn't intended for your character to visit that neighborhood, knowing where she won't go can pay off later in the story.

4. CREATE A REASON FOR CHARACTERS FROM DIFFERENT NEIGHBORHOODS TO MIX. Almost no one sticks to his or her neighborhood. Most people live and work in different parts of town. Certain kinds of entertainment, like movie theaters and ball games, draw people from across a city, as do places like universities and courthouses.

What places do this where your story or novel is set? Where do characters encounter people from other neighborhoods?

5. CREATE AN OPPORTUNITY FOR CHARACTERS TO CROSS INTO DIFFERENT NEIGHBORHOODS. Certain tasks (buying turf and flagstone or picking up cardboard boxes for a move or renting a car) can only be done in certain parts of town. The bars, parks, restaurants, grocery stores, and libraries in one part of town are not like their counterparts in another part. Why does your character leave his or her neighborhood?

6. ATTACH EMOTIONS TO THIS INTRA-NEIGHBORHOOD TRAFFIC. How does the character feel about going into a specific neighborhood: scared, excited, resentful, snooty? Does the character know his or her way around? Does the character need a guide (a friend, a taxi driver, a coworker) to enter this place? To go there, does your character need to try to fit in? Is fitting in even possible?

The goal is to make the information about setting active, to make it a source of tension and conflict, rather than simply *the place where stuff happens*. Don't be like my students, claiming they're from a generic place called Houston or the Valley, answers designed to shut down conversation. The more particular you get, the more there is to write about. My wife and I sent our kids to preschool in a much wealthier part of town than where we live. When we talked to other parents, inevitably they'd ask where we lived. They meant, what street. When we told them, some of them would look away. "Oh," they'd say. End of conversation. That story isn't possible if all you know about me is that I live in Austin. Specific details create story. Generalities kill it.

GONE GIRL   *Gillian Flynn*

. . . just delighted to arrive at the tail-end of a cocktail hour across town so he can guzzle a drink and head home with his wife. George shows up about twenty minutes later—sheepish, tense, a terse excuse about work, Insley snapping at him, "You're *forty* minutes late," him nipping back, "Yeah, sorry about making us money." The two barely talking to each other as they make conversation with everyone else.

Nick never shows; no call. We wait another forty-five minutes, Campbell solicitous ("Probably got hit with some last-minute deadline," she says, and smiled toward good old John, who never lets last-minute deadlines interfere with his wife's plans); Insely's anger thawing toward her husband as she realizes he is only the second-biggest jackass of the group ("You sure he hasn't even texted, sweetie?").

Me, I just smile: "Who knows where he is—I'll catch him at home." And then it is the men of the group who look stricken: *You mean that was an option? Take a pass on the night with no nasty consequences? No guilt or anger or sulking?*

Well, maybe not for you guys.

Nick and I, we sometimes laugh, laugh out loud, at the horrible things women make their husbands do to prove their love. The pointless tasks, the myriad sacrifices, the endless small surrenders. We call these men the *dancing monkeys*.

Nick will come home, sweaty and salty and beer-loose from a day at the ballpark, and I'll curl up on his lap, ask him about the game, ask him if his friend Jack had a good time, and he'll say, "Oh he came down with a case of the dancing monkeys—poor Jennifer was having a 'real stressful week' and *really* needed him at home."

Or his buddy at work, who can't go out for drinks because his girlfriend really needs him to stop by some bistro where she is having dinner with a friend from out of town. So they can finally meet. And so she can show how obedient her monkey is: *He comes when I call, and look how well groomed!*

Gillian Flynn, excerpt from *Gone Girl.* Copyright © 2012 by Gillian Flynn. Used by permission of Random House, an imprint and division of Penguin Random House, LLC.

GIVE SETTING A HUMAN GEOGRAPHY

THE STRATEGY

Ask people about their favorite city, and they may mention the architecture or landscape, but they're just as likely to mention the culture or atmosphere. This is particularly true of Austin, a city whose main attraction is a vibe (Keep Austin Weird), a soundtrack (Live Music Capital of the World), and a lifestyle (shorts, sandals, margaritas on the patio). Ask someone the difference between Austin and Dallas, and landscape probably won't get mentioned at all. Instead, they'll talk about how Dallas restaurants and clubs have dress codes, whereas in Austin you can show up almost anywhere in a tank top and cutoff jeans. Or they'll talk about Dallas's impressive art museums versus what Austin's street art and galleries housed in former warehouses. In each case, setting has less to do with physical place and more to do with the people living there.

Good fiction treats setting the same way, and it's an approach you'll find in spades in Gillian Flynn's blockbuster *Gone Girl*.

The novel charts the elaborate and thrilling dissolution of Amy and Nick's marriage. Much of the book takes place in Missouri, where the couple moves for economic reasons, but early in the book, they're living in Brooklyn and there's a scene when Amy meets some friends for dinner and cocktails. It's a Tuesday night, "so we aren't gearing up for a big night, we are winding down, and we are getting dull-witted, bored."

Then, the women's husbands begin to show up, which is where this page picks up.

The scene offers a kind of sociological study on marriage among Brooklyn's middle class. One husband shows up "just delighted to arrive at the tail-end of a cocktail hour across town." Another shows up "*forty* minutes late" and says, "Yeah, sorry about making us money." When Amy's husband never arrives, everyone feels a kind of smug pity. It's this reaction that causes Amy to explain the social geography of the setting:

> Nick and I, we sometimes laugh, laugh out loud, at the horrible things women make their husbands do to prove their love. The pointless tasks, the myriad sacrifices, the endless small surrenders. We call these men the *dancing monkeys*.

Next, we get examples of the *dancing monkeys*: Jack, who cancels on a ball game because "poor Jennifer was having a 'real stressful week' and *really* needed him at home." Another guy cancels on drinks so that he can meet her friend. Their wives, Amy explains, want "proof that you love me best." It's a public display, a "female pissing contest."

Amy is showing the reader how people behave in this place—at least in Amy's view. It's possible that other characters would describe these events and this behavior differently, and that's necessary and important. When it comes to social settings, perspective is crucial. The idea that men act like dancing monkeys matters because Amy despises it—or claims to. She's responding to the social setting by clarifying her own personality and philosophy and the behavior that results from both.

We do this in real life. In Austin, East Sixth Street is known for being a hipster hangout. But how you define *hipster* is pretty subjective. It's probably fairer to say that the crowd is mostly twenty- and thirtysomethings, young but older than the college students and tourists on Dirty Sixth. Both phrases (*hipster* and *Dirty Sixth*) imply a social geography, allowing people to say, "Oh god, I never go to Dirty Sixth anymore" or "I'm not a hipster like *those* people."

This is the advantage of focusing on the human element of setting (how people in a place behave). Characters will have opinions about the behavior they see. They will tend to categorize it and respond to those categories with strong attitudes—which goes a long way to helping create a character's voice.

THE EXERCISE

Let's give our narrative a human geography and give a character the opportunity to respond to it, using *Gone Girl* by Gillian Flynn as a guide.

1. GIVE YOUR CHARACTER BEHAVIOR TO OBSERVE. Just as people who buy cars or have babies tend to pay close attention to other cars and other parents with babies, all people/characters tend to notice certain behaviors more than others. The question is this: What concerns are on your character's mind? Someone who just bought a car, for example, is worried about buying the best/cheapest/safest one. What decision has your character made or what decisions must the character make on a daily basis? The rationale for those decisions will likely cause the character to notice people with the same rationale or, perhaps, who make different choices.

2. ALLOW THE CHARACTER TO CATEGORIZE THE BEHAVIOR. Flynn's character uses the term *dancing monkeys.* She's observed a behavior (women calling their husbands to join them) and gives it a name. We do this all the time in real life. Before taking their first drink of alcohol for the night, people sometimes use the phrases "beer thirty" or "Miller time." An article in the *New York Times* discussed "mom hair." These names reflect a lot about the mindset of the people using them, which is the goal in fiction. So, let your character name the behavior. Don't be afraid the make the name snide or full of some other emotion.

3. LET THE CHARACTER PLACE HERSELF WITHIN THESE CATEGORIES. Just as *Gone Girl*'s Amy tells herself that she is different—and has a different sort of marriage—than other women, you can let your character say, "I'm not like *those* people." This gives your character the opportunity to explain *how* she's different and *why* she's different. The *how* and *why* are a great way to create conflict—as you may have experienced firsthand if someone has ever explained *why* and *how* they disagree with your behavior.

4. MAKE THE CATEGORIZATION MATTER. In *Gone Girl*, we have a sense, even early on, that Amy doth protest a bit too much. Her observation about *dancing monkeys* matters because her own monkey isn't dancing for her. But it also matters because identity matters. If you don't believe me, try calling a Texas A&M Aggie a Longhorn. See what response you get. In your fiction, you'll squeeze more juice out of a scene if you attach a kind of moral righteousness to the categories perceived by the characters: they're *that*, but I'm *this*, and *this* is morally correct.

The goal is to transform setting from the place a story occurs to a reflection of the people who inhabit it—creating conflict as a result. It's a strategy that works when a character's at home, talking about dancing monkeys, or when she moves away and feels loathing for the Missouri people she's suddenly surrounded by, as is the case in *Gone Girl*. When you use setting to confirm or bolster a character's identity (They're *that*, but I'm *this*), you create distinctions and distance, which creates the opportunity to make a character uncomfortable. Just close that distance. Put her next to one of *those people*.

"WAITING FOR TAKEOFF" *Lydia Davis*

We sit in the airplane so long, on the ground, waiting to take off, that one woman declares she will now write her novel, and another in a neighboring seat says she will be happy to edit it. Food is being sold in the aisle, and the passengers, either hungry from waiting or worried that they will not see food again for some time, are eagerly buying it, even food they would not normally eat. For instance, there are candy bars long enough to use as weapons. The steward who is selling the food says he was once attacked by a passenger, though not with a candy bar. Because the plane had been delayed so long, he said, the passenger threw a drink in his face, damaging one eyeball with a piece of ice.

Reprinted from Lydia Davis, "Waiting for Takeoff," *Can't and Won't* (Farrar, Straus and Giroux, 2014), 214.

MANIPULATE CHARACTERS WITH SETTING

THE STRATEGY

I spent certain summer afternoons on my father's farm carrying manhole-cover-sized blocks of manure and straw across the slab of a hog building and tossing them into a lagoon. The job's metaphoric qualities were clear. You can't sink much lower than hauling shit, and we all knew it. My dad liked to tell us that Hercules had done the same kind of work for one of his seven tasks. Of course, he'd cleaned out his stables by rerouting a river through them. We had to settle for less-heroic methods, hauling chunk after chunk for hours and days on end. Your mind tends to wander. My dad sometimes said, dreamily, "What if they had a farming Olympics, and this was one of the events?" This was during the 1996 Olympics, and my daydreams mostly focused on the U.S. women's gymnastics team. As I lugged those bricks of manure, I thought, "If this was an Olympic sport, I could meet Kerri Strug and Dominique Dawes." (Google it, young people.) "They'd see me carrying this enormous slab of manure, balancing it on the pitchfork, my arms shaking with the effort, and they'd swoon." I'm pretty sure most other 15-year-olds weren't thinking those exact thoughts, and so when I'm in a writing workshop and someone says, "Setting is character," I'm tempted to respond, "Yes, I've noticed."

"Setting is character" is one of those workshop maxims that we implicitly understand to be true—in life and in the stories all around us. It's the reason Emma Donoghue used the title *Room* for her novel about a woman and her son held captive in a sicko's backyard shed. Nothing mattered more to the characters than that room. Try to imagine the film *Snakes on a Plane* or the novel/film *Mutiny on the Bounty* without the setting named explicitly in the title. My favorite book and film as a kid was *Treasure Island*, a novel that Robert Louis Stevenson could have titled *Long John Silver* or *The Black Spot*—all very good titles. But he didn't. Because setting, when done well, exerts real force. I can't count the number of times my father quoted *The Treasure of the Sierra Madre*, a film in which the setting and situation transform the characters before the viewers' eyes.

But how can we make our own story settings as powerful as snakes on a plane?

Lydia Davis' story "Waiting for Takeoff" demonstrates how.

The story leads with setting: "in the airplane so long, on the ground, waiting to take off." In this case, as with *Snakes on a Plane*, *Mutiny on the Bounty*, *Treasure Island*, and *Treasure of the Sierra Madre*, the setting is tied to situation. If the first line was changed to "in the airplane so long, on a transatlantic flight," the effect wouldn't be the same. There's nothing unexpected about the situation; if a character gets angry about the time required to fly to London, that says more about the character than the setting. But in this case, the situation is out of the ordinary, and *all* of the characters are transformed by the setting and situation. At first, they're transformed together, in agreeable ways. They begin to form a group identity: they're all in this together. They make wisecracks and eat terrible food. The distinction between passengers has eroded; the most basic identities on the plane have been partially stripped away by the fact of the plane stuck on the ground.

That's part one of the story, and it's the moment where a lot of beginning writers might struggle to figure out what happens next. It has all the hallmarks of a real-life anecdote: one time I was on a plane that was grounded for hours, and everybody pulled together, and I met the nicest people. It's the sort of anecdote that might make someone think, "I should turn that into a story." But on its own, it's not enough. Situation isn't story. This is where Lydia Davis' genius enters. She has written herself into a place where setting has transformed her characters into a single unit. Take another look at what comes next:

> "The steward who is selling the food says he was once attacked by a passenger, though not with a candy bar. Because the plane had been delayed so long, he said, the passenger threw a drink in his face, damaging one eyeball with a piece of ice."

It's not enough for setting to influence and transform characters. Or, it's only a beginning. The drama begins when the transformation is so complete that something extraordinary happens, something that disrupts everything that's been built up to that point. The steward's story cuts through the group identity on the plane, everyone grousing and joking together. Suddenly, it's everyone for themselves, as in *Lord of the Flies*.

In workshops I've taught, especially with college undergraduates, this is the piece that's missing from so many stories. Care and effort is spent building a world and the characters who fully inhabit it, and the result can *feel* complete. Robert Stone liked to compare a short story to a pitch, as "one continuous movement" as he said in an interview with Dwight Garner at *Salon*, and I've heard this quoted many times. The problem is that we focus on the "continuous movement" part and forget the rest of his metaphor: "It's one continuous movement that ideally has to, like a pitch, break and then with a kind of retrospective inevitability end up in a catcher's mitt." The *break* is the most important part. A story gathers all its momentum into one direction—and then must suddenly seem to hinge and run away from itself. Because of the brevity of "Waiting for Takeoff," that hinge stands out. Davis keeps pushing on setting. First, it transforms the individuals into a group. Then, when the situation persists and pressure builds, that group identity begins to break apart.

So, if you're feeling stuck, trying making your setting more disturbing. It can upset your characters enough that they'll do something, and that *something* is what pushes your story into motion. Building a story means building something that you'll eventually break and perhaps completely destroy. That destruction is the plot. As Davis shows, it can be created from setting alone.

THE EXERCISE

Let's make setting disturbing, using "Waiting for Takeoff" by Lydia Davis as a model:

1. START WITH A PRONOUN. Davis' story begins with *we*. It's impersonal; *we* could be anyone. By the end of the sentence, it's clear that the identity of *we* is wholly contingent on the setting. *We* are the people on the airplane. Nothing else about them matters. So, give yourself a pronoun: we, he, she, us, they, it. Don't use a name. Avoid nailing down details for now. The point is to give your story a warm body, nothing more.

2. INTRODUCE SETTING AND SITUATION TOGETHER. The setting is *the airplane*, and the situation is *on the ground, waiting to take off*. There are probably thousands of variations on this: *at the park with our screaming babies* or *in front of the classroom in his underwear* or *next in line as the gas pump runs dry*. In each case, the setting influences the behavior of the characters the same as a hill influences the wheels of a skateboard. When you introduce characters in charged situations, readers automatically begin making guesses about what will happen next.

3. SHOW ACTIONS THAT RESULT FROM THE SETTING AND SITUATION. Davis's first sentence ends with two actions: a woman makes a smart-aleck remark and another woman chimes in. The first action is a predictable consequence of the setting and situation. The second action does something interesting: it creates a group dynamic. What follows are actions taken by the passengers en masse: buying and eating food. It's almost always useful to put characters together, because a character in solitude has a limited capacity for dramatic action. So think about the pronoun you chose and the characters that exist around it or within it. When one character acts, what other actions follow? Are they acting together, in concert, or individually, against or in spite of one another?

4. CREATE CONSEQUENCE. If characters act without consequence, there's no story. We've all heard anecdotes like that. They peter out, the audience says, "And then what?" and the storyteller just shrugs. Stories like that aren't advancing beyond setting and situation. You

need consequences. The story needs to break what it has built. To get that break started, Davis moves from the group dynamic ("eagerly buying it, even food they would not normally eat") to a singular action ("The steward who is selling the food says . . ."). The story he tells is about another singular action in the midst of a group. And that action had consequences. Try this: If you're working with a group dynamic, focus on one individual within that group and ask, "What happens when this character gets pushed too far? What is required to make her unravel?" Or, if you're working with a singular dynamic (every man and woman for themselves), ask what happens to the group— or what happens if some of those unraveling individuals begin to act collectively. Then what? (Hint: *Lord of the Flies.*)

The goal is to use setting and situation to build the foundations for a story that will grow until the moment it falls in on itself. You're using the forces present in the setting and situation to transform the characters into something new. It's how almost all war stories work (the war zone transforms characters until they behave in ways that would have been impossible at the beginning of the story). It's also the structure used by many crime stories, most famously *Les Misérables.* Hunger drives Jean Valjean to steal bread, prison conditions drive him to escape, the bias against convicts forces him to change his name, the threat of death to an innocent man forces him to reveal his identity, and so on, with French society and Javert applying adding pressure to both Valjean and the French people. The many reversals in the novel are really just the story destroying something that it's built due to the increased pressure applied by the setting and situation. By the end of the novel, of course, almost everything has been destroyed.

Davis and Victor Hugo are doing the same thing. One wrote an epic novel, and the other has written a paragraph-long story, but both use setting and situation to push their characters into action.

HOW TO

CREATE

COMPELLING

CHARACTERS

THE REGIONAL OFFICE IS UNDER ATTACK! *Manuel Gonzales*

The problem with having a mechanical arm nearly impervious and super fast and super strong, comprised of hyperadvanced nanorobot technology and looking no different than her regular arm, was that people always assumed just because Sarah had the ability to crush metal with her armored grip that, when faced with a situation not to her liking, her first reaction would be to crush something with her mechanical fist.

Or if crushing weren't possible, smashing.

The elevator control panel, for instance. People seemed to always be waiting for that moment when, impatient with the often glitchy elevator, she would throw her fist into the elevator control panel, or the glass wall of her office, or through one of the interns.

A number of people seemed to be waiting for her to throw her fist through an intern.

Jacob, perhaps.

Not many people in the office would have blamed her for throwing her fist through intern Jacob.

All of which was only made more frustrating and disappointing when you woke up one day to find all that potential squandered by time and inaction and an inability to risk losing what you loved to gain something more.

Reprinted from Manuel Gonzales, *The Regional Office Is Under Attack!* (New York: Riverhead, 2016), 86.

CREATE CHARACTERS WITH A SINGLE, DEFINITIVE TRAIT

If you want to insult a book, claim that it engages in caricature, not characterization. Caricatures are cartoonish exaggerations, usually of a single trait (a nose, ears, teeth), whereas *characters* are lifelike and complex. In high school literature classes, we're taught that main characters should be round, not flat. They shouldn't be reduced to one trait; characters that are meant to represent real people in all their dimensions shouldn't be flattened into caricature.

I'm not arguing with this logic. Much has been written about Mark Twain's classic *The Adventures of Huckleberry Finn*, which is famous for its sympathetic portrayal of Tom, the escaped slave, but which also frequently portrays him with the racist caricatures of the day. Shylock from William Shakespeare's *The Merchant of Venice* is another character reduced, at times, to traits that are anti-Semitic caricatures. We rightly abhor such descriptions today.

And yet caricature can be a powerful and essential (and lifelike, realistic) tool for creating characters. In fact, it's a natural part of how we interact with and remember people in the real world. For example, what physical trait do you associate with Abraham Lincoln? I'll bet it's his height, his beard, or his stovepipe hat. Or, when you're telling someone about your friend whom they've only briefly met and they say, "Which one is that again?"—what do you say? It's probably some version of "You know, the tall/short/fat/funny one with the red hair/big nose/glasses/crooked ear." I do this all the time with my kids. I have five siblings, and when I tell stories about them to my kids, they often say, "Which one is that again?" I have one-phrase answers for each sibling. We reduce people to single traits and characteristics all the time, out of necessity and compulsion.

Great works of fiction do the same thing. In "The Man I Killed" from Tim O'Brien's *The Things They Carried*, the narrator keeps seeing a dead Vietnamese man's wrist and the hole where his eye had been. At times, the rest of the body disappears completely, with the wrist and the hole standing in for the entire man. This strategy verges on metonymy—the literary device in which one part of a thing refers to the whole (like the term *suits* for *businessmen*). In a way, caricatures do the same thing. One trait is singled out and expanded until it becomes the central focus. Sometimes, the other traits become completely hidden. The Russian writer Nikolai Gogol, for example, wrote a story, "The Nose," about a man whose nose leaves his face and claims an identity of its own.

Even if your story doesn't go so far as to reduce a character completely to one body part or trait, it's useful to make one trait more noticeable or prominent than the others. This is precisely what Manuel Gonzales does in *The Regional Office Is Under Attack!*

The novel is an example of a style that combines literary and genre elements, building on the work of writers like Donald Barthelme, Aimee Bender, and Angela Carter, who wrote (and write) surreal fairy tales and fables. Gonzales adds the genre elements of a later generation (superheroes, monsters). These aren't straight literary stories with some genre elements sprinkled in. They're true mixtures, producing something new. As a result, it's common to see writing strategies that might feel more appropriate to, say, comic books.

For example, Gonzales's book is about a fighting force composed of highly trained women assassins. One of them, Sarah, has a mechanical arm, a trait that is highlighted on this page. The trait starts out as a kind of caricature element, but Gonzales uses it to create a complex portrayal of the character. The complexity is found in how other characters react to her:

People seemed to always be waiting for that moment when, impatient with the often glitchy elevator, she would throw her first into the elevator control panel.

Now we're learning about the psychology of the characters around her. We also get a sense for the incongruity between the technology of her arm and the lack of technology in the elevator, which tells us something about the nature of the novel's world. We learn the assumptions that people around her make:

> People always assumed just because Sarah had the ability to crush metal with her armored grip that, when faced with a situation not to her liking, her first reaction would be to crush something with her mechanical fist.

Finally, we learn the hopes that people have for her:

> Not many people in the office would have blamed her for throwing her fist through intern Jacob.

By this point, we've learned a wealth of complex information about the character and the world. The mechanical arm was the vehicle that delivered it, and now the arm feels like a piece of her character, not the sum total of it.

Once you've created the defining characteristic, you can play with the way it stands out. Very often, the way we view a trait depends on circumstance. If Sarah found herself in a room full of women with mechanical arms, her own wouldn't stand out anymore. Some other trait would be needed to quickly identify her. The caricature would change—and so would our understanding of the character behind it.

THE EXERCISE

Let's create a character with caricature, using *The Regional Office Is Under Attack!* by Manuel Gonzales as a model:

1. GIVE YOUR CHARACTER A DEFINING TRAIT. It can be something physical like size, hair color, or an odd body part; in Homer's *Odyssey*, the Cyclops, as everyone remembers, has one eye. You can make the trait behavioral: a tic or disorder (as in *The Curious Incident of the Dog in the Night Time*), a pattern of behavior (laughing at the worst moments), or a temperament (rage, kindness). You can also use a piece of clothing or accessory; everyone knows that the Monopoly man has a cane and top hat.

2. MAKE THE TRAIT IMPOSSIBLE TO IGNORE. In *The Regional Office Is Under Attack!*, everyone stares at Sarah's mechanical arm. Why? Because it's unusually powerful. Why would people stare at your character? To answer that question, you may need to revise the trait you've chosen. In Austin, where I live and where you can walk into any restaurant in a tee shirt, I have, more than once, worn a button-down shirt to a party and people have said, "What's the occasion?" The shirt was noticed because of where I wore it. Elsewhere, no one would have paid it any mind. So, think about your setting, the people in it, and the trait. How can you combine elements that cannot coexist peacefully?

3. HOW DO CHARACTERS REACT TO THE TRAIT? Staring is only one possibility. As anyone with children knows, if you carry a very small baby through a store, someone is likely to walk up and admire the baby. If you get into an elevator with someone with strong body odor, people are likely to make faces. How do characters react to the trait you've chosen?

4. WHAT ASSUMPTIONS DO THEY MAKE? What do they infer about your character based on the trait? In Gonzales's novel, the characters assume that Sarah is short-tempered because she is powerful, that she'll crush things because she can.

5. WHAT HOPES AND FEARS DO THEY ATTACH TO THE TRAIT? Again, in *Regional Office*, the characters hope that Sarah will crush something—or someone. The fact that it's an intern named Jacob reveals a lot about the characters and the setting—the mundane tedium of it and the way small annoyances can become outstanding. What do the hopes and fears that your other characters attach to the trait reveal about them?

6. WHAT WOULD MAKE THE TRAIT NOT STAND OUT? We're moving beyond the page at hand, but it's not hard to imagine a scenario in which the mechanical arm is suddenly not so singular. (Minor spoiler alert: a scene like that eventually arrives.) If you can imagine a place or scenario where your chosen trait wouldn't stand out, then it's a great idea to take the character there, if only to explore what effect it has. Most athletes can tell you the moment they jumped from one level to another and realized everyone else was just as talented as them; it's a powerful realization that affects behavior. What would happen to your character in that situation?

The goal is to explore a character's presence—the impact that a character has on others—by focusing on one trait. When you pay attention to that trait, training your eye on it and around it, you begin to learn the presence it has in the world, how people react to it, and how the character with the trait responds to them. The trait becomes an entry to the complex character behind it.

HALF-RESURRECTION BLUES
Daniel José Older

The old floorboards creak under my boots. Every step feels like a chore. All I want is for that buzzing to cease and that creepy little panting laughter to never trouble me again. I can't even tell you why it's so disturbing. Some otherworldly ngk magic, surely, that cuts right to the core of a man; my very soul is irritated.

It gets worse when I round the corner. The big old room, gray in the late-afternoon shadows, is completely empty except for a tiny figure in the corner. I don't want to get any closer, but I know I have to if I'm going to end this plague of hideousness. The buzzing, the grunting, the chuckle—it's all coming from this sinister little thing, this ngk. It only reaches up to just above my ankle. Pale, greenish skin stretches in wrinkly folds across its bony little body. That face—an alarming grin reaches from one side of its head to the other. The frail lips are parted slightly, and its wormy tongue reaches out between tiny, uneven teeth. And, perhaps most unnerving of all, the ngk is riding what appears to be an exercise bike of some kind. It just cycles and cycles and cycles and pants and chuckles and grunts, not even registering that a tall half-dead Puerto Rican has entered the room.

Reprinted from Daniel José Older, *Half-Resurrection Blues* (New York: Roc, 2015), 27.

MAKE YOUR CHARACTERS INTO SOMETHING NEW

THE STRATEGY

There's an old idea that goes like this: all stories are basically the same. If you break them down into their essential parts (whatever you determine those to be), you get a handful of basic outlines. Some version of this idea pops up on Facebook at least once a year, usually accompanied by a chart resembling an EKG that claims to reveal how every novel in history follows one of a handful of structures. You've almost certainly heard of some of these outlines and structures: stranger comes to town, man goes on a trip, man versus self, man versus man, man versus nature, man versus society, the hero's journey, man blows up Death Star. One of my high school English teachers liked to say, "Nothing new has been written since Shakespeare."

The saying is inarguably true. People have been telling love stories, ghost stories, quest stories, and revenge stories for as long as stories have been told. And yet this isn't very useful to writers. In fact, it can be discouraging. After all, what fun is there in telling a story that has already been told a million times? It's not helpful to readers, either, and can seem downright false. When we read a good novel, we don't think, "Hey, this is just like *Hamlet*." Even if the similarities are striking, a good writer can make us forget them. To learn how this works, it's useful to look at genre fiction, where these outlines are called conventions. Crime fiction returns to the same elements over and over, as does science fiction/fantasy and westerns and so on. That continuity between stories is the appeal of genre fiction. A crime novel by a famous literary novelist like Denis Johnson or Thomas Pynchon may have some weird touches but it's a crime novel nonetheless.

One of my favorite genre writers is Joe Lansdale, whose *Hap and Leonard* series tells the adventures of a crime-fighting duo. (You may have seen the television adaption of the series on *Showtime*.) It's detective fiction, which means the stories all follow the same basic structure, but we don't care because they're so well done. Why? In large part, it's because the series is set in East Texas and Hap is a white draft dodger and Leonard is a gay black Vietnam War veteran—and both are martial arts masters. The pleasure in the novels is how the conventions of the plot create the space to build wonderful, new characters. Their friendship and sense of humor have appealed to readers for more than a dozen volumes. (You can read more on Lansdale's techniques in the How to Write Scenes section. See "Give Your Characters Space to Be Themselves," page 91.)

Something similar is going on in Daniel José Older's novel (and first in a series) *Half-Resurrection Blues*. Like Lansdale's series, this book contains a character you've probably never seen before: a monster called an ngk. It's suitably monstrous with its "pale, greenish skin" and "wormy tongue" that "reaches out between tiny, uneven teeth." But what makes the monster *new* is the fact that it's riding an exercise bike. Instead of piling gruesome detail upon gruesome detail, Older has added something totally unexpected. A reader can't help but stop and pay attention.

This is particularly useful for villains. A lot of the great ones have been written in a similar way. In *Star Wars: A New Hope*, we're introduced to Darth Vader in a menacing suit, but one of his early scenes puts him at what is essentially an Empire board meeting. A guy makes a snide comment about the Force ("your sad devotion to that ancient religion"), and then Vader has one of his best lines and moments, telling the guy, "I find your lack of faith disturbing" while using the Force to choke him.

J. K. Rowling did something similar with her greatest villain—not, in my opinion, He-Who-Must-Not-Be-Named, but Professor Snape. Here's our first view of him: "greasy black hair, a hooked nose, and sallow skin." A character says, "He knows an awful lot about the Dark Arts, Snape." Then, our next view of him is in a classroom, waxing eloquent about "the beauty of the softly simmering cauldron with its shimmering fumes" and calling the students "dunderheads." Snape, we begin to realize, is definitely a nerd and kind of a dork.

And, of course, perhaps the greatest villain in literature, the witch from *The Wizard of Oz*, starts out the film on a bike, just like Older's ngk. In all of these cases, it's the juxtaposition of unexpected things that creates the sense of newness: scary-looking guy at meeting room table, scary-looking guy geeking out on potions, scary-looking woman pedaling a bicycle with a basket, and monster on a stationary bike.

Once a character feels original, we'll follow it closely through the usual conventions of a genre. For example, we later learn that the ngk is one of a horde that is, according to a "very old Welsh text," summoned to bring about an end to the world as we know it. Apocalyptic monsters are hardly something new. But because we encountered the ngk riding an exercise bike, the revelation of this formulaic role seems more interesting. It's difficult to predict what will happen next to characters we've never encountered before.

THE EXERCISE

Let's create new, unexpected characters, using *Half-Resurrection Blues* by Daniel José Older as a guide.

1. IDENTIFY THE TYPE OF CHARACTER. It's no secret that characters fall into types: heroes/villains, protagonists/antagonists, detectives/criminals, butt-kickers/butt-kickees, and lovers/love interests. Think about the role your character plays. Is she the one going on a trip? The stranger coming to town? For just a moment, think about your story in terms of those outlines we're all familiar with. Which one are you writing?

2. DESCRIBE THE CHARACTER AS IT'S USUALLY WRITTEN. If you're not sure, here's an easy way to figure it out: Google your character's role in the story (detective, doctor, swordfighter, dragon master, etc.) and search Images. The results will probably show a pretty clear pattern. Your character needs to move beyond these patterns, but first, understand what they are. Make a list of the traits that readers might expect from your character.

3. JUXTAPOSE WHAT IS EXPECTED WITH SOMETHING THAT ISN'T. A caveat: avoid predictable juxtapositions, which are often based on the hoariest character clichés. Making a young female character pretty *and* fierce isn't surprising. It's subverting very old character tropes in a way that's been done about a hundred times before. When you start building a character with adjectives, you often get in trouble. They're too general. Instead, work with physical things. Think practically. If your character needs a car, don't give him a yellow Plymouth Barracuda. Instead, force him to drive a Fiat. Better yet—make him *love* his Fiat.

4. FORCE YOUR CHARACTERS INTO A GROUP OF CHARACTERS JUST LIKE THEM. Older does this later in the book. A bunch of ngks get together, and it's not nice. They swarm like, well, anything that swarms. They're indistinguishable from one another. But the opposite can also be true. When characters are put into a group or situation with other similar characters, they might begin to differentiate themselves from each other. The way characters respond to seeing others like themselves can be pretty revealing.

The goal is to create characters that deviate from the norm—whatever that is—so that even familiar stories seem fresh and new. This requires imagination and work, but the rewards are rich, for readers, of course, but also for writers. There's not much that's more magical than seeing a character click together in an unexpected way. You can feel it deep in your subconscious, and soon new ideas come streaming out onto the page.

"MY VIEWS ON THE DARKNESS"

Ben Marcus

To me it's strikingly obvious that we should seek to be supported by matter on all sides, a suit of earth, as Frehlan put it, whether in person-sized cavities or elsewhere. Altitude, even as a concept, has failed. Evolution teaches in the negative, but we are terrible students of the future.

—*Is it the Anchorites you side with?*
—Who said that if you want to watch someone die, befriend an Anchorite? There's a narcissism to people who flee to the mountains, and I'm not just singling out my father. The flight of the Anchorites is self-centered and historically minded—in the worst way—and to me they are like characters auditioning for a novel. Pick me, pick me! They are begging to be noticed and they cry when wounded. The preening quality of their isolation has no appeal to me. They have a fondness for exposure, and we might as well watch them decay before our eyes. But my opinion on this is merely personal. I care about results. In terms of efficacy, which is what matters, Anchorites die. Six of them will die during this conversation.

—*Is that your final measurement for people, whether or not they die?*
—That measurement predates me, and it will outlast me, too. I'd be curious to learn of a more revealing criterion.

—*You've given up many things in pursuit of the cave: your family, your home, your job.*
—I'll have those things again. They might not take the same shape or form, it might not be the same family, home, or job, but those things will return to me even stronger because of my survival work.

—*But do you miss your actual family?*
—I feel relief. Relief and gratitude.

Reprinted from Ben Marcus, "My Views on the Darkness," *Leaving the Sea* (New York: Vintage, 2014): 122.

DEFINE YOUR CHARACTER'S EMOTIONAL RESPONSE TO CONFLICT

THE STRATEGY

Perhaps no writer has more willingly donned the mantle of "experimental writer" than Ben Marcus. The stories in his first book, *The Age of Wire and String*, read like entries from an instruction manual for human relationships written by a bot programmed by a sadist. Many of the sentences resist understanding in a single read. The stories are mostly one paragraph long, with titles like "Snoring, Accidental Speech" and "Sky Destroys Dog" and "Died." I first encountered this book in grad school, where my classmates either loved it with the intensity that some people have for the Tom Waits songs that never get played on the radio, or they threw it across the room in frustration. The fans tended to believe that Marcus, like other "experimental" writers, was breaking conventions to create something new. His detractors claimed that the stories were intellectual exercises lacking in human drama. As someone who hadn't read much experimental writing, I couldn't make heads or tails of the book. But these days, when I read his most recent stories in the *New Yorker*, I'm struck by how even his least conventional writing contains a clear emotional charge and well-defined characters. "My Views on the Darkness" is a perfect example of this.

It's clear from a glance that "My Views on the Darkness" is working in a nonstandard form: an interview during an apocalyptic crisis with a man who's chosen to bury himself for safety. There is much that is unclear: the nature of the apocalypse, who the Anchorites are, who the interviewer is, and how exactly the man is burying himself. But the story gives absolute clarity to the man being interviewed, and on this page, he becomes sharply defined.

First, we're shown his attitude toward a group with whom he disagrees, the Anchorites. His answer about them begins with a rant:

> They are begging to be noticed and they cry when wounded. The preening quality of their isolation has no appeal to me. They have a fondness for exposure, and we might as well watch them decay before our eyes.

What do we learn from this rant? The man is angry, and his anger is personal ("I'm not just singling out my father"). The stakes are high, as the references to death make clear. With such high, personal stakes, the man feels the need to cloak his anger. In real life, people do this with passive-aggressiveness, too-kindness, sullenness, fake levity, practiced scorn or nonchalance, and many other disguises. This man uses pomposity, evidenced by his pseudo-academic euphemisms ("person-sized cavities") and rhetoric ("as Frehlan put it").

But he does more than rant. At the end of his answer to the question, *Is it the Anchorites you side with?*, he says, "I care about results. In terms of efficacy, which is what matters, Anchorites die. Six of them will die during this conversation." This is cold. He's no longer ranting. Instead, he's insulating himself with rationalism. As anyone prone to rants knows, you eventually wear yourself out, and when the fire dies out, you're left with a brittle shell that is easily cracked. The man knows this, and so he protects himself with a reasoning that seems, to him, to be the opposite of emotion.

And yet, that is not his only reaction to the events unfolding around him. When asked about the things he's lost (*your family, your home, your job*), he says, "I'll have those things again. They might not take the same shape or form, it might not be the same family, home, or job, but those things will return to me even stronger because of my survival work." The answer is a mixture of hope and honest awareness of what he's lost.

Of course, he immediately distances himself from this honest emotion when asked if he misses his family: "I feel relief. Relief and gratitude."

This is more posturing. He has lowered his guard and now must raise it again.

There is so much emotion and complex psychology on the page that it's possible to forget just how weird it is, that many readers would take one look at it and close the book. When they do, they miss seeing how even the most experimental fiction contains the same elements as traditionally written stories. Human characters, if well developed, will behave in complicated, compelling ways, no matter the fictional structure they're dropped into.

THE EXERCISE

Let's define character with emotion and attitude, using "My Views on the Darkness" by Ben Marcus a guide.

1. SKETCH THE OUTLINES OF THE CONFLICT. Marcus's story uses the genre of apocalypse. People on earth are dying in seemingly large numbers. Not much else is revealed—and we don't need much else. People are dying, and the living are searching for ways to survive. That's the conflict. So, begin by stating your story's own conflict in a sentence or two: _____ is happening, and this causes _____ to happen. This structure works for intimate conflicts as well as apocalyptic ones:

   - X had an affair, so Y _____.
   - X got sick, so Y _____.
   - X owed me money, so I _____.
   - X fell in love with Y, and Y _____.
   - X did ___, and so her best friend Y _____.

2. IDENTIFY YOUR CHARACTER'S APPROACH TO THE CONFLICT. It's important to define conflict. X had an affair is not a conflict. X had an affair, and so Y (had an affair, stalked the lover, brought home a stray dog, bought a Corvette) is a conflict. The story develops out of what happens next. In Marcus's story, people are dying, some people called the Anchorites are responding in a particular way, but the narrator is doing something different: burying himself alive. How does your character respond to the conflict?

3. LET THE CHARACTER JUSTIFY HIS ACTIONS. Part of the brilliance of Marcus's story is that its unusual form reinforces traditional story elements. Someone asks the narrator, why are you doing this? It's a great question to ask your character. The answer will be revealing. The key is to force the character to keep talking. Don't rely on a single emotional state. Most of us are quite savvy when protecting ourselves from things that hurt us. What does your character sound like when angry? When blaming someone else? When distancing himself from the conflict? What sort of language or attitude does the character cloak his arguments in?

4. GIVE THE CHARACTER A CHANCE TO DROP HIS GUARD. What does it sound like when the character is being honest with himself? When he's not on the defense? Certain moments can create this opportunity. For example, wear the character out through a fight or by making him walk for help after running out of gas. When the character doesn't have the energy for resistance, what gets said?

5. RAISE THE GUARD AGAIN. Such moments of honesty are dangerous to our sense of self. For many of us, if all our enemies disappeared, our sense of identity would vanish as well—and then we'd have to figure out who we *really* are. That's a difficult question to answer, and so we tend to walk around with our defenses up most of the time. So, find out why being honest is a danger to your character. Once you understand that danger, you'll know why he raises his guard again—and also how the writer must continue to ratchet up the conflict that has caused him to raise that guard.

The goal is to discover your characters through what they're *opposed* to, what they must defend themselves against. The rationale they use can tell you a lot about their personality and what they view as most dangerous, which tells you what the stakes are in the story. But the stakes are only the beginning. By pushing characters to defend their views and actions, by pushing until they become defensive, you learn about their private hopes, fears, and regrets and how they insulate themselves from that mental anguish. In other words, you develop a story's world and its characters.

"PROVING UP" *Karen Russell*

The Sticksels have met every Homestead Act requirement, save one, its final strangeness, what Pa calls "the wink in the bureaucrats' wall": a glass window.

Farther south, on the new rail lines, barbed wire and crystal lamps and precut shingles fire in on the freight trains, but in the Hox River Settlement a leaded pane is as yet an unimaginable good. Almost rarer than the rain. Yet all the Hox settlers have left holes in the walls of their sod houses, squares and ovals where they intend to put their future windows. Some use waxed paper to cover these openings; the Sticksels curtained up with an oiled buffalo skin. The one time I slept at their dugout that hide flapped all night like it was trying to talk to me: *Blah blah blah*.

"I know you don't belong here," I replied—I was sympathetic—"but there isn't any glass for that empty place. There's one Window in this blue-gray ocean of tallgrass, and it's ours."

"Now, Miles," both my parents preach at me continually, in the same tone with which they recite the wishful Bible rules, "you know the Window must benefit every settler out here. We are only its stewards." Pa long ago christened it the Hox River Window and swore it to any claimant in need. (I sometimes think my parents use me to stimulate goodness and to remind themselves of this oath, the same way I untangle my greedy thoughts by talking to the animals, Louma and Nore—because it's easy to catch oneself wanting to hoard all the prairie's violet light on the Hox panes.) He says our own walls cannot wear the Window until we prove up—it's too precious, too fragile. So we keep it hidden in the sod cave like a diamond.

Reprinted from Karen Russell, "Proving Up," *Vampires in the Lemon Grove* (New York: Knopf, 2013), 87.

GENERATE TENSION BY GIVING CHARACTERS UNEQUAL ACCESS TO AN OBJECT OF DESIRE

THE STRATEGY

When I was studying writing as a MFA student, I had the good fortune of taking a class from Tim O'Brien, one of my literary heroes as I mentioned in "How to Turn a Premise into Drama," or the Percival Everett chapter (see page 35). He was the first person I saw break down a passage in the way that I do in this book, explaining how it was put together, sentence by sentence. One of the things he preached in almost every class was the importance of knowing a character's desire. Characters need to want something; the way they pursue that desired thing is almost always the basis of the plot of every story and novel.

What does Gatsby want?

Daisy.

What do Jim and Huck want?

To get free of the place they're from, though they're running from different things, and they have different consequences for getting caught. The degree to which Huck understands this difference drives a lot of the drama in the novel and creates its structure. The risks that Huck faces as a runaway are severe, but they're not death or slavery. It's also easier for him to hide than it is for Jim, which is why Huck is able to leave the raft for chapters at a time while Jim just sits there, waiting. Huck also has more choices available to him. He can choose to help Jim, or not. Jim, however, is tied to Huck whether Jim likes it or not. Once he sets off with Huck, his choice is mostly irreversible. In *The Adventures of Huckleberry Finn*, it's not enough to say that it's a novel about wanting freedom. It's also a novel about the degrees to which characters can pursue that freedom.

The same is true of Karen Russell's story "Proving Up." It's set on the Nebraska prairie during the hard years of the Homestead Act, a world that will be familiar to readers of Willa Cather's novel *O Pioneers!* or Laura Ingalls Wilder's novels. One of the requirements for settlers trying to earn a 160-acre homestead was that they improve the land they had settled, which meant, among several things, owning a window made of glass—a real requirement, not something Russell made up; I actually stopped reading the story in order to look it up, which is a testament to Russell's imaginative eye. Among the talismans, human silkworms, and vampires in *Vampires in the Lemon Grove*, the collection in which this story appears, a window can seem equally fabulous and unreal.

So, the first lesson offered by "Proving Up" and Russell's work in general is to find those elements of a story that strike us (writers, readers) as remarkable.

The second lesson is to how to take the element that is most remarkable and desired and gives some characters more access to it than others. This page offers a clear demonstration of both lessons.

Russell establishes why the object (the window) is desired: it is "the wink in the bureaucrats' wall." The window is a requirement not because it is essential, like crop harvests, but because some lawmaker in Washington D.C. decided that it represented something important.

Next, she makes the window a relative sign of wealth, not a universal one. Homesteaders in other places have access to greater emblems of wealth: "barbed wire and crystal lamps and precut shingles." But in this place, the window means the difference between success (proving up) or failure, and so while the window may be a hill of beans, so to speak, for other homesteaders, it's crucial for the characters in this story.

Next, Russell describes the experience of *not having* the desired object. Waxed paper and oiled buffalo skins make poor substitutes for glass, as we see when the narrator sleeps at another dugout and "the hide flapped all night like it was trying to talk to me."

Russell then builds a philosophy and ethics around the window. Because it is so important, the people who possess it also possess great responsibility. The story revolves around the way that responsibility is born out: the narrator is asked to carry the window to neighbors so that they may temporarily install it in order to fool an inspector and fulfill the requirements of their homesteading claim. But such responsibility is not easily born, which is why the narrator thinks, "There's one window in this blue-gray ocean of tallgrass, and it's ours." It's why his parents need a reminder of their oath to share the windows with neighbors.

Finally, Russell lets the desired thing make requirements of its possessors. They must earn the right to display the window, one version of the "proving up" of the story's title.

Desiring something is only the first step in creating the groundwork for a story. You must also invent restrictions, limitations, rules, and obligations around the object of desire. This framework will often rely upon inequity. For example, watch any romantic comedy. There is almost always a character with no shortage of romantic options—all of the girls or guys want to be with this character—and so he/she doles out advice to the main character, who struggles to find someone to date/marry/love. As a result, love becomes more precious to the one who can't find it than to the one who has it in abundance, which almost certainly directs how the story plays out. Usually the tables will turn: by the end, the tough-luck lover becomes beloved and the much-loved character can't find anyone to commit. The same is true in sports stories, in which the less-talented characters often win out. Imbalance—who has what, and in what quantity—matters.

THE EXERCISE

Let's create inequality and a character's sense of obligation around an object of desire, using "Proving Up" by Karen Russell as a model:

1. IDENTIFY THE OBJECT OF DESIRE. The object is often named in the title: *The Treasure of the Sierra Madre*, *The Lord of the Rings*, *The Goldfinch*. Or the object is implied by the genre: love, vengeance, the solution of a mystery. In most cases, the object is set before a character as a prize, but it's only over time that the object gains personal importance to the character. This is most true in mysteries: someone gives the de-

tective a job, and at some point, that job becomes personal. (Sometimes there's even a line: "Now it's personal!"). So, even if the object seems a bit dry at the start, you're at least giving yourself something to work with, a direction to point your character in.

2. GIVE THE OBJECT RELATIVE IMPORTANCE. Some objects, like money and love, will always have importance, but the amounts may vary. A thousand dollars can seem a fortune or a pittance depending on the situation. Russell uses an external force to accomplish this. The bureaucrat in Washington, D.C., says the object matters, and since the government has the final say in the Homestead Act, that person's decree matters. Is there someone who says what matters in your story? Is there a way to highlight aspects of the situation that make it clear why the object matters?

3. CREATE INEQUITY OF ABUNDANCE OF THE OBJECT. Some people will have the thing, and some won't. Or, some people will have even greater objects ("barbed wire and crystal lamps and precut shingles"). Even if it doesn't really matter in the long run that others have more of the object or even greater wealth, you're beginning to personalize the object to the story and the characters. It's not just love or money but this *particular* love and money.

4. CREATE AN INEQUITY IN THE ABILITY TO PURSUE THE OBJECT. This is the *Huckleberry Finn* example. Huck can pursue freedom with more, well, freedom than Jim. In "Proving Up," the people living closer to the railroad have more ability to acquire wealth and, thus, have easier means to acquire a window than the people living in the isolation of the Hox River settlement. In your story, who finds it easier to pursue the object? Why is it easier for them?

5. CREATE AN ETHICS AROUND THE OBJECT. What does it mean to have the object? In *Star Wars*, there is an entire religion (sort of) around the Force. The same is true of the Ring of Power in *The Lord of the Rings*; in fact, several pivotal scenes are built around disagreements about how and when to use the ring. Ethics almost always play an important role in romance stories: how far will a character go to find love? In your story, what is ethically acceptable in the pursuit of the object? And, once the object is acquired, what ethics determine how one possesses the object? (If you read the rest of "Proving Up," you'll see that not every character subscribes to the same ethical code, which becomes a major plot point.)

6. CREATE A SENSE OF OBLIGATION ASSOCIATED WITH POSSESSING THE OBJECT. This is the logical next step in the issue of ethics. This entire page of "Proving Up" centers on the obligations the narrator's father believes accompany possession of the window. The father has a sense of fairness, of trying to level the playing field. In any story, it's a good idea to examine what characters feel is fair or unfair and then do the opposite of this story's father and *tilt* the field toward unfairness. A great example of this is Stephen Crane's poem "A Man Said to the Universe," in which he famously wrote that the universe feels no sense of obligation to the people in it. His story, "The Open Boat," dramatizes that lack of cosmic obligation: the four men on the lifeboat will live or die without regard to strength, intelligence, or virtue, and the main character mightily resists this realization. In your unfair story, who feels obligated to level the playing field? How can you turn that obligation into action?

7. LET THE OBJECT DEMAND REQUIREMENTS OF ITS POSSESSOR. If your object is viewed as precious, what superstitions or rules have characters created around it? When can it be displayed (as the window can or cannot be displayed)? By making it harder for characters to possess the thing (even when they possess it), you're creating opportunities for drama.

The goal is to create plot, suspense, and stakes by creating an imbalance around an object of desire. It's basic human nature to grapple with that imbalance, so characters will seek to understand and accept it, until a philosophy and ethics develops around the object. Your job as a writer is to create plot complications that challenge those philosophical and ethical codes. In this story, you'd better believe that the narrator's parents tell him that they are the window's stewards, Russell is going to make it exceedingly difficult to carry out that stewardship. A story, then, defines its characters' sense of right and wrong and then introduces a plot that makes it a lot easier for them to do wrong than right.

HOW TO

WRITE

SCENES

HONKY TONK SAMURAI

Joe R. Lansdale

I let the fart ease out, I did it quietly, not wanting to frighten the dog. I left the fart where I had laid it like a rotten egg and moved away from the smell.

"Who the hell are you?" the man said to Leonard.

"I'm the man fixing to put that leash on your neck and kick you all over this goddamn yard like a soccer ball."

"You're trespassing," the man said.

"That's just where I start," Leonard said. "How about I put one of your goddamn eyes out?"

Appeared like a start to a fairly ordinary day for us.

I stayed at the curb while Leonard stood in the yard talking. I was waiting patiently, ready to stop Leonard from the death blow, which I was fairly certain might be coming.

"Take two of you to do it?" said the man, checking us both out. He was a pretty big guy, about Leonard's height, wider than both of us, bigger belly than us put together. He had the air of someone who had once run with a football and thought that gave him an edge for life. Maybe he should get with his neighbor who went to the gym, get some diet and exercise tips. Still, he was big enough to cause problems, even if it was just falling on you.

"No," Leonard said. "Just one of us."

I said, "And you can choose which one. Just for the record, I can hit harder. But I was thinking I'd rather not get all worked up. The heat, you know."

"He can't hit harder," Leonard said. "Faster, but I actually hit a little harder."

"He's a braggart," I said. "We both know I can hit harder, and I'm faster, too."

"You don't neither one of you look so tough to me," he said.

"Why don't you show us how tough you are?" Leonard said. "You do pretty good with a defenseless dog wants to please you, but we don't want to please you. Right, Hap?"

"Right," I said.

Reprinted from Joe R. Lansdale, *Honky Tonk Samurai* (New York: Mulholland Books, 2016), 6.

GIVE YOUR CHARACTERS
SPACE TO BE THEMSELVES

The film *The Sixth Sense* was released when I was a freshman in college. The end of the film left me so stunned that I spent the rest of the evening talking it over with my friends, piecing together the clues that I'd missed. Eventually, I went home. My parents rented the film, and I sat with them, watching their faces, waiting to see their jaws drop. About fifteen minutes into the movie, we paused it to make popcorn, and I asked, "Well? What do you think?"

My dad shrugged. "Bruce Willis is dead."

There are many ways to group the people on earth, and one of them is almost certainly into Those Who Saw the End Coming in *The Sixth Sense* and Those Who Didn't. It might be tempting to draw conclusions about us based on these groups. Since I'm blind to context clues, I probably love genre fiction, especially mysteries, right? And since my dad can't be surprised, he probably avoids mysteries, right?

This makes sense, but it's completely wrong. We both like mysteries. Two of the books on my parents' bookcase during my childhood were the collected Sherlock Holmes and the collected Father Brown mysteries. As a family, we watched the PBS mystery series *Cadfael*, about a twelfth-century mystery-solving Welsh Benedictine monk. All three of these series follow the same basic episode/story arc: discovery of crime, investigation, a moment where all seems lost, and then victory for the detectives. Even if you can't foresee the end (or if the author/director won't let you), if you watch or read enough of these, the plots begin to feel familiar and predictable. Yet this is like saying the appeal of fried chicken and hot tubs is predictable. Sure, but let's have that discussion while I enjoy some chicken in a Jacuzzi.

In the chapter on Daniel José Older's book ("Make Your Characters into Something New"), I talked about how the greatness of "predictable" stories often comes from the originality of the characters. The plots of detective novels, for example, may be the same, but the detectives aren't. For example, Joe R. Lansdale's Hap and Leonard series takes place in East Texas, with a white draft dodger and a gay black Vietnam veteran who are both martial arts experts. You'll read nothing else like them. But once you've created interesting characters, then what? The MFA-workshop answer is to gradually reveal their complexity, which is a fine answer for some books, though it's not really what mystery series do. Instead, the stories and novels are built around scenes that continually invent new ways for characters to be their old selves. In fact, many of the best scenes in detective novels have nothing to do with solving a crime or fighting bad guys. Instead, they're character studies in which characters do nothing but talk. It's a long tradition that goes back to Raymond Chandler's brisk, witty, risqué dialogue.

In this page from Lansdale's book, we've just been reintroduced to Hap and Leonard. They're surveilling a house as part of a new job as private investigators. Nothing's happening, it's the last day of the job, and so, basically, they're just sitting there, being themselves. Then something happens: "A man had a dog on a leash and the dog was cowered on its belly and the man was kicking it." This is where our page picks up.

Hap farts (because he's Hap). Leonard threatens a guy (because he's Leonard). As Hap says, "Appeared like a start to a fairly ordinary day for us."

The series of events that follow is not really the point. Leonard pummels the man. The police arrive. One of the officers knows Hap and Leonard, and so things turn out okay, though this does turn out to be the start of a larger mystery. On a plot level, the book does exactly what it must. The reason that it's the twelfth book in the series is because of the characters: their friendship and banter. It's no surprise, then, that we get that in spades:

"Just for the record, I can hit harder. But I was thinking I'd rather not get all worked up. The heat, you know."

"He can't hit harder," Leonard said. "Faster, but I actually hit a little harder."

"He's a braggart," I said. "We both know I can hit harder, and I'm faster, too."

Even in the prelude to a fight, they're giving each other crap—and that is the point. In page after page of the novel, Hap is either having fun with Leonard or talking about Leonard, and Leonard is doing the same. The scene and circumstance doesn't matter. Here are just the first few in the novel: fight with the dog abuser, talking with the police, taking the dog to Hap's house, talking with the official Dame in Distress who hires them for a job, and pretending to be rich car buyers as they talk to a transgender man who runs a prostitution ring. In all of them, Hap plays it cool, Leonard gets wound up, and both make wisecracks. The plot chugs along, of course, and plenty happens (like, a battle with an entire motorcycle gang deep in the East Texas Piney Woods), but the appeal is the character back-and-forth, the chance to see Hap and Leonard act like themselves.

Like most novels, this one comes with blurbs, and on the front cover is one from Dean Koontz: "Reading Joe Lansdale is like listening to a favorite uncle who just happens to be a fabulous storyteller." The reason that uncle's your favorite is because of his personality and the way he talks. He's a pleasure to be in a room with. A good mystery novel is the same way: the plot is just an excuse to sit in a room with the characters.

THE EXERCISE

Let's sit in a room with your characters, using *Honky Tonk Samurai* by Joe Lansdale as a model:

1. DISTILL YOUR CHARACTER'S PERSONALITY TO ONE OR TWO TRAITS. Some writers may resist this; their characters are too complex to be distilled to a few words. And yet we do this all the time in real life. We say, "That so-and-so is such a ____." People who subscribe to

astrology will say, "He's such a Virgo." Try filling in the blank. What sort of temperament or personality does your character have?

2. IDENTIFY HOW YOUR CHARACTER RESPONDS TO CONFLICT. In *Honky Tonk Samurai*, Hap gets friendly and laid-back. Leonard gets aggressive. Some people laugh nervously. Others will actually seem to change personality. Think about how your friends and family respond to stress. Do they get snippy? Become weirdly Zenlike? Get the burps? Go into a shell? Take charge? Figure out what your character does.

3. IF POSSIBLE, PAIR YOUR CHARACTER WITH ANOTHER CHARACTER WITH A DIFFERENT PERSONALITY AND RESPONSE TO CONFLICT. There's a reason that buddy comedies are so popular and why relationships are so memorable in fiction (*The Odd Couple*, *Laverne and Shirley*, Holmes and Watson, Hap and Leonard). We love watching unlike characters play against each other. Hap's laid-back demeanor stands out because he's accompanied by a guy who prefers action to talk.

4. CREATE SITUATIONS FOR THESE TRAITS AND APPROACHES TO CONFLICT TO ENTER. This will seem natural to anyone with a difficult family member or friend, the sort of person who keeps everyone else on pins and needles. When someone has a usual response to a situation, everyone else feels the suspense: When will Uncle Bill go off? Even if he keeps his act together, everyone knows it's just a matter of time before he loses it. Treat your characters the same way. Every situation can become an opportunity for the character to do what he or she always does. Focus on the moments before or after a dramatic scene. In this case, Lansdale shows us Hap and Leonard before they beat up a guy. After they're done, he lets them talk about what just happened. While the fight drives the story forward, it's the banter that keeps us reading. If you're still early in the stage of a story or novel, make a list of pivotal scenes. As you write, use the moments immediately before and after those scenes to let your character yak it up.

5. FIND A TRIGGER IN A SCENE. You're searching for the exact moment when your characters quit yakking (or whatever it is they do when they're not caught up in high drama) and starting kicking butt (whatever that might mean in your story). Because you've already defined their traits in response to conflict (as discussed in this exercise and also "Define Your Character's Emotional Response to Conflict,"

you can now put those traits into action without explaining to the reader what they are.

6. CREATE RESISTANCE TO THE CHARACTER'S USUAL RESPONSE. With your awkward Uncle Bill, there's usually a reason everyone hopes he doesn't explode, some reason it'd be better if he didn't. The same is often true for Hap and Leonard. It would be better if Leonard didn't hit someone or better if Hap *did* fight. It's also the case that Hap is a little more self-aware than Leonard. Hap will often sense the possible consequences in a moment and how he ought to respond; Leonard is more rash. As a result, many scenes play out with Hap trying to keep Leonard calm or Leonard rushing in and forcing Hap to do something he doesn't want. So, the resistance to your character's usual response can be another character or heightened stakes that force a character's hand.

The goal is to create a typical behavior for your character and a trigger in every scene that sets off that behavior. The thrill for readers is anticipating the moment when a character does exactly what we know he or she will do. This is overly simplified, but you can think of scenes as having two jobs: driving the plot forward and building character/setting. If you've just written a scene in which the plot jumped forward in an exciting way, use the next scene to do something different. The reader is hooked and wanting to know what will happen, so slow down and show the characters being themselves. This contradicts, I suppose, my advice in the setting chapters to avoid descriptions of things (setting, characters) for their own sakes, to use those elements to drive a story forward. To paraphrase Walt Whitman, "Do I contradict myself? Very well, then I contradict myself. Fiction is large and contains multitudes." Remember what drew you to a story in the first place. When you get the chance, particularly after hooking the reader, take a moment to revel in whatever element you love. If you write it well, the readers will likely love it, too.

"ENCOUNTERS WITH UNEXPECTED ANIMALS" *Bret Anthony Johnston*

Lambright couldn't figure what she saw in his son. Until the girl started visiting, Robbie had superhero posters on his walls and a fleet of model airplanes suspended from the ceiling with fishing wire. Lambright had actually long been skeptical of the boy's room, worrying it looked too childish, worrying it confirmed what might be called "softness" of character. But now the walls were stripped and all that remained of the fighter fleet was the fishing-wire stubble on the ceiling.

Two weeks ago, one of his wife's necklaces disappeared. Last week, a bottle of her nerve pills. Then, over the weekend, he'd caught Robbie and the girl with a flask of whiskey in the backyard. She'd come to supper tonight to make amends.

Traffic was light. When he stopped at the intersection of Airline and Saratoga, the only headlights he saw were far off, like buoys in the bay. The turn signal dinged. He debated, then clicked it off. He accelerated straight across Saratoga.

"We were supposed to turn—"

"Scenic route," he said. "We'll visit a little."

But they didn't. There was only the low hum of the tires on the road, the noise of the truck pushing against the wind. Lambright hadn't contributed anything to the animal discussion earlier, but now he considered mentioning what he'd read a while back, how bald eagle nests are often girded with cat collars, strung with the little bells and tags of lost pets. He stayed quiet, though. They were out near the horse stables now. The air smelled of alfalfa and manure. The streetlights had fallen away.

The girl said, "I didn't know you could get to Kings Crossing like this."

They crossed the narrow bridge over Oso Creek, then came into a clearing, a swath of clay and patchy brush, gnarled mesquite trees.

He pulled onto the road's shoulder. Cliché pinged against the truck's chassis. He doused his headlights, and the scrub around them silvered, turned to moonscape. They were outside the city limits, miles from where the girl lived. He killed the engine.

"I know you have doubts about me. I know I'm not—"

"Cut him loose," Lambright said.

Bret Anthony Johnston, excerpt from "Encounters with Unexpected Animals" from *The Best American Short Stories 2013*. Originally in *Esquire* (March 2, 2012). Copyright © 2012 by Bret Anthony Johnston. Reprinted with the permission of the author.

USE REPETITION TO INCREASE TENSION TO AN UNSUSTAINABLE LEVEL

THE STRATEGY

I have two kids, and they have an intuitive sense for how to be annoyingly funny. My five-year-old, for example, will say, "I'm going to poop on your face," in his five-year-old voice, which is sort of cute and funny (as long as he's saying it to me and not Grandma). After all, he understands the same thing that Friedrich Nietzsche claimed in "On Truth and Lies in a Nonmoral Sense": we organize language so that good/evil, truth/lies, and beauty/ugliness are on different ends of a spectrum. As a result, if you say, "Up is down," we know it's a lie because those words occupy different parts of the spectrum, as do "poop" and "face." Smashing these categories is funny and often necessary in order to say anything interesting (but also, sometimes, to lie). So, I try not to discourage my kids too much in their linguistic play. I get it. I'm a writer. I break rules.

And yet my kids aren't satisfied with saying, "I'm going to poop on your face," only once. They watch my reaction and say it again. And again. And again. With variations involving other pieces of my anatomy or my wife's anatomy that meet most people's definition of obscenity. So, I tell them to stop, again and again, until I lose my mind and pretend to call the bouncy house emporium and cancel their birthday party.

As writers, we should follow my kids' lead. To create tension, do the same thing over and over. This is what Bret Anthony Johnston does in his story, "Encounters with Unexpected Animals."

In the story, a man offers to drive his son's girlfriend home after dinner. He thinks she's a bad influence on his son and intends to break them up. In terms of plot, the story is pretty simple: the man gets fed up and drives the girlfriend into the middle of nowhere, where he intends to tell her what's what—and then something bad happens. In terms of structure, though, Johnston uses my kids' strategy over and over.

The first time occurs when the story is explaining what has led to the dad driving the girlfriend home:

> Two weeks ago, one of his wife's necklaces disappeared. Last week, a bottle of her nerve pills. Then, over the weekend, he'd caught Robbie and the girl with a flask of whiskey in the backyard.

When creating this list of infractions, it might have been tempting to make each one worse than the last, but that's not what happens. Drinking whiskey isn't more severe than taking pills; in a way, it might even be more socially acceptable. Instead, the whiskey is the proverbial straw that broke the camel's back: the father's patience has been exhausted and he's forced to act. In this case, the repetition creates tension until conflict erupts.

The same strategy is used again on this page:

- The father drives through the intersection where he should have turned.
- He drives into the country, past horse stables.
- He drives over a narrow bridge in the middle of nowhere.
- Then he parks.

In each reference to the father's driving, the basic action is the same. Instead of driving the girl home, he drives her somewhere quiet and secluded. Each reference takes them farther into the country, so there is a progression, but that progression is less important than his intention. If he'd stopped outside the horse stables, where the "streetlights had fallen away," the scene would still be creepy; but, it would be less effective because it's only the second reference. There's a reason parents count to three when waiting for their children to do what they're asked. The extra beat allows tension to increase.

The repetition also allows Johnston to flesh out the scene. Imagine if, instead of repeating the driving passages, he'd written this: "He debated, then clicked it off. He accelerated straight across Saratoga and drove out of town, into the dark. Finally, he pulled over onto the shoulder." The situation is still the same, but a lot has been lost: the dialogue with the girl, the sound of the tires on the road and smell of the alfalfa, and the memory of the conversation about animals and the fact about cats' collars in eagles' nests. Spacing out the repetition creates room for resistance to what is happening ("We were supposed to turn—") and internal details that reveal mindset ("now he considered mentioning what he'd read . . .").

Doing the same thing over and over again can force characters to act but also draw out the moment before that action occurs—which is, in a way, the very definition of structure.

THE EXERCISE

Let's use repetition to create tension and suspense, using "Encounters with Unexpected Animals" by Bret Anthony Johnston as a guide. First, we'll unleash our inner five-year-old and use repetition to create motivation:

1. FIND A DETAIL THAT CREATES SOME EFFECT. This is a good strategy to use in revision. Read through a scene and find some detail that is charged negatively or positively. For example, Johnston could have started with the disappearance of the wife's necklace. That detail alone is enough to upset his character. In your scene, what makes your reader happy, sad, or angry?

2. REPEAT THE DETAIL. The easiest way to do this is to simply repeat it verbatim, the way my son repeats "poop on your face." But we're more advanced than five-year-olds (or so we like to think), and so you can build on that repetition. What variations can you add? The result can be surprising. For example, a character might like receiving flowers, but if flowers are delivered three times in a row in short succession, that pleasure might turn into annoyance. Or, I like carrot cake, but if I eat three slices, my enjoyment is diminished by my stomachache. Conversely, locking your keys in the car is frustrating, but if you do it three times in a row, you might begin to laugh at the situation (or you might try to break the window with your belt buckle). In fiction,

unlike in life, moderation isn't a virtue. What happens when you max out on something, good or bad?

3. MOVE THE CHARACTER TO ACTION. The goal is to move your character out of inaction. So, if I lock my keys in my car or eat too much cake, I'm not likely to continue on as before. Drive your character crazy, whether it's the good kind or not.

Now that the character has decided to act, let's use repetition to create plot. (Plot, of course, is not a Point A or Point B but the space between.)

1. FIND A DECISIVE ACTION. In Johnston's story, it's the father driving out of town instead of to the girl's home. Your action can be anything: whatever seems momentous to your characters. Going on a diet could be an action, as could remodeling a bathroom or taking chemotherapy. Find a moment where your character has decided to act with a goal in mind.

2. CLARIFY THE INTENTION. In other words, make the goal clear. In each repetition, this stays the same. What does your character hope to achieve?

3. REPEAT WITH SLIGHTLY DIFFERENT DETAILS. Johnston uses the basic setting around the father's car: stoplight, horse stables, bridge. In the same way, a character on a diet could not eat cupcakes, fried chicken, and cheese cubes. The basic action is the same, but it looks slightly different.

4. EXPLORE THE AREA AROUND EACH REPETITION. What do people say? How do they act? What do they think? What do they sense or feel? What do they remember or predict? In short, what is the range of human experience that can be revealed with each repetition?

The goal is to create plot by forcing characters to act and to create suspense by delaying the end result of that action. This can happen in each scene or within scenes—the term is flexible and really means, for my purposes, a unit of space and movement in a story, almost interchangeable with the word *passage*. When you think of a story as a collection of scenes or passages, with each one creating plot and suspense, you can begin to see how tension is built and released multiple times over and why repetition is a great tool to do it.

THE FLAMETHROWERS *Rachel Kushner*

One night, motorcycles converged on the corner beyond the café, motors revving, goggled grins exchanged among the cyclists. No one had clued him in.

What was happening?

"A race, pal."

The young people smoking at the outdoor café tables cheered. Someone threw a full bottle of Peroni, which smashed in the paved intersection, leaving a great wet stain that glittered with broken glass.

The drivers all backed out simultaneously and squealed off down the Corso.

Two men crossing the avenue with evening newspapers under their arms and a woman in a black toque carrying packages were all sent diving for the curb. A tram came, and the brakeman had to pull the lever and let the gang of motorbikes pass. Pedestrians and vehicles halted for these renegades, their cycles growling like a convoy of hornets. The atmosphere had changed. The quick looks, the retreats to the secret meeting room, there was none of that. This was an open celebration, and Valera, too, was lifted by the festive spirit. He felt that he was part of it, even as he wasn't sure what they were celebrating.

Twenty minutes later he heard the far-off noise of cycles accelerating in sync. The racers, returning.

The motorbikes came screaming down the Corso, their light beams diffused by fog into iridescent halos, each a perfect miniature of the colored ring that appeared around the moon on rare occasions, an effect of ice crystals in the clouds. Scores of moon rings laced and interlaced. Valera knew they were cycles with riders, but all he saw as glowing rings.

Rachel Kushner, excerpt from *The Flamethrowers*. Copyright © 2014 by Rachel Kushner. Reprinted with the permission of Scribner, a division of Simon & Schuster, Inc. All rights reserved.

WRITE ACTION SEQUENCES WITH MINIMAL CHOREOGRAPHY

THE STRATEGY

When I was in middle school, one of my friends owned a Nintendo, and during sleepovers, we'd stay up for hours playing *Mortal Kombat*. It was a simple game: two fighters in a ring, beating each other up. There was little strategy. Even if you didn't know how to play, you could get lucky by simply pressing the buttons on the game controller as fast as possible. An effective sequence looked like this: down forward B, back back forward, down down up, forward back back back A. On the screen, you'd see this: Shoot Lightning, Flying Thunder God, Teleport through the Ground, and Fatality. As a game experience, it was addictive and exhilarating. But if you to read a novelization of *Mortal Kombat* that consisted of only the fighters' moves, you'd quit before the end of a single page.

When we're talking about scenes, one of first types that people may think about is action scenes. To be successful, they must offer more than the choreography of punch, punch, kick. In fact, any sequences that rely on a dance-step approach will be deadly dull, no matter how high the stakes. Yet this strategy is almost always the default for beginning writers—and even some good ones.

Rachel Kushner's novel *The Flamethrowers* offers a different approach. In this page, a young man, Valera, is living in Milan in 1912, and eavesdropping on some dashing young men who gather in a coffee shop to talk politics and art. In this scene, a motorcycle race breaks out. For a moment, imagine how this scene could have been written: the motorcycles could have gunned their motors, raced down the street, swerved around people and cars and trashcans, and driven up ramps and soared over piles of explosives (if Michael Bay was directing the film). In other words, how tempting it would be to focus on the motorcycles, the sexiest of all vehicles. But that's not what Kushner does. In fact, we barely see the bikes. Here's how the race begins: "The drivers all backed out simultaneously and squealed off down the Corso."

That's it. No wheelies, swerves, or crashes. Instead, Kushner focuses on the action *around* the bikes:

- People "were sent diving for the curb."
- A tram's brakeman has to "pull the lever and let the gang of motorbikes pass."
- "Pedestrians and vehicles halted for these renegades."

Instead of showing the movement of the bikes, Kushner portrays the disruption they cause. The result is a much more engaging scene. This strategy is the same reason why we watch football games from cameras high above the field and not on helmet cams worn by the ball carrier. A wide angle sometimes shows more than a narrow one. This runs counter to the current trend in film, in which fights are filmed through close-up shaky cams, and so it must be said that the suggestion to pan out is probably as much an aesthetic preference as a craft issue. I can't stand those action close-ups. They make me dizzy and confused about basic aspects of the fight, like who's winning. But, of course, those filmmakers are getting millions of dollars to finance their films, so they must be doing something right. That said, I still think Kushner's description of the scene *around* the motorcycles is masterful and something to emulate.

The paragraph closes with this terrific comparison between the bike race and the meetings in the coffee shop:

The quick looks, the retreats to the secret meeting room, there was none of that. This was an open celebration, and Valera, too, was lifted by the festive spirit. He felt that he was part of it, even as he wasn't sure what they were celebrating.

Again, we're not shown the motorcycles. Instead, the general sense of the race is described: it's open and festive rather than closed and hushed.

The energy of the race spreads to the onlookers, which is the real impact and the source of drama. Without the effect of the race on the crowd (and especially on Valera), the riders might as well be zipping around on empty streets.

THE EXERCISE

Let's write an action sequence, using *The Flamethrowers* by Rachel Kushner as a guide.

1. SUMMARIZE THE ACTION. While you don't want the final scene to resemble a transcript of *Mortal Kombat*, you do need to know what happens. It can be involved (numbers of kicks and punches) or general, as it probably was with Kushner (motorcycles ride through the streets, out of sight, and then return). Also, action doesn't only mean fights and chases. If a character walks from one place to another, that's an action sequence. Washing dishes, building a fort, and fishing are also action sequences, as if anything that can descend into a list of actions: cast, reel, cast, reel, etc.

2. FIGURE OUT WHO'S WATCHING. Who will the scene impact? In Kushner's scene, the racing motorcycles directly impact the actions of pedestrians and automobiles. If no one is impacted, consider who observes the action. Think of fan reactions to famous sports moments: when an outfielder leaps for a home-run ball, the reaching fans and diving are as interesting as the player himself. Or, think of Alfred Hitchcock's film *Strangers on a Train*, the camera shot that shows the crowd at a tennis match watching a volley, their heads turning together, back and forth—except for one man, whose head is still. Reactions to action are often more telling than the action itself.

3. SEE WHAT ELSE IS PRESENT. You may ask, what if no one is present except the people involved? In that case, you could describe the impact on inanimate objects in the room or area: plates broken, keys thrown, doors slammed. So, take stock of what is present (people or things) in addition to the people involved in the action sequence.

4. DESCRIBE IN TERMS OF DISRUPTION. Describe the action in terms of the way it disrupts the place where it occurs. To do this, you may

need to set the scene: show how things are *before* the action takes place. For example, if a fight breaks out in an apartment, it'd be useful to know how neat or messy the apartment was before it was trashed. However, some scenes require no setup. For example, in *The Flamethrowers*, Kushner doesn't need to tell us how pedestrians usually cross the street or how a tram usually drives. We know this already through experience. As a result, Kushner can simply tell us that pedestrians "were sent diving for the curb."

5. DESCRIBE IN TERMS OF GENERAL EFFECT ON CROWD AND ON AN INDIVIDUAL. So far, you've focused on disruptions to people and things. Kushner ends her action sequence by describing the *general* effect: "This was an open celebration, and Valera, too, was lifted by the festive spirit." So, try making a statement about the *kind* of sequence we've just witnessed. Start with adjectives: joyous, tragic, angry, fierce, mild. You can also compare the effect of the sequence to the usual state of affairs, as Kushner does, comparing the race to the furtive meetings in the coffee shop. Finally, how are people or a specific individual affected? Are they lifted, as in *The Flamethrowers*? Are they depressed, scared, freaked out, made skittish, or energized?

The goal is to show an action sequence without relying on the blow-by-blow details of the action itself. By describing the impact or effect of the sequence on the surrounding people or setting, the scene can be dramatized and invigorated. Think about it in terms of physics and the transmission of energy. In Kushner's scene, the energy is generated in the café, moves to the motorcycles, and is then transmitted into the crowd, and so it feels natural for the writer's camera to follow that path. When you're writing your own scenes, consider where the energy starts and the path it travels away from that source.

OPEN CITY *Teju Cole*

There had earlier been, it occurred to me, only the most tenuous of connections between us, looks on a street corner by strangers, a gesture of mutual respect based on our being young, black, male; based, in other words, on our being "brothers." These glances were exchanged between black men all over the city every minute of the day, a quick solidarity worked into the weave of each man's mundane pursuits, a nod or smile or quick greeting. It was a little way of saying, I know something of what life is like for you out here. They had passed by me now, and were for some reason reluctant to repeat that fleeting gesture.

We were in the day's last light, and the street was largely in shadow. It was unlikely they would have recognized me again even in strong daylight. Still, I was unnerved. And it was in the middle of that thought that I felt the first blow, on my shoulder. A second, heavier, landed on the small of my back, and my legs gave way like sticks. I fell to the ground. I don't recall if I cried out, or if opening my mouth I was unable to make a sound. They began to kick me all over—shins, back, arms—a quick, preplanned choreography. I shouted, begging them to stop, conscious of a man on the ground being beaten. Then I lost the will to speak, and took the blows in silence. The initial awareness of pain was gone, but now came the anticipation of how much it would hurt later, how bad tomorrow would be, for both my body and my mind. My mind had gone blank except for this lone thought, a thought that made my eyes sting, a prospect more painful, it seemed, than the blows. We find it convenient to describe time as a material, we "waste" time, we "take" our time. As I lay there, time became material in a strange new way: fragmented, torn into incoherent tufts, and at the same time spreading, like something spilled, like a stain.

Teju Cole, excerpt from *Open City*. Copyright © 2011 by Teju Cole. Used by permission of Random House, an imprint and division of Penguin Random House, LLC.

MAKE INTERIORITY THE FOCUS
IN ACTION SCENES

THE STRATEGY

I want to stick with action scenes a little longer. In the last exercise, I wrote, "Action sequences must offer more than the choreography of punch, punch, kick." In *The Flamethrowers*, that *more* is the view of the world around the action—the pool balls scattering from the break rather than the cue ball that sends them rolling. But there is another approach to action scenes, one that is typified by writers like Sheila Heti, Ben Lerner, and Teju Cole, whose novels contain little action and are, instead, about the thoughts and impressions of the narrators. These books are often hailed for their newness, as in this *New York Times* review of Lerner's *10:04*: "Formally "10:04" belongs to an emerging genre, the novel after Sebald, its 19th-century furniture of plot and character dissolved into a series of passages, held together by occasional photographs and a subjectivity that hovers close to (but is never quite identical with) the subjectivity of the writer."

But this isn't quite true. Henry James made a career out of dissecting and analyzing human consciousness (and the subjectivity of the main character, if not the writer), especially in *The Beast in the Jungle* and *The Turn of the Screw*. The difference is that writers like Heti, Lerner, and Cole are writing in a world with a new sense of consciousness. Like James, we experience and see things, think about them, and then, if we're very self-conscious, think about what we thought. But we also post our thoughts on Twitter, and the feedback from social media becomes something new to consider, and that feedback loop shapes our thoughts. As a result, most of us have multiple consciousnesses and identities, and the distinction between our "real" and "digital" selves is often blurry. This will come as no surprise after you've watched someone who is walking and staring at a phone a same time. When they step blithely into a busy street or into a sign, it's clear that the action around us isn't always foremost on our minds.

That focus on interiority, and its interaction with action, is clearly at work in Cole's *Open City*. Even in a scene with a lot of movement, the novel emphasizes what's going on inside the character's head.

In the novel, the narrator spends most of his time walking through New York City. On this page, he encounters two men after having seen them earlier; instead of walking by as they did previously, they mug him. It's a violent scene, and yet the focus is on the narrator's thoughts as much as on the beating he takes.

The scene begins with the narrator thinking about the glances he shared with the men earlier and what such glances mean, the social function they serve. He's buried deep in this thought and barely registers his surroundings (a street "largely in shadow"), thinking *about* the men more than seeing them ("It was unlikely they would have recognized me again even in strong daylight"). Next, he describes his mental state in general: "I was unnerved." When action occurs, it's into this interiority that it intrudes: "it was in the middle of that thought that I felt the first blow, on my shoulder."

Now, we're into the action and given a brief blow-by-blow account, a sequence that is described in straightforward terms. But the narrator's internal life quickly reasserts itself: "The initial awareness of pain was gone, but now came the anticipation of how much it would hurt later." Appropriately for such a self-conscious narrator, the thought of future discomfort is "more painful, it seemed, than the blows." From this point, the narrator's thoughts dominate, moving beyond thoughts about the beating he's taking to a more philosophical discussion of "time as a material." Only a brief mention of the situation ("As I lay there") keeps us grounded in what is happening outside the narrator's head.

You can find this same strategy of focusing on perception and contemplation rather than action in the writing of Henry James. In the opening scene of *The Beast in the Jungle*, for example, the main character encounters a woman that he feels that he remembers, though he isn't sure why.

For pages, he examines her and his memory of her, trying to place her, eventually moving from memory to fantasy:

> He would have liked to invent something, get her to make-believe with him that some passage of a romantic or critical kind *had* originally occurred.

When they finally get the chance to talk, her words ("I met you years and years ago in Rome. I remember all about it.") do not get their own paragraph. They're stuck in the middle of a page-long passage of the main character's thoughts. His inner life takes precedence over the exterior world around him. As with the Kushner example, this is a matter of aesthetics as much as craft. If you're writing an action thriller, you most important parts of the book probably aren't the wanderings of the main character's mind. That said, it can be useful to be able to move inside the character's head when necessary. Even a *Bourne* novel isn't one-hundred percent action. You can think of action scenes as existing on a spectrum, with Robert Ludlum's novels on one end and Teju Cole's novel on the other. Figure out where your novel sits on that spectrum and dial in the appropriate level of interiority or action.

THE EXERCISE

Let's write an action sequence with a focus on interiority, using *Open City* by Teju Cole as a guide.

1. SUMMARIZE THE ACTION. What is the basic sequence of events? What was happening just before the action began? Since you're going to be working inside the character/narrator's head, it's useful to keep a plan in mind to avoid getting caught up and lost in thought. Develop a map of the action before you discover the impact of that action.
2. BEGIN WITH OBSERVATION. Give the character or narrator something to see/hear/touch/taste/smell. It can be something obvious, like a woman leading a tour of a house, as in *The Beast in the Jungle* or two men on a street, as in *Open City*. What's important is that the observation initiates the action and resonates with the character. James's character sees the woman and tries to remember where he's seen her be-

fore. Cole's narrator sees the men and remarks on the glance they share as young black men. In short, the observation should quickly lead to thought or analysis: I saw _____ and thought/was reminded of _____.

3. CHARACTERIZE THE MENTAL STATE. Cole does this plainly: "I was unnerved." A line like this is helpful for a couple reasons. First, it offers a filter for the thoughts. Aimless contemplation risks losing the reader. There should be a goal, an aim, a point. A character who is unnerved, angry, stunned, thrilled, relieved, or anxious has an end or desire in mind. Secondly, the mental state sets the stage for the action. Cole's narrator is unnerved for good reason, as it turns out. He's unnerved, and so are we.

4. MAKE THE ACTION INTRUDE ON THE THOUGHTS. Try using Cole's structure as a guide: As I was thinking _____ when I felt/heard/saw _____. Something should knock the character out of her head and force her to pay attention to what is happening. It's a natural transition to the action itself: a quick summary of what is taking place.

5. LET THE CHARACTER REFLECT ON THE ACTION. To do this, Cole uses a version of a tried-and-true rhetorical strategy: "what's really important is . . ." He writes, "The initial awareness of pain was gone, but now came the anticipation of . . ." His narrator begins to think beyond the moment to its consequences. This is not so different than thinking beyond the moment to wonder what's on Facebook or, as anyone with anxiety can attest, thinking beyond the moment to worry what might happen in the next moment. To get started, consider a version of this sentence: "After a while, it occurred to me that _____." Whatever occurs to the character should lie outside the frame of the immediate action. You can remind the reader what's going on ("As I lay there"), but the focus returns to what's most important and pressing to the character—the narrative inside her head.

The goal is to write an action sequence (fighting, washing dishes, driving, eating dinner) with the focus on the character's internal monologue or, as is sometimes the case, dialogue with herself. As in real life, characters who are self-conscious spend a lot of time observing and often find themselves on the edge of dramatic action. The tension in a story rises when those characters are pulled into the action, and this strategy is a way to avoid a jarring transition from mostly thought to mostly choreography.

HOW TO

MAKE

DIALOGUE

SNAP

NW *Zadie Smith*

Felix spotted a customer through a mullioned, glittering window sitting on a leather pouffe, trying on one of those green jackets, waxy like a tablecloth, with the tartan inside. Halfway up, the window glass became clear, revealing a big pink face, with scraps of white hair here and there, mostly in the ears. The type Felix saw all the time, especially in this part of town. A great tribe of them. Didn't mix much—kept to their own kind. THE HORSE AND THE HARE.

"Good pub, that pub," said Felix. It was something to say.

"My father swears by it. When he's in London it's his second home."

"Is it. I used to work round here, back in the day. Bit of film work."

"Really? Which company?"

"All about. Wardour Street and that," Felix added and regretted it at once.

"I have a cousin who's a VP at Sony, I wonder if you ever came across him? Daniel Palmer. In Soho Square?"

"Yeah, nah . . . I was just a runner, really. Here and there. Different places."

"Got you," said Tom, and looked satisfied. A small puzzle had been resolved. "I'm very interested in film—I used to dabble a bit in all that, you know, the way narrative works, how you can tell a story through images . . ."

Felix put his hood up. "You in the industry, yeah?"

"Not exactly, I mean, no, not at the moment, no. I mean I'm sure I could have been, but it's a very unstable business, film. When I was in college I was really a film guy, buff, type. No, I'm sort of in the creative industries. Sort of media-related creative industry. It's hard to explain—I work for a company that creates ideas for brand consolidation? So that brands can better target receptivity for their products—cutting-edge brand manipulation, basically."

Zadie Smith, excerpt from *NW*. Copyright © 2012 by Zadie Smith. Used by permission of Penguin, a division of Penguin Random House, LLC.

CREATE A POWER IMBALANCE

THE STRATEGY

If you take a writing workshop, at some point, you'll hear this statement about dialogue: characters should talk past each other. There are many ways to phrase this advice: characters should speak from different levels or planes, or they should talk *at* each other rather than *to* each other. Whatever the version, here's the takeaway: if characters are talking about the same thing, in the same way, with the same understanding of the thing being discussed, then the dialogue is bound to be boring. As with all things dramatic, boring is bad.

So, how can you write dialogue so that the characters *aren't* on the same level? One approach is to create a power imbalance. This could mean exploring the racial, gender, and class structures implicit in your novel's world and using them to create plot obstacles. But power structures aren't limited to political stories. Has there ever been a sports film made that wasn't about underdogs, with one team/athlete better funded and trained than the other? And what about our national film, *The Godfather*? All Mafia movies are about people leaning on other people, their plots driven by the suggestion and eventually the raw demonstration of what happens to characters who don't do what they're told. When Vito Corleone says, "I'll give him an offer he can't refuse," he is saying, "You'll do what I say because I can make you."

Of course, most of us aren't writing about good fellas, so how can we introduce power dynamics into other types of fiction?

Zadie Smith offers a primer in the nuances of power and class in her novel *NW*. It's set in a neighborhood of London, in a housing project where the four main characters were raised. As adults, they've achieved varying levels of financial and personal success, and those levels are dramatized on almost every single page. In this one, Felix has gone to buy a car from Tom, a "tall, skinny white boy, with a lot of chestnut fringe floppy in his face. Drainpipe jeans, boxy black spectacles." Felix is black and from the housing project. Almost every single word out of their mouths reflects the characters' differences.

- When Felix says, to fill the silence, "Good pub, that pub," Tom reveals that his "father swears by it. When he's in London it's his second home." We learn that Tom's father travels and that, when he's in town, he spends most of his time in a place where people like him—"big pink face, with scraps of white hair here and there, mostly in the ears"—keep to their own kind.
- When Felix reveals that he used to work in film in the area, Tom immediately says that he knows a VP at Sony and wonders if Felix ever met him. When Felix explains that he "was just a runner, really," Tom looks satisfied, as if a "small puzzle had been resolved." The puzzle, of course, is how a black guy buying a used car that won't run could have worked in film. The answer, to Tom's mind, is that Felix didn't, really, at least not in a way that is meaningful to Tom
- Tom says, "I'm very interested in film," and then uses the word *dabble* and academic phrases like "the way narrative works" and "tell a story through images." Felix's response? He is aware of the power dynamics and the fact that he's just been dismissed as irrelevant. He can't exactly walk out, since he wants the car. But he still manages a physical sign of his annoyance: He puts up his hood. Then he calls Tom out. "You in the industry, yeah?" But Tom isn't in the industry, and so he is forced to come up with some explanation for why not: "it's a very unstable business, film."

Keep in mind: they haven't discussed the car once on this page. They're just *talking*, which can be the most difficult dialogue to write if you're only thinking about plot and the basics of character desire, in this case *buy a car* and *sell a car*. This entire conversation exists because Felix is a poor black guy and Tom is a rich white guy and they've met in the rich white guy's turf. The power imbalance is the story.

It's also possible, in part, because we know they'll eventually get to negotiations over the car. It's a bit like the Joe Lansdale example of two characters sitting in a room together. Because we know something dramatic will happen, we're willing to wait, which provides opportunity for dialogue like this.

THE EXERCISE

Let's create a power imbalance, using *NW* by Zadie Smith as a guide.

1. CHOOSE WHICH CHARACTER TO SIDE WITH. If the scene between Felix and Tom had been told from Tom's perspective, the understanding of even basic facts and details would have very different. Perspective matters. Take any bit of dialogue you've already written—or that you want to write—and decide in advance to privilege one over the other. This doesn't mean we need to like or approve of the character's every action or word, only that the scene will be viewed through that character's sense of what is happening.

2. KNOW WHAT THE CHARACTER IS TOUCHY ABOUT. In *NW*, Felix is sensitive about the fact that he used to work in film and that he currently doesn't. He knows that he has little money. Tom knows that his job is hard to explain ("creates ideas for brand consolidation") and senses, in the generic way of many white people, that his life is somehow less authentic than the life of a poor black person's, that his struggle is less "real." Both characters become defensive about these things. What does your character become defensive about?

3. TILT THE SCENE SO THAT IT FAVORS ONE CHARACTER OVER THE OTHER. In *NW*, the setting is a bar where rich white men go. The scene centers on the sale of a car—a car in such bad condition that it must be towed. It's a transaction that involves a wealthy person selling something to a person with little money. So, set your scene on one character's turf. Create a transaction. This doesn't require selling something. Most conversations are transactional: someone is trying to

elicit information or approval or agreement, which means that one person has information or approval or agreement to give. What is at stake in the scene, and how can the setting make it easier or more difficult to achieve?

4. USE MUNDANE DETAILS TO REVEAL THE POWER IMBALANCE. Think about money, of course, but also sex appeal, race and ethnicity, wealth and the appearance of wealth, clothing and the assumptions we make about it, and the urgency of situation (it's cold and one character has to pee). All of these are subtle clues that characters can pick up on—or not. What would each character notice?

5. MAKE ONE CHARACTER MORE AWARE OF THE IMBALANCE THAN THE OTHER. If you've ever sold an item at a negotiable price, you understand that the price can change for a variety of reasons. How would your character leverage his or her power—whatever it is—to gain the best deal? What does one character know but the other doesn't? Or, what does one character hope the other doesn't realize?

6. LET A CHARACTER CALL OUT THE OTHER CHARACTER—BUT SUBTLY. If one character is hoping something goes unnoticed, let the other character notice it—and say that she's noticed it. If a character is bluffing, call the bluff, as Felix does to Tom when he says, "You in the industry, yeah?" If one character assumes more credibility or knowledge than he actually possesses, call him out. But do it subtly. Felix doesn't say, "You don't really work in film, do you?" Instead, he goes along with what Tom says and gives Tom the room to keep talking. The problem for Tom, though, is that he has nothing left to say except that he knows a guy. So, think about the one-liners, the shtick, that your character tends to use. Let the other character recognize it as a line and push the conversation beyond what is rehearsed or practiced. Felix's quote is a good one to adapt: "Oh, yeah? Tell me about it."

The goal is to accentuate the power imbalances that are present in almost every interaction between characters. Use them to create conflict and drama, which will add texture to the bare bones of the plot and give a scene more to do and characters more to talk about. You can also play with the amount of awareness that characters have of the imbalance. For example, even if Tom understood that he was being a rich jerk, he probably wouldn't be able to stop himself. He'd still namedrop his cousin who's a VP at Sony, but when Felix didn't know the guy, Tom might instead apologize or act awkward instead of looking satisfied. He might say something like, "Right, I don't even know him very well. Distant cousins and all that." Being aware of a power imbalance doesn't make the imbalance go away. Money, access, prestige, education, geography are real things, and the power that they give is just as real. Put them into your fiction, and drama will inevitably unfold.

PULL ME UNDER   *by Kelly Luce*

These kids ought to be suspended. I heard her arguing with my father. He was dismissive. Discipline didn't work like that in Japan.

My mom made rash decisions. As soon as Hiro left for Tokyo the next day, she dragged me to see the vice principal, Miura-san. We sat down across from him in his office and in her stumbling Japanese, my mom explained that I was being teased. Miura-san listened, expressionless.

My face burned. The shame of being bullied was nothing compared with this. My mom deserved a pretty daughter, one who danced lightly with her hair that flowed like water, a thin-limbed girl everyone could celebrate.

When she was done, Miura-san looked past her and said, "There is nothing we can do about children teasing one another. It is a natural thing every child must endure."

The color rose in my mom's cheeks. Miura-san avoided her eyes. I could see that her beauty embarrassed him.

"That's ridiculous. This is worse than teasing. She comes home crying. She draws violent pictures." To my horror, she produced my latest work, an image of a well-dressed boy's head exploding. It had taken a long time to sketch every bit of brain material.

Miura-san looked impassively at the drawing. There was an international school in town, he said. Perhaps I would fit in better there.

"She fits in fine here!" my mom yelled in English. Fear flickered across Miura-san's face and was quickly replaced by annoyance.

"We will investigate the matter," he said, rising and looking at his watch. "In the meantime, I'm sure your daughter will do her part to solve the problem." He gave her figure a nod. "As you have obviously done for yourself, Mrs. Akitani."

Reprinted from Kelly Luce, *Pull Me Under* (New York: Farrar, Straus and Giroux, 2016), 116.

TURN DIALOGUE INTO NARRATION

THE STRATEGY

The nice thing about living in Austin is that the city is home to several great bookstores, including BookPeople, the largest independent bookstore in the state. There's a nice reading space on the second floor and a marquee outside announcing which author is reading that day. As a result, I get to meet a lot of great writers and hear the smart things they have to say, many of which have informed the exercises in this book. For example, I recently attended a reading by Owen Egerton (whose story was discussed in "Give Your Characters What They Wish For"). Because Egerton has written both books and films, he was asked about the difference between the two. The answer wasn't one that I'd heard before.

People often compare books to films or, because we live in the golden age of television, series like *Breaking Bad*. You'll hear the word *cinematic* to describe a book or the word *Dickensian* to describe a series, as critics did incessantly with *The Wire*, and it's considered a compliment to say about a book, "It's written so vividly that I can see it." Sometimes the two mediums seem interchangeable. Stories told on the screen are often drawn from books, as with *The Handmaid's Tale* and *Game of Thrones*, and critics and audiences will argue about which version is better. The assumption used to be that books always won out, but I've heard enough people claim otherwise with *Game of Thrones* that the screen may finally have overtaken the page. But that seems unfair. They're two completely different art forms, even as they're formed in the writer's mind, as Egerton reminded everyone. (And I can quote him word for word because the reading was broadcast on Facebook Live!)

He said, "When I'm making a film, I'm very much thinking that I'm crafting something. I want this to happen, beat beat bam, so that the audience screams or laughs. When I'm writing a book, there's a little less of that. I'm getting lost in something."

I think this difference in process, the fact that books start out as dreams and daydreams that the writer chooses to dive into, is an essential part of differences between the ways that screenplays and books work on the page.

In a film, everything is on the surface. This doesn't mean that films are superficial, only that almost every scene is happening in real time, in the narrative here-and-now. The contents of a character's head aren't available to the audience except through dialogue and body language, and once a scene with dialogue begins, it's difficult to speed it up or slow it down. Good filmmakers can create exceptions to these rules with cuts and sequencing, of course, but even those directors can't do something as simple as what Kelly Luce does with dialogue on this page. Words on the page offer their own inimitable strategies.

The page begins in the middle of an argument between the narrator's mother and father. The mother says, "These kids ought to be suspended," and her father replies, "Discipline doesn't work like that in Japan." Except that's not exactly true. The characters don't actually speak those lines. They're delivered as part of the narrator's voice, her narration of the story and scene. Most readers will pass over this paragraph and not even realize what a deft piece of craft it is—and how it is very difficult, if not impossible, to accomplish in film.

Luce uses the same strategy twice more.

In the next paragraph, she takes the narrator to see the vice-principal of her school and tells him "that I was being teased." When the mother pulls out a drawing, the vice-principal says, "There is an international school in town. Perhaps I would fit in better there." But, as with the example at the top of the page, he doesn't say these lines in direct dialogue with quotation marks.

Luce goes on to use three different strategies for showing speech without dialogue (no quotation marks):

- She introduces a line of speech with a description that makes it clear who is speaking: "He was dismissive."
- She uses a speaking word to indicate that a line is a summary of a bit of speech: "my mom explained that I was being teased."
- She uses an attribution ("There was an international school in town, he said") without quotation marks.

In all three examples, the indirect method of showing speech, as opposed to direct dialogue ("I rule," he said) speeds up the scene. Imagine if all of this speech had been shown through direct dialogue. If Luce followed the usual rules of dialogue (new speaker = new paragraph), the opening paragraph would become two or three paragraphs. The paragraph in which they arrive at the vice-principal's office would also become multiple paragraphs. In this new version, the prose that currently fits on one page would likely fill at least a page and a half.

That length matters. In books, you must always contend with the ticking clock of the reader's attention span. Research—and, no doubt, your own experience—has shown that readers often put down books and never return to finish them. It's a big difference between prose and film. For most people, a film has to be truly awful for them to turn it off or, in the case of theaters, walk out. If a scene goes on too long (Peter Jackson, I'm looking at you), readers will adjust their butts in the seats and stick with it. Novels and stories don't have the luxury of a captive audience. Writers cannot simply give the blow-by-blow of a conversation, at least not through direct dialogue. You speed up whenever possible to get to the essential parts—and then you slow down. Luce slows down to show us, several times, the way the vice-principal looks at the narrator's mother because those looks count. They increase the tension in the scene and advance our understanding of the action. It's the move of a writer who knows what she's doing and what's important in her story. Luce creates space for the good parts and speeds through the connective material that holds them together.

THE EXERCISE

Let's speed up dialogue by turning it into narration, using *Pull Me Under* by Kelly Luce as a model. We'll try out the three approaches used by Luce:

1. INTRODUCE A LINE OF SPEECH BY DESCRIBING THE SPEAKER. Luce writes, "He was dismissive" and then follows with a close, though probably not exact, summary of what he said: "Discipline didn't work like that in Japan." You can try this by writing the dialogue first and then figuring out the speaker's tone. Then, go back and write a sentence along the lines of "He/she was _____ [insert appropriate emotional adjective, like *dismissive*]." Or, you can start with the tone. Ask yourself, what would the character's emotional response be to what was previously said? State the emotion and then summarize the dialogue that might follow.

2. USE A SPEAKING WORD TO INDICATE THAT A LINE IS A SUMMARY OF WHAT SOMEONE SAID. Luce uses the word *explained*: "my mom explained that I was being teased." This releases Luce from any obligation to show us *exactly* what the mother said. It doesn't really matter. The point is that she's laying out the facts. The more interesting scene is the one that follows: how the vice-principal responds to those facts. So, study your dialogue for passages that are informational, whose purpose is to set up another piece of dialogue or action. Rather than slowing down to show us the entire passage, use a word like *explained*, *told*, *described*, or *related*, or any other speaking word to introduce a quick summary of what was said.

3. USE AN ATTRIBUTION WITHOUT QUOTATION MARKS. Luce writes this: "There was an international school in town, he said." Notice that there are no quotation marks in the passage in the book. (Mine, of course, show that I'm quoting Luce.) For whatever reason, this strategy makes it easier to switch back and forth between speakers within a single paragraph. Maybe it's because too many quotation marks confuses the reader—I don't know. The important thing is the effect. Luce doesn't switch, but she could have if she wanted. You'll see other writers do this quite often: mixing these strategies in order to switch speakers in a paragraph and speed along. It works even with specific

lines of dialogue that are delivered rapid fire, as in a David Mamet play. So, simply take any piece of dialogue and remove the quotation marks. Then, you can switch speakers or—as Luce does—personalize what gets said next: "Perhaps I would fit in better there." The *I* adds to the emotional impact of the suggestion.

The goal is to speed up dialogue by removing quotation marks and, when necessary, summarizing what was said instead of stating it exactly. This gives the writer more flexibility in determining the focus of the scene and in directing where the reader should look and feel about what is happening. To continue with the film analogy, it's as if a filmmaker had the power to speed up and slow down the actual speed of the film. Again, this isn't impossible. Good filmmakers have all sorts of tricks. But it's something that prose does so much more naturally. The movement through space and time in novels and stories is unique to the form, and it's imperative that writers learn the tools of the trade. We'll discuss them in detail later in the aptly named chapter "How to Move through Time and Space."

CARTWHEEL *Jennifer duBois*

"You're boring, you know."

He raised his eyebrows. "Am I?"

"You are."

"Say a little more about that," he said, refilling her glass.

Lily took another sip. "You're boring because I know exactly how you're going to react to every single thing I say. You're going to look for the least sincere response possible, every time. You're like an algorithm."

Sebastien gave her a look of incredulous amusement. "So all I would suggest—if you're open to suggestions—"

"Please. Humility is a virtue."

"I would suggest that you mix it up a little. You should occasionally say things that have an unexpected relationship to reality. You could even throw in some things you mean, from time to time. Nobody's going to know. It will make you more interesting."

Sebastien's eyebrows were still raised. He did have beautiful eyes—so green and humane and, weirdly, so expressive. He'd get far with those eyes, she thought. Then she told him so. Then he kissed her.

His kiss was more vigorous than Lily would have expected—not that she'd expected him to kiss her, necessarily, though then again here she was, drinking wine, in his house, so really, what did she think? She was grateful for the swiftness of his approach; she thought with chagrin of many an awkward windup, staggeringly embarrassing advance-and-retreats, faces too close to do anything else, and then not quite, and then finally the clink of tooth on tooth, the tepid warmth of another person's mouth. Awful. She felt confident enough once the whole business was under way, but the first kiss gave her pause. It was just so odd, when you thought about it.

Sebastien pulled back and looked at her gravely. "Thank you for the suggestions," he said.

"See?" said Lily. "You're doing it. I have no idea what you mean. You're more interesting already." She'd meant it, teasingly, but it came out a little flat, a little mean, she thought, though Sebastien didn't seem to care. He smiled.

"That roommate of yours," he said.

Jennifer duBois, excerpt from *Cartwheel*. Copyright © 2014 by Jennifer duBois. Used by permission of Random House, an imprint and division of Penguin Random House, LLC.

CRITIQUE HOW A CHARACTER TALKS

THE STRATEGY

When my wife and I were first married, we'd get into fights about the sort of things that drive people nuts when they're not used to sharing the same space all of the time. We lived in an 800-square-foot duplex with a postage-stamp backyard filled with dirt and dog turds. To get out of the house, we'd sit out front in folding lawn chairs in the driveway. Our landlord lived next door, and he'd walk over with a Heineken and a story about how, before he became a firefighter, he was a hippie with long hair, living with a rich woman he met while playing beach volleyball. It was weird and great—unless you wanted to be alone. If we were mad at each other for some reason, we had no choice but to sit and listen to the guy's crazy stories and, when he was gone, sit there and not look at each other, talking about mundane things, tense but not sure about what. Usually, I'd be the one to lose it, and not in a subtle way, causing my wife to respond like this:

"What?" she'd say. "All I said was 'I'm going to bed.'"

"It's not *what* you said, it's how you said it."

As a rule of thumb, you won't win any points in an argument by imitating the way your partner just said something, even if you follow it with "I was just trying to show you what you did."

Now that we have two kids, I watch them do the same thing, mocking each other by copycatting phrases in whiny voices. They do the same thing to me, too. "This is how you sound, Dad." You'd think I'd get smarter with age.

Instead, I've learned that it's smart to do the same thing in fiction. Jennifer duBois gives a perfect example of how to let a character critique the way another character talks. As in real life, it's a strategy that's great for creating drama.

The novel is about a college student, Lily, who travels to Buenos Aires for a semester abroad. She stays with a host family, along with a roommate, and starts hanging out with the mysterious guy living across the street in a mansion. Eventually, the roommate ends up dead, and the question is, who did it? In this scene, Lily has gone over to the mansion to drink wine with the guy, Sebastien. It's both a perfect and difficult space for dialogue because the characters are just sitting there, just talking. Think back to your initial dates with someone, worrying what you'd talk about, how you'd fill the hours. The same is true in fiction. When plot's out the window, what do characters talk about?

In this case, they talk about how they talk.

> "You're boring, you know."
> He raised his eyebrows. "Am I?"
> "You are."
> "Say a little more about that," he said, refilling her glass.

She then proceeds to describe the way he acts and talks:

> "I know exactly how you're going to react to every single thing I say. You're going to look for the least sincere response possible, every time. You're like an algorithm."

And she tells him how he ought to act and talk instead:

> "I would suggest that you mix it up a little. You should occasionally say things that have an unexpected relationship to reality. You could even throw in some things you mean, from time to time. Nobody's going to know. It will make you more interesting."

In the scene, context is everything. If they were fighting, this exact same dialogue could lead to a blow up. But they're flirting, and so it leads to a kiss. (Side note: How great is that description of kissing?) After he pulls away, he says, "Thank you for the suggestions," which is mostly sincere, at least a little bit, which means he's taken her advice.

Next, the scene does something really cool. Lily tells him, "You're more interesting already," and immediately begins critiquing the way she spoke and her tone in almost the same way that she critiqued Sebastien, except that now she's not joking. She's self-critical. As a result, the moment becomes a little more tense. Instead of reveling in the kiss, she's doubtful—and so are we.

By focusing the dialogue on *how* things are said rather than *what* is actually said, the scene is able to fill those vast potential silences, build character and tension, and create a sharp back-and-forth—everything you could possibly want in a work of fiction.

THE EXERCISE

Let's write dialogue by focusing on *how* characters speak, using *Cartwheel* by Jennifer duBois as a model:

1. PUT TWO OR MORE CHARACTERS TOGETHER IN A SPACE WITH VAST TIME AHEAD OF THEM. Urgency can be great in dialogue, but it also restricts the sort of dialogue available to a writer. Police and crime dramas are a great example of scenes with characters having nothing to do but kill time: They're on a stakeout or, in the terrific show *The Wire*, standing on a corner, waiting for something to happen and talking to each other until it does. Of course, you may not be writing a crime novel, but plenty of real-life scenes force characters to chat until something happens: dates, car rides, family dinners.

2. ESTABLISH THE TONE OF THE SCENE. Are characters on the verge of a fight? Recovering from a fight? Flirting? Excited about something? Worn down? Curious? As we see in *Cartwheel*, context matters. The same dialogue can lead to shouting or kissing. Know what the situation is with your characters.

3. MAKE ONE CHARACTER MORE ASSERTIVE THAN THE OTHER(S).
   In this scene, Lily drives the conversation forward while Sebastien
   plays along. This is almost always the case in fiction and real life when
   characters begin to critique how someone speaks. Someone takes
   charge while someone else tries to lie low. In your scene, who is who?

4. DECIDE WHAT ONE CHARACTER FINDS ANNOYING, AMUSING,
   MADDENING, CHARMING, OR ALL OF THE ABOVE ABOUT HOW
   THE OTHER ONE TALKS, DEPENDING ON THE CIRCUMSTANCE.
   This happens in real life all the time. The reason *Saturday Night Live*
   cast members can imitate and mock presidential candidates is because
   those candidates, like all of us, possess particular tics and traits that
   become recognizable once you watch them long enough. I'll bet everyone reading this can impersonate a family member: voice, mannerism,
   sentence structure. The way we feel about that person in the moment
   often determines how we feel about their personal speaking style: "It's
   how you said it" and "Would you stop doing that?" What traits does
   your character notice about the other? What traits can be predicted?

5. LET THE CHARACTER CRITIQUE THAT TRAIT. The tone determines
   how this critique sounds, whether it's lighthearted or cutting.

6. LET THE OTHER CHARACTER RESPOND. Again, the tone matters. Is
   the character playing along or battling?

7. LEAD UP TO ACTION. Flirting leads to kisses, and fighting leads to
   slammed doors. What is the inevitable action that will follow the back-
   and-forth about how a character speaks?

8. RETURN TO DIALOGUE. It's easy to end a scene too soon. This page
   could have shown the kisses and faded to black. But it doesn't. They
   kiss, but still those vast hours lay before them. They kiss—and then
   what do they say? The same is true for fights. After a door get slammed,
   keep your literary camera rolling. What comes next? Let the characters acknowledge what was said previously, which is what duBois does
   when Sebastien says, "Thank you for the suggestions," and Lily says,
   "See? You're doing it."

9. TURN THE STRATEGY INTERNAL. Once a character becomes hyper-
   aware of how someone else is speaking, it's not a stretch to make them
   aware of their own speech patterns and tones. In a precarious scene,
   let them critique their own words. We do this naturally, immedi-

ately replaying the scene and asking ourselves, "Did I make a fool of myself?"

The goal is to create the substance of a novel—the tissue that hangs on the bones of plot—by letting characters talk about how they talk. You'll notice that this is a running theme in the book: what to do in the moments when a story or novel isn't driving the plot forward. In novels, this space might be several pages long. In a story, it might last for a few paragraphs. Either way, there are opportunities to do whatever it is that you love, whatever seems interesting with the story's world and characters. It's a little bit like when you were a kid and learned that the start of school was delayed for two hours due to weather: free play time. In fiction (and maybe in your childhood, too) if you play around in certain ways, your characters (or you and your siblings) end up feeling tense, ready to fight. In fiction, all roads lead toward conflict.

THE PERIPHERAL *William Gibson*

"Why'd they call?"

"Because they want to know what happened, on the shift. But I didn't know."

"Why don't they know? Don't they capture it all?"

"Don't seem to, do they?" He drummed his fingers on the wheel. "I had to tell them about you."

"They going to fire you?"

"They say somebody took out a hit on me tonight, on a snuff board, out of Memphis. Eight million."

"Bullshit. Who?"

"Say they don't know."

"Why?"

"Somebody thinks I saw whatever you saw. You see who did it? Who did you see Flynne?"

"How would I know? Some asshole, Burton. In a game. Set her up for it. He knew."

"The money's real."

"What money?"

"Ten million. In Leon's Hefty Pal."

"If Leon has ten million dollars in his Hefty Pal, he's going to hear from the IRS tomorrow."

"Doesn't have it yet. He'll win a state lottery, next draw. Has to buy a ticker, then I give them the number."

"I don't know what Homes did to you, but I know you're crazy now."

"They need to talk to you," he said, starting the car.

"Homes?" And now she was frightened, not just confused.

"Coldiron. It's all set up." And they were headed down Porter, Burton driving with the headlights off, his big shoulders hunched over the fragile-looking wheel.

Reprinted from William Gibson, *The Peripheral* (New York: Berkley, 2014), 73.

RESIST CONCLUSION

THE STRATEGY

Let's end our discussion of dialogue by returning to that workshop truism that characters should talk past each other, that their words shouldn't connect. The problem with this advice is that it leads to dialogue like this:

"My wife left me today."
"I've been thinking about vegetables. Did you know that baby carrots aren't actually young carrots?"

Such dialogue could work if meant for comic effect, or if you *mean* for the character talking about carrots to do everything in his power to avoid the subject at hand. However, if every conversation between these characters involved Person 1 saying something meaningful and Person 2 changing the subject, the story would quickly become about that avoidance, which is fine if you're writing "Bartelby, the Scrivener" but not great if the avoidance isn't the point of the story.

So what are other ways for characters to talk past each other?

Gibson offers a great example of this kind of dialogue. In this scene, the first speaker is asking a question ("Why'd they call?"), and the second speaker is giving an answer ("I had to tell them about you.") that has dramatic implications. A pattern is set. One character knows something the other character doesn't. That difference in knowledge initially drives the dialogue, as the less-informed character asks questions to find out what's going on:

"Why don't they know? Don't they capture it all?"

This structure (question and answer to gain information) is useful but has limits. Once both characters are informed, the scene is over, a fact that can lead to very short conversations, like this:

"Do you have a gun?"
"Yes."

Now what? Gibson solves this problem by making the less-informed character unsatisfied with simply learning what's going on. In fact, she resists the information she's given:

"They say somebody took out a hit on me tonight, on a snuff board, out of Memphis. Eight million."
"Bullshit. Who?"

She continues to resist, moving beyond basic questions to observations that cast doubt on the information she's given:

"The money's real."
"What money?"
"Ten million. In Leon's Hefty Pal."
"If Leon has ten million dollars in his Hefty Pal, he's going to hear from the IRS tomorrow."

The scene has taken on an extra dimension. It's not simply structured around delivering information but, now, getting the character to accept it. When she does, the scene is over. Gibson handles this moment with the page's first line that *isn't* dialogue: "And now she was frightened, not just confused."

An emotional shift has occurred, which means she's begun to accept the information: he's told her something, and now she's scared. Once that change happens, the scene can end.

THE EXERCISE

Let's write dialogue that conveys and resists information, using *The Peripheral* by William Gibson as a guide.

1. CREATE A SCENARIO IN WHICH ONE CHARACTER KNOWS MORE THAN ANOTHER. This situation can be used in any genre. Obviously it's a staple of detective stories: the interrogation. It's also common in horror and fantasy fiction: "What are you going to do me, young sexy vampire?" But it's also found in more realistic scenarios: "Tell me the news, doctor," or "Why is my TV showing nothing but static?" It's easier to start with two characters, but the scene can contain more.

2. PROVIDE INFORMATION THROUGH DIALOGUE. In short, answer the questions. Let one character tell the other character what she wants to know. This may involve some back-and-forth to clarify the information (What do you mean *zombies*? I thought there was just one").

3. GIVE THE LESS-INFORMED CHARACTER A REASON TO RESIST THE INFORMATION. As parents know, resistance drives most of the dialogue in our lives: "But I *want* a Popsicle. Why can't I have one?" Desire is key to the resistance. We don't question answers that give us what we want. Rather, we resist information we don't want to receive. In the case of Gibson's novel, the woman doesn't want to believe that her brother is in trouble ("Bullshit. Who?"). So, figure out why your character wouldn't want this information to be true.

4. GIVE THE CHARACTER DIFFERENT WAYS TO RESIST. You can use defiance: "No, it's not." Or wheedling: "But I *want* a Popsicle." Or valid-seeming observations: "If Leon has ten million dollars in his Hefty Pal, he's going to hear from the IRS tomorrow." Make the character savvy in his or her resistance. Of course, the way that better-informed character responds to this resistance will reveal a lot about their relationship.

5. END THE SCENE WHEN THE CHARACTER ACCEPTS THE INFORMATION. This acceptance can be voluntary ("Oh, okay.") or it can be impossible to fight, like bad news from a doctor. You're searching for a moment of emotional change. What does that moment look like? Does the character sit back and sigh? Does the character resolve to im-

prove the situation? Does the character decide to run away? Or does the character, as in *The Peripheral*, simply begin to understand the implications of the information she's been given? When you find yourself writing this moment of change, the scene is likely over.

The goal is to create and draw out a dramatic moment with nothing more than the delivery of information. When the scene ends, the reader will likely be anticipating what comes next.

HOW TO

MOVE

THROUGH

TIME AND

SPACE

"NOBODY YOU KNOW"   *Elizabeth Tallent*

The town has gone ahead without her: a new traffic light on Highway 1, a McDonald's painted a shade of blue sanctioned by the Coastal Commission, a hotel at cliff's edge where once a grove of towering shaggy eucalyptus had sifted the wind. In a dim room smelling of latex paint she opens the window for the evening breeze and leans out: yes, tatters and coils of beige-green bark litter the margin of bare ground between cliff and raw hotel. Ximena slides between the newish sheets, and after a time realizes that she has been awake far too long. After such a long drive sleep is rightfully hers, but this paint-stinking room withholds it, the rustle of clean sheets repels it, impersonal pillows offend it. She tosses and moans and scratches fleeting itches, waking in wan eleven A.M. light with a headache and a weird chemical taste in her mouth.

Reprinted from Elizabeth Tallent, "Nobody You Know," *Mendocino Fire* (New York: Harper, 2015), 107.

SLIDE BETWEEN THE
PARTICULAR AND GENERAL

THE STRATEGY

When you read enough slush-pile manuscripts and student drafts of stories, you learn a few things about what makes a narrative work. Most of them aren't a surprise: conflict is intriguing, scenes are engaging, and voice is compelling. But it's also true that a story can have all three of these elements and still not work. Sometimes we blame aesthetics, the fact that you and I like different kinds of prose styles and narratives. Or we write it off as a matter of genre conventions that we don't understand. But this is too easy. The truth is there are certain traits of good writing that are hard to describe.

One such trait was revealed to me in rather dramatic fashion in a workshop led by Tim O'Brien. We were discussing a story, and he pointed at a word and asked us to circle it every time it appeared on a specific page. We were shocked (or, at least I was) to find that the word had been used more than ten times. It was a lesson in *unintentional repetition*. A writer can repeat a word for effect, but when that word pops up over and over unbeknownst to the writer, it's a signal that the prose has gone flat. So, writers should be alert for such repetitions and cut them. To make clear, this isn't a solution but, rather, a step toward one. Cutting those words creates a hole in your paragraph or page, and something must be invented to fill it.

For some, *unintentional repetition* isn't news, but I found it remarkable, just as I was excited to learn about filtering (the excess words in *I saw the dog bark* compared to *The dog barked*). These aspects of sentence craft could be learned, even if your imagination took the day off, and were as mechanical as righty-tighty, lefty-loosey. A writer whose prose reflects a knowledge of these craft lessons demonstrates a kind of professional competence, less flashy than voice but just as necessary.

In writing, competence can reveal itself through any skill (dialogue, setting, etc.), but the truest test may be in the writer's ability to move through time and space. Novice writing plods along, minute by minute. Chapters begin with characters waking up and end with them going to sleep (or losing consciousness in other ways). The prose is a prisoner of the march of time. If this describes you, don't despair. We all start out writing this way. Then, slowly or all of a sudden, we learn how to leap through time and across geographic distances as vast as a hemisphere or intimate as a couch cushion the way that Neo learns to leap off of buildings in *The Matrix*. Words are not matter, and writers are not bound by the rules of physics.

There are few writers who understand this better than Elizabeth Tallent. In so many of her stories, she breaks the "rules" of workshop: shifts in point of view, changing tenses, and characters whose behavior can change radically. She can do all of this because she is smart and perceptive and talented, sure, but also because she's exceedingly effective at moving through time and space. She can move a character (and, therefore, the reader) from a street to a hotel room window (as she does on this page) so easily that you don't even realize it's happened. As a result, you read along without questioning what is happening on a craft level. And when a reader doesn't question, the writer can pull off anything she wants.

Look how easily she manipulates time and space in that paragraph.

It starts generally in the town: a streetlight, a McDonald's, a hotel. In the next sentence, we're in the hotel room with the character, a fact that most readers probably don't even notice because it happens so smoothly. Think, though, at what that shift doesn't include:

- We don't see the character get out of her car, though that's where she presumably was as she passed the traffic light and McDonald's.

- We don't see the hotel parking lot or lobby or the desk clerk or the character checking in.
- We don't get a sentence that says some version of "She walked into the room."
- She doesn't put down her bags or think, "Boy, I'm tired."

Instead, the prose jumps from "shaggy eucalyptus had sifted the wind" to "a dim room smelling of latex paint." The first action that we see in all of this is the character opening the window and leaning out to look at the ground. Again, consider what that means: Two sentences full of movement do not start with the word *she*, as in *She drove through town* or *She looked at the hotel and sighed*.

How does she do it?

First, the passage delays settling into the character's perspective (looking through her eyes), and so it's able to avoid the trap of showing us every single thing she sees or does. Tallent also uses images to carry the reader from one place to another, from "sifted the wind" outside the hotel to "the evening breeze" coming in the window of the room. Also, even though the passage moves us into the room, it lingers outside with the breeze and the bark from the trees we just saw littering the ground outside the window.

Tallent moves through time just as quickly. The character gets into bed, a movement that takes place in a clearly defined moment of time, but then time becomes general. It's the reverse of what happened at the beginning of the paragraph, when the prose moved from a general location to a specific room. Tallent uses the phrase "after a time" to slide into the unmeasured hours of sleeplessness. The actions become general as well:

> this paint-stinking room withholds it, the rustle of clean sheets repels it, impersonal pillows offend it. She tosses and moans and scratches fleeting itches.

Finally, the prose moves back into a specific moment in time when she wakes at eleven in the morning light. These shifts from specific minutes and places to a more general sense of time and geography allow Tallent to skim along the surface of the world she has created. This may sound less lofty and artistic than the way we sometimes imagine writing to be. It's not a matter of singing muses or light bulbs flashing above our heads. But without these mechanical skills, a story—no matter how brilliantly conceived—will fail to keep a reader engaged past a page or two. The devil is in the details, the saying goes, but so is the genius.

THE EXERCISE

Let's slide between particular and general senses of time and place, using "Nobody You Know" by Elizabeth Tallent as a model. For this exercise, you can start from scratch or revise a scene that plods along, minute by minute, mired in uninteresting details.

1. BREAK FREE FROM THE CHARACTER'S EYE SOCKETS. This works for close third-person point of view as well as first-person. Imagine if a film was shot entirely through the literal gaze of one of its characters, the way certain scenes in *Being John Malkovich* are filmed. You'd be driven mad. Another way of thinking about it is with the concept of *filtering*. Cut the character out of the descriptions of what is seen, heard, etc. Skip straight to the descriptions themselves. Try Tallent's approach and begin a sentence with the thing being described and the character in a secondary position, merely along for the ride: "The town has gone ahead without her . . ." Here are some other versions: "The _____ lay still around her," "The ___ grew dark/lighter around her," "The sound enveloped her," or "The chair seemed to stiffen beneath her." The point is to make the thing active, not the character observing it.

2. SWEEP THE DESCRIPTION IN A CLEAR DIRECTION. Tallent moves us down a street: streetlight, McDonald's, hotel. There's also a small-to-larger progression. Once we arrive at the hotel, the sweep slows, dwelling on the trees before moving inside. Think of the narrative eye like a camera on a film shoot. If the camera jerks around randomly, the viewer becomes dizzy and disoriented. You don't always need to follow a street or some other physical line, but there should usually be a smooth movement in one direction, the way one's eyes move in real life.

3. CARRY PARTS OF THE DESCRIPTION FORWARD. Tallent does this with the breeze. It's present outside and then inside the hotel. It's easy to do this with temperature, humidity, smell, and sound. As a character moves from one place to another, certain aspects of the setting persist or follow along. You can also try the opposite: negate what was previously described. Tallent does this as well when she moves from "shaggy eucalyptus" to "smelling of latex paint." The room becomes the antithesis of the nature in the previous sentence: chemical and unpleasant.

4. CHOOSE A MOMENT IN TIME AND THE ACTION IT CONTAINS. In "Nobody You Know," the character opens a window and looks out of it. She slides between the sheets. We don't see her moving between the window and bed. In a film, we'd likely see that movement across the room, but it's not necessary in prose. Instead, the writing gives us flashes of the action as if the room is dark until suddenly illuminated so that we can see what is happening. Readers are able to fill in the blanks in their minds. So, try illuminating your own scene in the same way. What is the character doing in those moments? What are the actions that seem most important to show?

5. SLIDE INTO THE GENERAL. Tallent uses the phrase "after a time," and there are doubtless many others that ease out of a moment in the same way: *after a while, gradually, eventually, by and by.* These words and phrases do the opposite work of the word *suddenly.* I know, of course, that many teachers hate the word *suddenly,* and you should be careful of overusing it and all of these phrases, but banning it altogether is like banning cuff links. They're unnecessary until you put on a shirt without buttons on its sleeves. Once you've slid into the general, choose actions that don't knock the reader back into the particular. Talent uses *tosses, moans,* and *scratches* but also makes the setting active ("the rustle of clean sheets repels it"). Think about the sort of activities that we naturally measure out in inexact lengths of time rather than minutes and seconds. And, of course, since the experience of time is relative, a minute can feel like an eternity, depending on the situation.

6. MOVE BACK INTO THE PARTICULAR. The most important parts of stories almost always take place in a particular moment, not a general one. General time moves the reader from one particular moment to an-

other. It's an easy move to make. Tallent uses a verb (waking) that occurs in a particular moment—or, at least, a more particular moment
than the verbs that preceded it (tossing, moaning, scratching).

The goal is to become light on your feet, to move quickly and easily
through time and from one place to another. This is one definition of narrative pace, the ability to speed up and slow down and not rely on the
tick-tock of the literal passing of time. In fact, it may be the only definition of narrative pace that matters. You're literally manipulating time
and geography. It's the ultimate power afforded by prose, and you should
learn to take full advantage of it.

"NIGHT OF THE SATELLITE"   *T. C. Boyle*

What we were arguing about that night—and it was late, very late, 3:10 a.m. by my watch—was something that happened nearly twelve hours earlier. A small thing, really, but by this time it had grown out of all proportion and poisoned everything we said, as if we didn't have enough problems as it was. Mallory was relentless. And I was feeling defensive and maybe more than a little paranoid. We were both drunk. Or if not drunk, at least loosened up by what we'd consumed at Chris Wright's place in the wake of the incident and then at dinner after and the bar after that. I could smell the nighttime stink of the river. I looked up and watched the sky expand overhead and then shrink down to fit me like a safety helmet. A truck went blatting by on the interstate and then it was silent but for the mosquitoes singing their blood song while the rest of the insect world screeched either in protest or accord, I couldn't tell which, thrumming and thrumming till the night felt as if it was going to burst open and leave us shattered in the grass.

"You asshole," she snarled.

"You're the asshole," I said.

"I hate you."

"Ditto," I said. "Ditto and square it."

Reprinted from T. C. Boyle, "Night of the Satellite," *T. C. Boyle Stories II: The Collected Stories of T. Coraghessan Boyle* (New York: Penguin, 2013).

CREATE SPACE FOR ALL OF YOUR NARRATIVE TOOLS

THE STRATEGY

In high school, I tried out for two plays. The first was a melodrama with a moustache-twirling bad guy and a damsel in distress, and, in the audition, the drama teacher asked me to speak in a British accent. "Um," I said. The teacher tried again. "How about an Australian accent?" I thought about it for a moment. "G'day?" Needless to say, I didn't get a part. A few years later, I *did* get a role (incidentally, the exact same role that, twenty-three years earlier, my father had in the same play on the same stage in my rural high school), and I remember in those early rehearsals hearing a word I didn't know: *blocking*. I learned that it meant, basically, where we stood, how we moved, and everything we did while delivering our lines. I'd been so focused on learning my lines that it hadn't occurred to me that the *words* were only a small part of what happened on stage. If our director hadn't choreographed each scene, we actors would have just stood there looking at each other.

The same thing is true on the page. Beginning writers know that a story or novel must have plot, characters, setting, dialogue, etc. But once you sit down to write, it's quickly evident that knowing a story's setting and characters and what they'll say and do isn't enough. On the page, you must execute these things not just one sentence at a time but moving those characters and the readers from one sentence to the next, through several sentences and across passages.

Hemingway's supposed advice that the key to creating a story is writing "one true sentence" is nonsense. Anyone can write a sentence about character or setting or a nifty piece of dialogue. The trick is fitting multiple sentences together. Good writers are able to execute paragraphs that mix multiple story elements. This is exactly what T. C. Boyle does on the first page of his story, "Night of the Satellite."

The story begins with conflict ("What we were arguing about that night") but takes a very long time telling us *what they were arguing about that night*. In fact, we don't find out for pages. The sentence could have said, "What we were arguing about that night was how we behaved during someone else's fight," which is, in fact, what they were arguing about. Instead, it tells us the time. Then, it tells us the *nature* of the conflict ("small thing . . . grown out of all proportion") and the context ("as if we didn't have enough problems as it was"). That's sentence one. The rest of the paragraph provides a lot more information that doesn't tell us what the fight was about:

- We learn how each character engages in the argument ("Mallory was relentless. And I was feeling defensive and maybe more than a little paranoid") and a major reason for their behavior ("We were both drunk").
- We're given the relevant locations (Chris Wright's place, the bar).
- Next is a longish passage about the setting, heavy on mood ("truck went blatting by" and "the mosquitoes singing their blood song") and one character's impression of it ("watched the sky expand overhead and then shrink down to fit me like a safety helmet").
- Finally, we get dialogue that tells us nothing new but clearly and sharply illustrates everything we've just been told: They both think the other one is an asshole.

We're introduced to conflict, time and place, character, context, close descriptions of setting, and dialogue in a single passage. Boyle manages to juggle all these elements by creating space for them within the initial moment promised by the first line ("What we were arguing about"). We're back to the idea we'll return to again and again—creating space for the good stuff. In this case, Boyle slows down the story to describe the moment, utilizing the many different tools available to him.

THE EXERCISE

Let's create space around a moment to describe it using different narrative tools, with "Night of the Satellite" by T. C. Boyle as a model:

1. START WITH CONFLICT. When in doubt, this should always be your move. A clear statement or suggestion of conflict refocuses the reader's attention. You can state some conflict outright (She threw a spitball at him) or suggest it, as Boyle does: "What we were doing . . ."

2. LOCATE THE CONFLICT IN TIME. Shakespeare did this constantly at the beginning of scenes, with characters stating the time, often more than once to make sure the audience got it. Boyle does the same thing, and with plain language: "it was late, very late, 3:10 a.m." He also locates the initial incident in time as well. So, state what time things are happening or happened.

3. DESCRIBE THE NATURE OF THE CONFLICT. Is it a big deal or not? Is it the last straw or the first volley? Was it premeditated or rash?

4. DESCRIBE HOW EACH CHARACTER ENGAGES IN THE CONFLICT. Often, but not always, characters will engage differently—with different energy levels, approaches, intentions, strategies, intentions, and goals. The differences can reveal a lot about a characters' temperament and personality. Again, don't be afraid to be direct, as Boyle is ("Mallory was relentless"). You can also give context for their behavior, both short-term ("We were both drunk") and long-term ("as if we didn't have enough problems as it was").

5. GIVE THE RELEVANT LOCATIONS. Think about the present location and any locations that are attached to the moments in time you stated earlier.

6. DESCRIBE A LOCATION FROM INSIDE ONE CHARACTER'S HEAD. It doesn't really matter, in "Night of the Satellite," that a truck drives by or that the river stinks. The setting doesn't really impact the events. What is important is *what the character notices*. The truck goes *blatting* by; it doesn't just drive past. The word choice matters. Boyle's entire passage about the setting has a consistent tone, and that tone suggests the character's claustrophobia. Even the sky seems to press upon him in that beautiful line about the safety helmet. So, dig into the setting you've given yourself. Given your character's state of mind, what details are noticed and how do they feel?

7. CUT DIRECTLY TO DIALOGUE. Boyle doesn't preface the dialogue with a line of physical description like "She took a deep breath." It's not necessary. What's great about the dialogue is that it reveals the intensity and, again, the nature of everything we've learned. If you've ever been in an argument with a significant other, you've likely had a moment like this, when you're no longer advancing your argument and simply trying to say something that hurts the other person's feelings. Great dialogue can be like that: it doesn't reveal new information but, rather, shows the depth of something we already know. So, think about your lines that stated how the character engaged in the conflict. Write dialogue that illustrates their approaches.

The goal is to expand your prose to include as many of the essential tools of narrative as possible. Keep in mind, though, that this often works best for passages that set up a scene. Once the scene kicks into gear, the writing often moves more quickly. Later in this story, for example, there's a crucial scene involving a missing object. The writing in that moment becomes stripped down. Boyle has already set up his pieces and now he focuses on their actions—on the conflict that he promised us at the beginning.

A BRIEF HISTORY OF
SEVEN KILLINGS *Marlon James*

The white man takes out his wallet—I only need ten minutes, he says. Damn Americans always thinking we're like them and that everybody is up for sale. Just once I'm glad the guard is such an asshole. But he's looking at the money, he's looking at it long. You can't help it with American money, getting 'round the fact that this piece of paper is more valuable than everything else in your purse. That if you whip out one you change the behaviour of a whole room. It just doesn't seem right, a piece of paper with no colour but green. Lord knows pretty money isn't the only pretty thing that's worthless. The guard takes one last look at the piling bills and walks away, over to the entrance of the house.

I chuckled. When you can't fight temptation, you have to flee, I say. The white man looks at me, annoyed, and I just chuckle more. Doesn't happen every day, a Jamaican who doesn't turn into a yes massa I going to do it for you now massa, whenever he sees a white man. Danny used to be appalled by it. Until he started to like it. Hell of a thing when white skin is the ultimate passport. I was a little surprised at how good it felt, me and the white man both being kept outside like beggars. On the same level in that regard at least. You'd think I'd never been around white people, or at least Syrians who think they're white.

—You fly all the way from America just to do a story on the Singer?

—Well yeah. He's the biggest story right now. The numbers of stars coming out for this concert, you'd think it was Woodstock.

—Oh.

—Woodstock was a—

—I know what Woodstock was.

—Oh. Well Jamaica is all over the news this year. And this concert. *New York Times* just did a story that the Jamaican opposition leader was shot at. From the Office of Prime Minister, no less.

—Really? That would be news to the Prime Minister since the opposition would have no reason to be at his office. Also that's uptown. On this very road. Nobody firing no bullets here.

Marlon James, excerpt from *A Brief History of Seven Killings*. Copyright © 2014 by Marlon James. Used by permission of Riverhead Books, an imprint of Penguin Random House, LLC.

MIX ACTION AND INTERIORITY

THE STRATEGY

It's possible to divide prose into two purposes: describing what is *happening* in a story and describing *what a character is thinking or feeling.* Like all blanket statements, this one is flawed by its generality, but it also highlights a problem faced by writers who are attempting their first stories or novel drafts. They tend to treat action and interiority as two different realms; they'll produce pages of a character thinking and feeling and then, separately, pages of bare-bones dialogue and mechanical descriptions of what the character is doing: fighting, running, hiding, walking, working, making a peanut butter sandwich, etc.

Does this contradict what I said earlier about driving plot forward and then carving out opportunities for characters to sit and be themselves? Yep. One of the beautiful things about fiction is there are no hard and fast rules. Sometimes you can chisel out space for play. Other times you've got to juggle ten balls at once. The best fiction captures the incredible complexity of real life, where basic ideas of right and wrong and how to be apply—until they don't.

So, sometimes it's important to mix the action of a story with a character's interior life, focusing more on action for a while and then shifting that focus to the characters' thoughts. (This is different from the way Teju Cole focuses almost entirely on interiority.) Beginning writers know this, but the mixing process is difficult. They'll write dialogue with each line interrupted by a chunk of interiority. The pace slows to a crawl. Or they try to mix every line in an action sequence (a fight or running/walking/ driving from Point A to Point B) with a line or two of interiority. Again, the result is that something that should happen quickly now happens at a snail's pace.

What is needed is a way to mix action and thought while keeping the prose light and quick.

Marlon James does exactly that throughout his excellent novel *A Brief History of Seven Killings*, and this page is a good example. The novel is about an attempted assassination of Bob Marley in 1976 and the lives afterward of the people involved. In this scene, the narrator, Nina Burgess, is waiting outside of Bob Marley's house, and a reporter for *Rolling Stone* has arrived for an interview, only to be turned away by the guard.

In the paragraph that begins "The white man takes out his wallet," watch how the prose jumps from exterior to interior:

EXTERIOR: "The white man takes out his wallet" and speaks.

INTERIOR: The narrator sees this moment and responds with strong emotion: "Damn Americans always thinking we're like them . . . Just once I'm glad the guard is such an asshole."

EXTERIOR: But perhaps the guard isn't an asshole after all? We see the guard "looking at the money . . . looking at it long."

INTERIOR: The narrator responds with a more tempered observation: "You can't help it with American money, getting 'round the fact that this piece of paper is more valuable than everything else in your purse."

EXTERIOR: The guard must make a decision, and so he does: "The guard takes one last look . . . and walks away."

This back-and-forth continues into the next paragraph in the same way except that now the narrator isn't merely a passive observer.

EXTERIOR: The narrator laughs and says, "When you can't fight temptation, you have to flee." This annoys the reporter.

INTERIOR: The narrator is amused by his irritation and thinks, "Doesn't happen every day, a Jamaican who doesn't turn into a yes massa I going do it for you now massa, whenever he sees a white man . . . I was a little surprised at how good it felt, me and the white man both being kept outside like beggars."

The dialogue that follows between the narrator and reporter contains no interiority at all—and no attribution (he said/she said). Here's the question: Why? Why do some passages mix action and interiority and others don't?

In part, the answer is *space*. When the narrator is observing, she has time to think. It's harder to think extended thoughts, however, in the middle of a conversation in which you're engaged.

But it's also a matter of attitude and point of view. The narrator has strong feelings about the encounter she witnesses between the guard and reporter. Those feelings matter for two reasons. One, they help us predict how the scene will play out and why. (Will the guard accept the bribe or not?) Two, they lay the foundation for the dialogue between the narrator and reporter—dialogue that contains plenty of attitude ("I know what Woodstock was.") and information that the narrator understands better than the reporter ("Really? That would be news to the Prime Minister"). Once her point of view and attitude are established, the dialogue can run without explanation.

THE EXERCISE

Let's mix action and interiority, using *A Brief History of Seven Killings* by Marlon James as a guide.

1. IDENTIFY THE QUESTION AT THE HEART OF THE SCENE. In James's scene, the question is whether the guard will accept the bribe and let the reporter enter. He will, or he won't. The moment of deliberation gets drawn out, providing the space for interiority. So, determine what set of possibilities exist in your scene. Think of the scene like one of those Choose Your Own Adventure Books: If ___, turn to page ___. But if ___, turn to page ___. What are the options in your scene?

2. IDENTIFY THE CHARACTER(S)' APPROACH TO THAT QUESTION. In *A Brief History of Seven Killings*, the reporter assumes that he can

influence the guard's decision with a bribe. The narrator also understands this to be a possibility, but she also understands that it's part of a larger issue. The reporter isn't just some weird guy doing weird things; the narrator has seen this same interaction before, and she has some feelings about it. So, what assumptions do your character act upon? What context can they draw upon to understand what they're witnessing?

3. LET A CHARACTER ACT. The reporter acts on his assumption about bribes. Let a character in your scene act on his or her assumptions or knowledge.

4. LET ANOTHER CHARACTER OBSERVE AND RESPOND EMOTIONALLY TO THAT ACTION. The narrator sees, understands, and responds emotionally to what she is witnessing—the attempted bribe. In short, she's expressing internally everything that we discussed in Step 2. Give your character a chance to do the same thing: respond internally by contextualizing, with emotion. Notice that James uses an explicit emotional phrase: "I'm glad . . ."

5. INTRODUCE AN ACTION THAT COMPLICATES THAT INTERNAL RESPONSE. The narrator thinks the reporter's bribe is being refused, and she rejoices in this refusal. But then the guard looks at the money. The action complicates her enjoyment of the moment. What action can a character (a third character, perhaps) add to the scene?

6. LET THE CHARACTER OBSERVE AND RESPOND TO THIS NEW INFORMATION. The narrator's emotional response changes from a kind of savage joy to bitter acceptance ("You can't help it with American money"). Let your character understand this new action and what it means. Let the character respond to it internally. Again, James uses an explicit emotional phrase: "It doesn't seem right . . ."

The goal is to add an internal element to a scene with action and dialogue. The thoughts and feelings can set the stage for and enhance what is said and done. This is very useful for writers working somewhere in the middle of the spectrum between Robert Ludlum's action-packed Bourne novels and Teju Cole's highly internal novel that we discussed in "Make Interiority the Focus in Action Scenes." Most writers will need to balance what's happening in a scene with what's going on inside a character's head, and the way James moves back and forth between the two offers a terrific model that can apply to almost any book.

SALVAGE THE BONES *Jesmyn Ward*

"I'm almost done." I bend over the sink and drink until I don't feel like throwing up anymore. Even after I turn the water off, I still keep swallowing. My tongue feels rolled in uncooked grits, but I still swallow. Repeat *I will not throw up, I will not throw up, I won't.* When I walk out of the door, I follow the baseboards.

"You okay?" Randall stands in my way.

"I rinsed the hair out the tub," I say. "Don't worry."

The sound of Daddy chugging the working tractor through the yard, I ignore. In bed, I pull the thin sheet over my head, mouth my knees, and breathe so hot it feels like two people up under the sheet.

When I wake up for the second time, the air is hot, and the ceiling is so low, the heat can't rise. It doesn't have anyplace to go. I'm surprised Daddy hasn't sent Junior in here to get me up by now, to work around the house and prepare for hurricane. Late last night, he and Junior carried some of the jugs in, lined them up against the wall while I made tuna fish. Daddy kept counting the bottles over and over again as if he couldn't remember, glanced at me and Randall as if we were plotting to steal some. If Randall's told him that I'm sick, he won't care. Maybe they've scattered: Junior under the house, Randall to play ball, Skeet in the shed with China and her puppies. My stomach sizzles sickly, so I pull my book from the corner of my bed where it's smashed between the wall and my mattress. In *Mythology*, I am still reading about Medea and the quest for the Golden Fleece. Here is someone that I recognize. When Medea falls in love with Jason, it grabs me by the throat. I can see her. Medea sneaks Jason things to help him: ointments to make him invincible, secrets in rocks. She has magic, could bend the natural to the unnatural. But even with all her power, Jason bends her like a young pine in a hard wind; he makes her double in two. I know her.

Jesmyn Ward, excerpt from *Salvage the Bones*. Copyright © 2011 by Jesmyn Ward. Reprinted with the permission of Bloomsbury.

CREATE SIMULTANEITY

THE STRATEGY

When I was a MFA student, one of the buzzwords in my workshops was *simultaneity*, the idea that stories need multiple things happening at once. The idea is to write a scene in which characters act or talk about one thing but think about a second thing, with that talking/acting/thinking being informed by a third thing. The result looks something like this: "I love you," she told Bill, while thinking of John, as the Jaws of Life snatched her from the burning wreckage of her unicycle.

This is hardly a new idea. James Joyce was obsessed with simultaneity and strove to create a prose style that resembled music: multiple layers present at the same time, even in the same word. But that's not the path we're on, unless you want to write *Finnegans Wake*:

> A way a lone a last a loved a long the riverrun, past Eve and Adam's, from swerve of shore to bend of bay, brings us by a commodius vicus of recirculation back to Howth Castle and Environs.

Is it beautiful? Absolutely. But if you try to keep reading beyond that passage, the prose begins to resemble static. So, we'll stick to simultaneity on the passage, paragraph, and sentence level.

This may seem obvious, but in order to have multiple things happening in any given passage in a story or novel, you need multiple things to draw from. When a narrative is too flat—when it hasn't been imagined beyond the most immediate aspects of character, plot, or setting—the writer finds herself facing a yawning blankness. In dialogue, for example, the characters will devolve into talking heads, and the writer, sensing this, will add random details: "I love you," he said, bending over to pick up a penny from the sidewalk. Where'd the penny come from? What does it add to the scene? Who knows? But the guy needs something to do, right? In "Take a Tour," the chapter on Nina McConigley's story (see page 42), we discussed one way to make setting meaningful in a moment of dialogue. But you can't always give a tour of setting. Another strategy is needed, and Jesmyn Ward supplies it. The problem in the scene with the guy picking up the penny while saying "I love you" is that there's only one thing going on. This isn't true of the page from *Salvage the Bones*. Look at how much is happening:

- The narrator is pregnant (which is why she's nauseous).
- A hurricane is coming (which is why the narrator's father is using the tractor to collect wood to nail over the house's windows).
- The father is an alcoholic (which is why he keeps counting the water jugs).
- One kid likes to hide under the house.
- Another kid loves basketball.
- A third kid has a dog that just birthed puppies.
- The narrator is really interested in her book about mythology.
- The family doesn't have a lot of money (which is why the house is so hot: no air conditioning).

Ward gives each of her characters a trait, preference, or hobby. She gives her narrator a conflict (pregnancy) *and* an interest (mythology), which means that the character isn't defined entirely by the conflict and won't become the pregnant girl from an after-school special. Ward gives the characters a conflict that affects them all (hurricane) and some limitations in how they can deal with it (poverty, the father's alcoholism, attachment to the puppies). All of this is present in *one single page*. The result is prose that doesn't get bogged down in any one conflict or character trait. Instead, it constantly moves from one thing to another. It's dynamic:

Repeat *I will not throw up, I will not throw up, I won't*. When I walk out of the door, I follow the baseboards.

"You okay?" Randall stands in my way.

"I rinsed the hair out of the tub," I say. "Don't worry."

The sound of Daddy chugging the working tractor through the yard, I ignore.

In this example, the prose moves from pregnancy to poverty (brother, only one bathroom) to hurricane (dad on the tractor). Ward has given herself details to include amid and around the dialogue. She isn't forced to write something like this: "I rinsed the hair out of the tub," I say, looking at my feet. There's nothing *wrong* with "looking at my feet," but it's not nearly as good as the simultaneity of hurricane, poverty, and pregnancy. James Joyce was trying to achieve the simultaneity of music, but Ward shows us the simultaneity of life.

There's always ten things happening at once. If you find that your story has only one thing going on, it might be a sign that you haven't fully developed the characters and their world. Everybody I know is juggling more balls than they can manage; it's part of being an adult—and also part of being a kid. My five-year-old can go from worrying about a missing library book to wanting to play a game to wanting me to read to him to wondering what happened to that toy from two years ago to getting mad at his brother to hugging his brother in a matter of two minutes, maybe faster if he's tired. I sometimes long for the days before clocks, when time was measured in hours and, maybe, quarter hours. Wouldn't it be nice to think of only one or two things at once? And wouldn't it be lovely to sit around, waiting for someone to meet you, nothing to do but think? But modern life doesn't work that way, and so neither should our fiction. Give your characters plenty to worry about. Use this exercise to juggle it all.

THE EXERCISE

Let's create simultaneity, using *Salvage the Bones* by Jesmyn Ward as a guide.

1. **CREATE A GENERAL CONFLICT.** In *Salvage the Bones*, this is the hurricane, a conflict so central to the novel that it's the first thing men-

tioned on the book jacket: "A hurricane is building over the Gulf of Mexico . . ." But it's also the backdrop to the real story, which is the drama between the characters. Almost every type of story has a general conflict. Road trips have *the road*. Love stories such as *Love in the Time of Cholera* often use societal conflict or, as in *Romeo and Juliet*, family feuds. Geopolitical thrillers use the geopolitical conflict of the moment: the Cold War, the IRA, and terrorism. This conflict is on the characters' minds but not always at the forefront.

2. LIMIT THE CHARACTERS' ABILITY TO DEAL WITH THE CONFLICT. Ward's characters live in the Mississippi Gulf Coast—but not *in town*. Instead, they live on a piece of land filled with trees and the ruins of old buildings that are salvaged when needed. The characters are poor. To get into town, they often must hitch a ride. These limitations are part of the setting, but they're also situational. Not everyone in this place lives the same way. So, consider the way setting *and* the characters' situation defines how they deal with the conflict. What is possible, and what isn't? What solutions lay at hand, and which are just out of reach?

3. GIVE AT LEAST ONE CHARACTER A PERSONAL CONFLICT. Ward gives her narrator pregnancy and a love that cannot be returned. This conflict exists independently of the hurricane. It has several roots: the narrator's personality, the way her identity as a woman is viewed in this place, and the options available to her because of the same things that limit her family's ability to prepare for the hurricane. Boiled down, the conflict looks like this: the character wants something she cannot have and needs something she may not get. Try giving your character a similar conflict based on wants and needs.

4. GIVE THE CHARACTERS PERSONALITIES. A personality can be created in several ways: through traits like funny or morose, through preferences like a favorite chair, through hobbies like basketball, and through interests like Greek mythology. When we say that a character is flat, it often means the character is defined entirely by conflict (pregnant girl) and lacks a personality. So, play around with different traits, preferences, hobbies, and interests for each character.

5. GIVE CHARACTERS VIRTUES AND VICES. Ward makes the narrator's father an alcoholic. She also makes the narrator's siblings loyal in various ways.

6. **JUXTAPOSE SOME OR ALL OF THESE QUALITIES IN A PASSAGE.**
   Finally, we've returned to this: *"I love you," she told Bill, while thinking of John, as the Jaws of Life snatched her from the burning wreckage of her unicycle.* Ward does something similar: *I'm pregnant, she thinks, while her brother pounds on the door and her father prepared for the hurricane.* Boiled down, it's this: *Personal Conflict, while another character expresses a need, in the midst of General Conflict.* If you write dialogue, instead of describing how the character talks, instead describe what is happening in the background (General Conflict). If a character is thinking about a personal conflict, add another character acting out his personality trait, preference, hobby, or interest. (This is why scenes with only one character can be so challenging to write.) In short, add layers to your prose. Juxtapose the elements of the story—General Conflict, Limitations, Personal Conflict, Personalities, Virtues and Vices—line by line.

The goal is to create simultaneity in your prose, which, as a side effect, makes it more dynamic. Instead of dwelling one thing, it can dart from thing to thing, character to character, and place to place. This is a trait of the most brilliant minds, a kind of restlessness and sideways movement from thing to thing. One of the pleasures of Vladimir Nabokov's *Lolita* is how swiftly Humbert Humbert's voice can change direction and subject. That novel—as horrible as the subject matter is—succeeds because the narrator is so smart. So, make your characters smart. In reality, everyone is. Or, they think they are. Give them too much to handle and think about, and then let them rise to the challenge.

LENSES

FOR THE

ARTIST'S

VISION

A WHILE BACK, I was at a reading series in Austin, talking with a man who mentioned that his wife was an artist. "She does fiber arts," he said. "They used to call it *quilts*, but that's not what it is."

I nodded politely, but the comment struck me as odd. His wife might have had a great reason for not using the word *quilt*. Fiber arts and quilting, after all, are not synonyms. But if she was, in fact, making quilts, why not call them that? Was it because fiber art sounds better (less folksy, less gendered, more serious) than quilting? Too often, the word *art* is used this way: to suggest that certain types of artistic creation are more valuable than others without any real basis for the distinction—or there is a basis, one that is rooted in biases that have nothing to do with the work of art.

Used in this way, *art* and *artist* become exclusionary, the domain of certain types of individuals but not others. The terms of that exclusion are why Charlotte Brontë, Mary Ann Evans, and Joanne Rowling were first published under male-sounding pseudonyms. It's also why a *New York Times* reviewer could write this about *Sula*, the second book by Nobel Prize–winning Toni Morrison:

"Toni Morrison is far too talented to remain only a marvelous recorder of the black side of provincial American life. If she is to maintain the large and serious audience she deserves, she is going to have to address a riskier contemporary reality than this beautiful but nevertheless distanced novel. And if she does this, it seems to me that she might easily transcend the early and unintentionally limiting classification 'black woman writer' and take her place among the most serious, important and talented American novelists now working."

All of this is to say, I don't care for the terms *art* or *literature*. But it's also true that I like some novels and stories better than others. Trying to explain that difference, though, without resorting to the bigotry of many definitions of *art* and *literature* can be tough. It's tempting to point to issues of craft as proof for our judgments, and reviewers frequently do this, highlighting clunky sentences to support their claims that a book isn't very good. But mechanics and craft issues (the sort of things this book is concerned about) can't really explain why we respond to some books but not others. In fact, books are often great in spite of glaring flaws. For example, I think the Harry Potter series is as good as any young adult fantasy series ever written, but I can't argue with Harold Bloom when he points out some of Rowlings tics:

"As I read, I noticed that every time a character went for a walk, the author wrote instead that the character 'stretched his legs'. I began marking on the back of an envelope every time that phrase was repeated. I stopped only after I had marked the envelope several dozen times."

It's a valid critique, but his conclusion seems a touch overwrought: "Rowling's mind is so governed by clichés and dead metaphors that she has no other style of writing."

What makes a novel or story great if not the quality of the sentences? It's a difficult question to answer. I could highlight any number of examples of great writing from Rowling's series, but I doubt it would make much sense to Bloom. On the other hand, I've read books whose clichés have made me quit reading. The best rationale I can give is that a poorly written sentence here and there doesn't bother me much when the book has captured my imagination. But when it hasn't, a couple of clichés can break the spell so completely that I'll give up.

To put it another way: all the writing ability and skills in the world won't make you a good writer. They help, of course. You can't write a story or novel without them. But vision and imagination are required to put those skills to good use. This is why some people claim that writing can't be taught. Because it's *an art*. But it's been my experience that artistic vision can be learned (and therefore taught) as much as any mechanical writing skill. The exercises in this unit can help you figure out the mechanics of vision: the shape a story takes, the details it focuses on, and the style its sentences take.

HOW TO

CREATE

STRUCTURE

"BOYS TOWN" *Jim Shepard*

You want to talk about sad: even after all I been through, one of the saddest things I ever saw was a year after I got home, when my mother pulled over at a stop sign, it must've been ten below, and she's got the window down and she's scooping snow from the side mirror and trying to throw it on her windshield to clean it. We'd gone about three blocks and couldn't see a thing before she finally pulled over. I'm sitting there watching while she leans forward and tosses snow around onto the outside of the glass. Then every so often she hits the wipers.

She did this for like five minutes. We're pulled over next to a Stewart's. They got wiper fluid on sale in the window twenty-five feet away. She doesn't go get some. She doesn't ask me to help. She doesn't even get out of the car and try and do it herself.

My hair started falling out. I found it on my comb in the mornings. I could see where it was coming from. Not that anybody gives a shit, but you put that together with the teeth and you have quite the package.

I came in from thirty minutes of sliding slush off the porch and there was my kid's voice on the machine. My mother was playing it over again and turned it off when I got inside. She went back to whatever she was doing at the sink.

"Were you gonna tell me he called?" I asked.

"You cleaned up all that ice already?" she asked me back.

"I didn't do the ice. I did the slush," I told her.

Reprinted from Jim Shepard, "Boy's Town," *You Think That's Bad* (New York: Knopf, 2011), 164.

INTERVIEW YOUR CHARACTER

THE STRATEGY

When I was in college, I applied to become an ambassador for the College of Arts and Sciences, a position that involved giving campus tours and standing behind a table during college fairs. I didn't actually *want* to do either of these things, but I figured it would look good on my résumé. To prepare for the interview, I studied a list of common questions, you know the type: Describe a challenge you faced and how you overcame it; What is your biggest weakness?; and If you were a tree, what kind would you be? Keep in mind, I grew up on a farm. Job interviews didn't exist. I worked for my dad, and when he needed help beyond his six children, he relied on references, calling people he trusted and asking if they knew anyone looking for work. If that person said, "Well, so-and-so is good when he's sober," my dad didn't bother calling so-and-so. When my dad found someone worth asking, the conversation didn't go much beyond "Are you interested?" He never asked anyone what sort of tree they'd be. When I saw the question, I thought it was a joke.

About halfway through the interview, the college senior running it asked, "If you could be a tree . . ."

Later, I would think of all sorts of funny answers, like "A Dutch elm. Because when I was a kid, I wiggled so much my dad always asked if I was wormy." In the moment, though, I think I only managed something like "A Christmas Tree. Because they're bright and shiny and people love them." I did not feel bright and shiny as I left, but somehow I got the position.

The point, of course, is not to be witty but, instead, to show that you're able to quickly organize your thoughts around a scenario or topic. The same thing is applicable when writing fiction. Many paragraphs and passages start with the equivalent of a bad interview question. Jim Shepard does this throughout his story, "Boys Town." The first line in the story is "Here's the story of *my* life," which is not so different than "Tell us about yourself." Elsewhere, he writes, "I had all kinds of jobs" (Tell us about your work history), "You get lonely, is what it is" (Describe a challenge you've met), and "There were a lot of things I wanted to do about my appearance but only so much I could get accomplished until I got certain things squared away" (What is your biggest weakness?). These opening lines create landmarks for what follows. No matter where the passage goes, the line orients the reader (and also the writer).

This is what happens on this page, with the line "You want to talk about sad: even after all I been through, one of the saddest things I ever saw was . . ." The brilliance of a line like this is that it works for every character ever written. It's a setup for character development through anecdote. What follows, the actual sad thing, is determined by who the character is and the writer's ability to imagine what that character would say next.

One of the things often said about Shepard is that he can write a story set anywhere, with any type of character. In the collection this story comes from, he writes about the first scientists to study avalanches, the first woman to cross the Arabian Desert, a soldier in Joan of Arc's army, and a top-secret operative at the National Laboratory in Los Alamos, New Mexico. He's able to write such diverse stories because he's a great writer, but also because he sets himself up for passages with great, character-revealing anecdotes. You might be wondering, what does this have to do with structure? It's another example of creating spaces within plot to build character and do all sorts of fun and exciting things that, at first, seem tangential to moving the story forward. Stripped of these moments, plot is no more than one thing after another. There might be momentum as a reader moves through the events, but beware any novel described as a roller coaster ride. Roller coaster rides are over in a couple of minutes. Unless you've got the writing chops to write with the brevity of

Lydia Davis, you'll need the narrative to last a lot longer than that. Ideally, you're filling that narrative with writing so good that readers won't ask why it's there.

In the anecdote on this page, about trying to clean a dirty windshield, notice how there is no explanation. The narrator doesn't say, "Here's what this story means" or "Here's how it felt." He only gives the details of what happened along with context ("They got wiper fluid on sale in the window twenty-five feet away"). He doesn't need anything else because the opening line ("one of the saddest things I ever saw") has done that work for him. It's told us how to read the anecdote that follows.

Earlier in the book, I quoted Dean Koontz's blurb that "Reading Joe Lansdale is like listening to a favorite uncle who just happens to be a fabulous storyteller." It's passages like this one from Jim Shepard that create that same "favorite uncle" effect. When you're listening to a great storyteller, you don't really care about plot. There are very few stories that you'll hear in your life that are riveting because of what happens. The reason people have been entertaining each other with stories from time immemorial is because of *how* they're told, the flavor that a storyteller adds to well-known plots. If you want your book to be remembered, find your own flavor. Here's an exercise to get started.

THE EXERCISE

Let's use an interview question to create space for an anecdote, using "Boys Town" by Jim Shepard as a model:

1. CHOOSE AN INTERVIEW QUESTION. A Google search will bring up hundreds of examples, but here are some common ones:

   - Tell us about yourself.
   - What's your greatest strength?
   - What's your biggest weakness?
   - Describe a challenge you faced and how you overcame it.
   - Describe a difficult colleague and how you worked with that person.
   - Describe your value system.
   - What are your pet peeves?

- Describe your work history?
- What is your preferred work culture?
- What was the best/worst/happiest/saddest moment of your life.
- If you could meet one historical person, who would it be?
- If you could return to one year of your life, which would it be?
- If you were a tree/animal/state/biosphere, what kind would you be?

Try picking an easy one and a hard one. Surprise yourself.

2. ANSWER THE QUESTION WITH A STORY. It's often a bad sign in an interview when the question is longer than the answer. When you're drafting a story, the goal is to get words onto the page. So, don't give a quick answer like, "He prefers to work alone." Instead, tell a story about a time that the character needed to work alone but couldn't or about a time when working alone was a great relief.

3. LET THE OPENING LINE DO THE WORK OF EXPLAINING THE STORY. If you tell the story right, with the right frame (which you've provided with the interview question), no other explanation is likely required. Adding more will likely bog down the story, leaving the reader thinking, "Okay, I got it already" and beginning to skim ahead.

4. FOLLOW THE PASSAGE WITH A CLEAR LINE ABOUT PLOT. Shepard follows his anecdote with the line "My hair started falling out." A few lines later, he finds his mom hiding a voicemail left by the narrator's young son. In short, we jump immediately from the anecdote into the main narrative. The result is that the emotion in the anecdote carries over into this new scene. So, place your interview question and its passage into the larger story. Use it as a break from the plot and a trampoline back into it.

The goal is to create the space for character-building anecdotes by using the sort of obvious conversation starters that we encounter almost every day. Don't over think the questions. Just start writing. Surprise yourself. There's much to be said for outlining (though you'll notice I don't talk about it in this book), but the real point of outlining (at least to the outliners I know) is to settle the question of what happens next so that the writer can focus on the good stuff. I hope you'll find plenty of good stuff to keep you going!

WHO DO YOU LOVE   *Jennifer Weiner*

His face was red and his eyes were watery as he put his arms on Andy's shoulders. "Andrew," he began. Then Lori had been in the room, throwing the door open so hard that it slammed into the wall with a sound like a gunshot.

"Get away from him," she'd said. "You don't get to speak to my son ever again."

When they were gone, his mother had stood with her hands braced against the front door, red nails vivid against the white paint, as if they might come back and try to push their way back through. Finally, she'd turned to Andy and in that terrible, low voice had said, *If they call, hang up the phone. If they ever come, you shut the door in their faces. As far as I'm concerned, you don't have any grandparents. We don't need them. We have each other. That's enough.*

But now Lori was gone and they were here. Andy could see the wrapped and ribboned boxes in their hands.

"Honey, please," his grandma said. The heavy gold earrings that she wore had stretched out her earlobes, and her red lipstick was smeared on her front teeth. He remembered how she always smelled good, and her soft sweaters, and cookies with sprinkles, and how he'd felt when she'd said, "Of course he's mine."

Andy's throat felt thick and his eyes were burning. "I can't," he said again.

His grandfather stepped forward until his chest was almost brushing the door, and Andy could smell him, Old Spice and cigars. He was a heavy man with iron-gray hair combed straight back from his deeply grooved forehead. He'd been a pipe fitter and worked in the Navy Yard, but now he was retired.

"Andrew," he said, in his deep voice. "We know we're not welcome here. But please, son. Whatever's going on between the two of us and your mother isn't your fault."

Jennifer Weiner, excerpt from *Who Do You Love*. Copyright © 2015 by Jennifer Weiner. Reprinted with the permission of Atria Books, a division of Simon & Schuster, Inc. All rights reserved.

JUXTAPOSE EMOTIONAL STATES

THE STRATEGY

You've probably heard of Jennifer Weiner for one of two reasons. One, she is a beloved writer whose books are almost assured of hitting the best-sellers list. Two, she has publicly called out book reviewers for not reviewing her books and other books like them. Like Rodney Danger-field, she feels that she gets no respect. She's a genre writer. In this case, her genre is women's fiction, an odd, catchall term that refers to novels with women at the center and (often but not always) a romantic storyline. Like romance novels, they usually end on a happy note, but on the way to that ending, they play around with structure and plot in ways that might surprise readers not familiar with the genre.

I say this because I think of myself as a literary writer, with stories in literary magazines; I'm as guilty as anyone of feeling a little smug when it comes to genre. Yet when I read *Who Do You Love*, I experienced an in-credible shock. I realized that the novel had an eerily similar premise to one I'd started and given up upon. In both, a troubled boy with a single mother gets arrested, causing his mom to give him an ultimatum. This page drops into that scene, one that is incredibly similar to a scene from my abandoned novel (the mom gets angry at her parents and forbids them to see her son). The main difference between the two is that Weiner's scene is far better than the one I wrote. When I tried to figure out why hers worked so well, I assumed its success had something with plot, one of Weiner's strengths, as it is for most genre writers. But I had my mind changed (and eyes opened) when I presented a writing exercise based on the scene to the Austin chapter of the Romance Writers Association. The writers at the meeting immediately pointed out ways that the scene succeeds in ways that have nothing to do with plot—but instead with a literary quality Harold Bloom might even approve of: its sentences.

In the scene, Andy is forced to choose between his mother and grandparents, and the toll it takes on him is clear; on the next page, his emotions boil over and land him in jail. The scene's power derives from the acute way that Weiner juxtaposes the emotions connected to the two paths Andy can take. On one hand, his grandparents are portrayed as tender and caring while, on the other hand, his mother's rage fills the room.

Watch how Weiner shifts from one hand to the other:

- The grandfather has tears in his eyes as he "put his arms on Andy's shoulders" and says his name.
  - But then: Andy's mom bursts into the room and screams, "Get away from him." She tells Andy to ignore and disown his grandparents: "We don't need them."
    - Then we jerk back: A sentence later, the grandparents arrive with armloads of Christmas gifts, his grandmother saying, "Honey, please." He remembers her good smell, soft sweaters, and cookies. We smell his grandfather's Old Spice and hear his deep voice.

This is powerful stuff. Andy is being pulled in two directions, and the forces pulling on him are significant and succinctly juxtaposed. The sweaters are so much softer for being next to his mother telling him to "shut the door in their faces." In case you think I'm making too much of this moment, I'd suggest you consider the most popular movie franchise in American history: Star Wars. The best of the films is the second one, *The Empire Strikes Back*, and it contains one of the most famous lines in history: "Luke, I am your father." Darth Vader goes from fighting Luke Skywalker to extending his hand, offering to pull him close, to mentor and father him. That image of the villain in all black, stretching out his hand and using the name *father*, is a stunning juxtaposition. When my kids began expressing interest in *Star Wars*, we borrowed a

library book that told the stories of the original three films, with photos. When we got to this scene and I said the famous line, my kids' eyes
bugged out. "That's his *dad*?" they said. Luke is torn between two clear
desires (help his friends, know his father) that are excruciating to choose
between. Weiner does the same thing, and Andy's reaction is like Luke's:
his "throat felt thick and his eyes were burning." The juxtaposition can
be seen on the sentence level, but it also dictates the structure that the
novel will take, built on that emotional conflict.

THE EXERCISE

Let's juxtapose emotional images, using *Who Do You Love* by Jennifer
Weiner as a model:

1. DETERMINE THE PURPOSE OF THE SCENE. This is something that
    may be easier for screenwriters, who often knowingly start a scene
    with one emotional state and end it on a different one. The purpose is
    to, basically, make things more intense for a character. This may be a
    better way of thinking about purpose. Ask yourself, what is the dra-
    matic result of this scene? Beware the word *realize*, as in *the charac-
    ter realizes* ____. Realization is important, but the realization should
    have consequences—even for mind-blowing realizations. For exam-
    ple, imagine a character realizing that she should be a boy, not a girl.
    That's a giant realization, but it's even more powerful if the character
    realizes this while on a date. In other words, the realization ought to
    make a situation more challenging. So, what challenge does your scene
    present to a character?

2. IDENTIFY TWO EMOTIONAL STATES WITHIN THE SCENE. In
    Weiner's scene, there's the grandparents' love for their grandson jux-
    taposed with the mother's hatred for her parents. But the emotions can
    also be located within the same person, as with my five-year-old son
    at any public place, torn between raw enthusiasm and his tired feet.
    The emotion can also be the same one but split like light through a
    prism: Andy loves his grandparents but also loves his mother. Try all
    three version: 1) juxtapose different emotions as felt by different char-
    acters (love/hate, anger/joy, enthusiasm/indifference, pride/embarrass-

ment, or any pair of unlike emotions), 2) juxtapose the different emotions with the *same* person, and 3) split one emotion so that it's felt in two different, conflicting ways.

3. DISTILL THE DUELING EMOTIONS TO IMAGES. Weiner does a great job of using the characters' movements to do this. So, the grandfather's "arms on Andy's shoulder" are juxtaposed with his mom "throwing the door open so hard that it slammed into the wall." She also focuses on specific body parts: we see Andy's mother's "red nails vivid against the white paint" of the door as she holds it shut and, in the next paragraph, his grandparents' hands holding "wrapped and ribboned boxes." We're also told about his grandmother's nice smell and soft sweaters and his grandfather's smell of "Old Spice and cigars." In short, Weiner is using the full range of sensory possibilities to convey emotion. So, try juxtaposing a) characters' movements and b) the differences between particular details about their bodies or appearance.

4. STEP OUT OF TIME IF NECESSARY. Weiner doesn't restrict herself to the present moment. The details about the grandmother's smell, sweaters, and cookies are remembered. They don't break the momentum of the scene because they're doing the same work (establishing emotional conflict) as the present-tense details. So, let your character recall something from the past that fits the same emotional frame that you decided on earlier.

5. REDUCE CONNECTIVE MATERIAL BETWEEN THE EMOTIONS AS MUCH AS POSSIBLE. By definition, juxtaposition only works if sharp contrasts are drawn. The more stuff that gets between the conflicting emotions and their images, the less effective the juxtaposition becomes. Weiner creates those contrasts with transitional words: The grandfather puts his arms on Andy's shoulders *and then* "Lori had been in the room, throwing the door open"; Andy's mother tells him to disown his grandparents *but now* "Lori was gone and they were here." The transitional words *then* and *but now* quickly pivot us from one emotion to the next. Try this: After a sentence with a clear emotional image, begin your next sentence with *then* or *but now*.

6. MOVE BACK AND FORTH MORE THAN ONCE. Weiner could have called it quits after the first paragraph on the page, which introduces us to tender grandfather and angry mother. Instead, she keeps moving back and forth between these emotional images, which heightens

the tension: which one will Andy choose? If there's any truism about writing, it's that once you find something that works, it's often a good idea to return to it again and again.

The goal is to create tension and reader engagement by structuring a chapter around conflicting emotions and juxtaposed images that distill those emotions to their strongest versions. I've written elsewhere (and you've almost certainly been told in writing classes) that characters must have strong desires, but it's truer to say that they should have *more than one* strong desire. A good story will force them to choose between them.

"THE LOST & FOUND DEPARTMENT OF GREATER BOSTON"

Elizabeth McCracken

The children knew nothing about palmistry, little about life, less about love, but they believed in life lines and love lines the way they believed in mercury thermometers: they meant something but probably you needed a grown-up to read them. "It means I'll write my own fate," Karen Blackbird would have said, if asked. The children, including her own son, didn't care that Karen Blackbird was forty-two: all of adulthood seemed one un-differentiated stretch of time. But the ages of objects excited them. When Karen Blackbird disappeared, the graphite in her palm was thirty-three years old.

In this case and no other, *Once upon a time* means *Late summer, 1982*.

Before her disappearance, Karen Blackbird lived in a ramshackle Victorian with her elderly father and teenage son. The son was seventeen but small: five-foot tall and eighty pounds. He hired himself out to rake leaves and shovel snow, he delivered the weekly *Graphic*—all the usual local-boy jobs. With his dark hair and his newsprint eyes, he looked like an enterprising orphan, though he dressed like a hippie, in jeans faded to gray and ragged slogan T-shirts. The grandfather didn't approve of how his daughter was raising his grandson. He believed childhood was the furnace in which men were forged: it couldn't be lukewarm. The grandfather had a head shaped like a bellows, wide at the temples, ears attached at slants, face narrowing down to a mean, disappointed, huffing mouth.

Look here: Karen Blackbird is standing on the front porch before she disappears. The house itself is a wreck, the brown asbestos tile weathered in teary streaks. A lawn mower skulks up to its alligatorish eyebrows in the yard.

Reprinted from Elizabeth McCracken, "The Lost & Found Department of Greater Boston," *Thunderstruck* (New York: Dial, 2014): 128.

REPEAT YOURSELF

THE STRATEGY

Once upon a time, a woman disappeared. She left behind a father and a son, and then the father died and the son was starving, so he stole a frozen pizza from a grocery store. He got caught. The authorities found him a new place to live, but the grocery store manager never forgot him and often wondered what happened to his mother. The boy grew up into a well-adjusted, happy adult.

That's the short version of Elizabeth McCracken's story, "The Lost & Found Department of Greater Boston." Condensed like this, it seems like a weirdly anti-climactic plot, one that might lose the reader after a few pages. And yet it's a long story that holds the reader's attention in dramatic fashion—and not because the premise has a ripped-from-the-headlines sensibility to it, as do so many of the other stories in the same collection *Thunderstruck*. The lurid storylines aren't really the appeal. If they were, the plots would be more complicated, with twists and turns and reversals. You'd spend pages wondering, "Who did it?" Instead, Mc-Cracken tends to tell us the same thing over and over again. It's a great lesson in what writers mean when they talk about story structure. These repeated lines affect the actual shape the story takes.

Here's the story's first sentence: "Once upon a time a woman disappeared from a dead-end street." That opening paragraph ends on the page we've just read, with the sentence, "When Karen Blackbird disappeared, the graphite in her palm was thirty-three years old."

And, then, two sentences later, this: "Before her disappearance . . ."

That's three references to the disappearance in less than two pages. It's not because McCracken thinks we're dumb and unable to remember what's going on. Instead, she understands the appeal of what she's got, a hook that can keep on hooking. It's not so different than the way reality TV shows milk their dramatic devices. How many times will such a show cut to commercial with the announcer saying, "Who will get voted off?" When the show returns from break, we still don't find out the answer, and yet we keep watching. Why? Because we want to know the answer.

In a way, plot and structure mean almost the same thing. If plot is the delivery of information (how fast or slow), structure is the way pieces of information are grouped together on the page. A good writer (or reality-show producer) can eke a lot of pages or minutes out of one good plot point. And what fills those pages? The good stuff. I've been talking about this throughout the book, and now here's the big payoff: a famous writer citing an even more famous writer in order to make the same point:

In his introduction to *The Adventures of Huckleberry Finn*, George Saunders claims that all writers have "The Thing This Writer Loves to Do, and Does Naturally" and that this thing, whether it's being funny or describing nature or whatever, is also the thing readers love. And yet doing nothing but that thing—for instance writing "[t]hree hundred pages of descriptions of rich people's houses"—will become boring for even the most smitten reader, and so the writer needs a device to move the story forward. That device, whatever it is, is plot. In this view of narrative, the plot is simply a mechanism that creates space for the good stuff. One plot structure that's perfect for this: repetition.

It's a strategy used in almost every story in the collection *Thunder-struck*. In reading those stories, it becomes clear that McCracken's true love is describing characters. She does it so well that each one seems like a mic drop—except that then she picks up the mic, delivers another killer line, and drops the mic again. For example, here is McCracken describing a woman in "Something Amazing": "Her clothes are unbleached cotton and hemp; an invalid could eat them." And here she is describing a woman and a rabbit in "Juliet":

The bunny eyed her with its usual unhappiness, another grubby pair of hands reaching into the cage. Human flesh gave our neurotic bunny the willies.

And, finally, this from the page in question:

> He believed childhood was the furnace in which men were forged:
> it couldn't be lukewarm. The grandfather had a head shaped like a
> bellows . . .

You might think, well, those descriptions are so great that there's no
need to make room for them. They step onto the page the way a good-
looking person slides into a crowded elevator just before the door closes.
The space creates itself. Yet anything beautiful grows dull when there's
no urgency to pay attention to it. Anyone who's visited a major art museum can attest to this: after an hour or two, your eyes glaze over, no
matter how spectacular the exhibits.

But repetition can be dull as well, which is why McCracken doesn't
simply repeat sentences word-for-word.

- "Once upon a time a woman disappeared from a dead-end street."
- "When Karen Blackbird disappeared . . ."
- "Before her disappearance . . ."

McCracken changes the basic the basic diction (*disappeared* and *disappearance*) and syntax by adding conditional words like *when* and *before*,
words that promise something new. The reader feels that the story is
moving forward, even if nothing has actually happened yet.

THE EXERCISE

Let's use repetition to create space for the good stuff, using "The Lost
& Found Department of Greater Boston" by Elizabeth McCracken as a
guide.

1. IDENTIFY QUESTIONS WITHIN YOUR STORY. These are moments
   that suggest something next: this and now *this:* a woman disappeared
   and then . . . Anyone hearing this story will ask, "And *then* what happened?" We naturally want to know, and our desire gives the writer
   great power. She knows we'll keep reading in order to satisfy our cu-

riosity. So, rather than immediately supplying the answer, she can de-velop the story in whatever what she wants and then pique our cu-riosity again by repeating the question. This holds true at any point in the story. In "The Lost & Found Department of Greater Boston," a character hangs up a *missing person* poster, and that action gets re-peated for several pages. Again, it's a moment that begs two questions: What happened next? Did they think it would work? If you can iden-tify these moments in your story, then you can repeat them.

2. STATE THE QUESTION AS SIMPLY AS POSSIBLE—AND AS A STATEMENT, NOT A QUESTION. McCracken doesn't write, "Will the woman be found?" Instead, she tells us that "a woman disappeared" and trusts the readers to ask the question themselves. In workshop, this is sometimes called "let the reader do the work," which is both true and aggravatingly vague. What work? In love stories, that work usually looks like this: The reader takes in the situation unfolding on the pages—X unable to take her eyes off Y—and makes an inference—it's inevitable that X and Y will go on a date. The questions are clear: How will the date go? Will Y like X back? Why does X like Y? State the hooks within your story as clearly as possible.

3. REPEAT THE STATEMENT BY ADDING CONDITIONAL WORDS. Cre-ate geographic space (what's literally around the statement) and time (what happened before and after). *When* they went on the date . . . *Be-fore* they went on the date . . . *During* the date . . . It's in the passages that follow that you have the opportunity to play around, to do your favorite things as a writer.

4. REPEAT THE STATEMENT BY ADDING STAKES. Imagine that your reader is constantly on the verge of leaving your story. A guest ed-itor for a best-of anthology once wrote that she selected stories that held her attention while sitting on a plane. So, if your reader is dis-tracted and uncomfortable, don't be shy about raising the stakes in your repetition: "What nobody knew about the date was . . ." "It was almost certain that the date would . . ." "The thing about the date that worried her most was . . ." You're creating space for the thing you love to do.

5. END THE REPETITION. Though it's theoretically possible to keep the repetition going until the very end of the story, most readers and most stories will require you to make good on what you've promised, that

you'll answer the question that you've posed. So, end it. Move on. If this happens in the middle of the story or chapter or novel, choose something new to repeat. You've got a list of things, remember? This is one way that plot works: introduce a ball, keep it aloft like a beach ball at a baseball game, and then let it fall. Introduce a new ball. While the ball is aloft, play.

The goal is to use repetition of dramatic statements to create the space to do what you love as a writer, whatever that is. It's one more example of carving out opportunities within plot to do the fun stuff.

THE MOOR'S ACCOUNT   *Laila Lalami*

Dorantes was telling Martín about our winter on the Island of Misfortune and about the raft we had found on the river the day before.

I know what happened to it, Martín said. I heard the story from the only survivor from that raft. After the storm, the comptroller's raft was marooned not far from this area, at the mouth of the river. The men walked a short distance to the bay, in order to feed on oysters and crabs, but once there they found the Narváez raft. So many men had died during the storm that both crews could have fit on one raft, but the governor refused to take the stranded men aboard. On the contrary, he ordered his own men to disembark and said that, henceforth, both crews would travel by land while he and his page would follow in the water along the coast. If they came upon a river, he promised, he would ferry the land crew across.

The comptroller rebelled, of course. And with an order like that, who could blame him? Once again, he complained, the governor was dividing the men into land and sea contingents. Had he learned nothing from his experience? Narváez immediately relieved the comptroller of his command and put one of his own men in charge of the land crew, a brute by the name of Sotomayor. So everyone was forced to walk along the shore, while Narváez sailed close by. The next night, while they were camped on a beach, Narváez slept on his raft, with his page and helmsman by his side. But the wind picked up in the middle of the night, and the raft was swept to sea. The rest of the survivors walked along the shore for several days, hoping to reach Pánuco on foot. When one of them died of disease, they ate his flesh. Before long, they began to kill and eat one another. The last man alive was Esquivel the welder, who was still feeding on Sotomayor when these Indians you see here found him.

The m-m-men t-t-turned into c-c-cannibals?

Yes, Father.

A-a-all of them?

That is the story Esquivel the welder told me.

No, the friar replied. No, no, no. He must have had the fever and was delirious. Or he made up the story just to frighten you. I knew Esquivel. He could not have done what he told you he did.

Father, who would lie about something like that?

Laila Lalami, excerpt from "The Story of the Three Rivers" from *The Moor's Account*. Copyright © 2014 by Laila Lalami. Used by permission of Pantheon Books, an imprint of Penguin Random House, LLC.

USE STORYTELLING TO EXPAND YOUR STORY'S WORLD

THE STRATEGY

Here's the dark side of creating space within plot for the good stuff: your novel or story goes off the rails. After a while, you realize that you have no idea how to get back on the rails or even what the rails look like. In the process in finding them, the story bloats to 15,000 words or you start telling yourself that many respected novels have been over 800 pages long. This is a natural problem to encounter. Our characters and plots exist within worlds, and as we develop our stories, we're also building the worlds around them. Like explorers in some strange new land, we see something fantastic and unexpected, and so we write it down. And as we write it, we get more excited, and soon the thing that we saw glimpsed in passing and wanted to write a few sentences about suddenly becomes an essential part of the story. Sometimes this is good. Sometimes it's just a bunch of stuff crammed into a book.

We need a way to fit the amazing discoveries from our narrative worlds into our stories without losing our sense of direction. An excellent example for how to do that can be found in Laila Lalami's novel, *The Moor's Account*.

The novel tells the story of real-life, historical Estebanico, a Moroccan slave who accompanied Cabeza de Vaca's expedition to Florida, through the American Southwest, and into Mexico. It's an adventure story with shipwrecks, monsters, and villains—so much cool stuff that it could easily lose its way, despite its clear narrative map (the expedition's route through the Americas). There are so many weird, compelling things for the characters and writer to notice that the novel could easily get bogged down or choose the wrong path. But Lalami manages to include those great details and keep the story going.

This page demonstrates one of her strategies.

It takes place in Texas, after the expedition has been shipwrecked on what is now Galveston Island, endured a winter of starvation and disease, and split into two different groups. Those groups have now reunited on the Texas mainland and encountered a man named Martin, who had deserted one group over the winter. This encounter gives Lalami a perfect opportunity to broaden the world of her novel. She does it by letting Martin tell a story: "I know what happened to it . . . I heard the story from the only survivor from that raft."

The story, as you can read, is the stuff of old-school, paperback adventure stories: a villainous leader, a brutish henchman, an almost-Godlike flood that washes the leader away, and, finally, cannibalism. That last detail is so good that a character literally trembles over it: "The m-m-men t-t-turned into c-c-cannibals?" It's a detail so provocative that its inspired stories for as long as people have been telling them. Herodotus, writing roughly around 450 BC, included cannibals in *The Histories*. One of the first English-language novels, *Robinson Crusoe*, has cannibals. One of the greatest American writers, Herman Melville, wrote about cannibals at least twice: in *Typee* and *Moby Dick*. We still find the idea provocative: think about the Donner party, Jeffrey Dahmer, the film *Alive*, and the films and novels about Hannibal Lecter. There's something about cannibalism that we respond to instinctually, and so when it appears in your story, you're almost obligated to include it.

But there's a problem: once you put cannibals on the page, it's hard to write about anything else. A story needs an out, and this is exactly what Lalami gives *The Moor's Account*. Martin tells his story about the cannibals, but when the story ends, the cannibals disappear. They're gone. The expedition and the novel's plot carry on without them, though the knowledge of their story will stay with the characters and inform—directly or indirectly—their decisions.

How does she keep the cannibals from eating up more of the story? In large part, it's that clear narrative thread I mentioned earlier, the expedition's trip/quest. The men have to keep moving, which means they'll encounter something else down the road and the plot will change accordingly. But the story also informs their experience of the road. It's one thing to walk down a path, worrying about dangers ahead and around you; it's quite another to worry about the people who are supposed to have your back. The story creates fear in the men. If it had no emotional effect, it wouldn't be worth telling.

When all else fails, use emotion as your guide to structure. Anything that makes you or your characters weep, tremble, laugh, or rejoice is worth expanding upon. Stories or details that lack that emotional punch can be cut. This is why the full name of William Goldman's novel *The Princess Bride* is actually *The Princess Bride: S. Morgenstern's Classic Tale of True Love and High Adventure, the "good parts" version,* abridged by William Goldman. Make all of your stories and novels just the good parts. If that means telling stories within stories, do it.

THE EXERCISE

Let's use storytelling to expand the world of a story or novel, using *The Moor's Account* by Laila Lalami as a model.

1. IDENTIFY THE AMAZING THING. You can often identify this in your writing because you've spent a lot of time rationalizing its existence, telling yourself, "It doesn't really fit, but . . ." Or, you've considered pulling it out of the novel/story and expanding it into its own narrative. You may have disappeared for hours or days down the rabbit hole of research, learning more about it. Or you tell people about the official story but quickly segue to this one minor part of it because it strikes you as so incredible. In other words, if you're honest with yourself, you probably already know what amazing thing is threatening to run your story off the rails.

2. REMIND YOURSELF OF THE MAIN PLOT THREAD. In other words, what are the rails running through your story? In *The Moor's Account*, it's the expedition's path through the Americas. Any road trip story will have a similar plot line. But most stories aren't about trips, and so it can be useful to formulate the plot thread as a question. For Lalami's

novel, that question might be "Will they reach their destination?" or "How many of them will survive?" Love stories have some obvious questions: Will they get together? Will they last? Coming-of-age stories tend to have this question: How embarrassing or uncomfortable will the situation get before the character gains some maturity? It's necessary to keep these questions in mind because you can occasionally ask yourself if what you're writing is relevant? If not, you may be too far off the rails.

3. FIGURE OUT THE IMPACT OF THE AMAZING THING ON THE PLOT. A story can leave the rails for a while if what happens affects the characters or the plot. In *The Moor's Account*, the characters now understand that it's possible for the situation to become so dire that they might resort to cannibalism. They've learned something about themselves—and, generally, characters learning about themselves is a good thing for a story. A tangent within a story can also impact characters decisions—what they must factor into the calculus. But, if the amazing thing leaves no trace, so to speak, then it might not be necessary to include in the story.

4. CHOOSE A CHARACTER WHO WILL INTRODUCE THE THING. Once you've decided the *thing* has a place in your story, you need to build a frame for it. Without a frame, the thing can sprawl like a Texas suburb and take over your story. One way to create a frame is to put the thing into a story that someone tells. In *The Moor's Account*, a character tells the story about the cannibalism that was told to him by someone who was part of it. Note: The story is told secondhand. It's not even told by someone who was there. That indicates how powerful the amazing thing—cannibalism—is. If it was told firsthand, it might still take over the story. So, the more powerful the thing, the more distance you need from it. The question is this: Who will tell the story? Is it someone who encountered or participated in the amazing thing? Or someone who heard about it from someone else? You can have the character tell the story in dialogue, as in *The Moor's Account*. Or, you can do the equivalent of the washy-screen thing that television shows do when fading into something that happened in the past: the character says, "I'm going to tell you a crazy story," and then there's a space break and the prose moves inside the story so that it's not being told through dialogue but, instead, through normal narration.

5. GIVE YOUR STORY A WAY OUT. The most obvious way to do this is to simply end the story that's being told. Or, let characters respond to the story. This is what Lalami does with the stammering priest. Once he talks, the story is over and the repercussions of the story take center stage—which is to say that the plot takes over again and the story gets back on the rails.

The goal is to use a story within a story to add great anecdotes or details to a narrative without them taking over. It may feel like the opposite of structure, like your novel is sprawling out of control, but if you've got a clear sense of direction, you can add in all sorts of asides and tangents as long as they pack a punch.

HOW TO

DRIVE PLOT

FORWARD

STATION ELEVEN *Emily St. John Mandel*

She ran a hand through her short gray hair. "There have been four times," she said, "in all these years, when Symphony members have become separated from the Symphony, and in every single instance they have followed the separation protocol, and we've been reunited at the destination. Alexandra?"

"Yes?"

"Will you state the separation protocol, please?" It had been drilled into all of them.

"We never travel without a destination," Alexandra said. "If we're ever, if you're ever separated from the Symphony on the road, you make your way to the destination and wait."

"And what is the current destination?"

"The Museum of Civilization in the Severn City Airport."

"Yes." The conductor was quiet, looking at them. The forest was in shadow now, but there was still some light in the corridor of sky above the road, the last pink of sunset streaking the clouds. "I have been on the road for fifteen years," she said, "and Sayid's been with me for twelve. Dieter for even longer."

"He was with me in the beginning," Gil said. "We walked out of Chicago together."

"I leave neither of them willingly." The conductor's eyes were shining. "But I won't risk the rest of you by staying here a day longer."

That night they kept a double watch, teams of four instead of two, and set out before dawn the following morning. The air was damp between the walls of the forest, the clouds marbled overhead. A scent of pine in the air. Kirsten walked by the first caravan, trying to think of nothing. A sense of being caught in a terrible dream.

They stopped at the end of the afternoon. The fevered summers of this century, this impossible heat. The lake glittered through the trees.

Reprinted from Emily St. John Mandel, *Station Eleven* (New York: Knopf, 2014), 138.

ADD PLOT ELEMENTS THAT CHANGE THE COURSE OF THE STORY

THE STRATEGY

When we talk about *the plot* of a novel, we often speak of it as a singular thing like *outer space* or *steak* or *happiness*. In reality, however, there usually isn't a single plot but, instead, a general *thing that the novel is about* and, within it, a series of storylines. For most of us, this makes intuitive sense with novels that build around quests and road trips. The general *aboutness* is the journey, and within that journey is a series of episodes built around encounters with strangers and sudden hardships (blizzards, flat tires, one-eyed giants). The result is that for stories likes these, the most memorable parts are just that: parts.

This is a very old way of thinking about narrative. Homer (or the countless bards whose stories have become the Homeric tales) recited his epic poems aloud, before audiences. He didn't start at the beginning and finish at the end. Instead, he'd tell the story of Odysseus and the Cyclops or Hector's duel with Ajax during the Trojan War, episodes that, strung together, were part of the general plots of *The Iliad* (war) and *The Odyssey* (getting lost while returning home from war).

Many contemporary novels are constructed in the same way. What are chapters if not episodes? Therefore, understanding plot in its full scope means not only figuring out both the general aboutness of the story, but also what drives the plot of each episode. Is each one a continuation of something we've already seen? Or is it something wholly new, causing all-new obstacles? This is why it's so difficult to discuss part of a novel in workshop; readers can't see the whole thing, and so they can't offer good feedback. It's an idea that depends upon our seeing novels as having interconnected strands like a rug or afghan blanket. If you're only looking at a four-by-four-inch square, you don't really know about the piece as a whole. Sometimes this is true—but not always.

Edgar Allan Poe famously argued for "the unity of effect" in his essay "The Importance of the Single Effect in a Prose Tale." He claimed that the first sentence of the story must work toward this effect, as must every episode of the plot. But he was talking about short stories. In a later essay, "The Philosophy of Composition," he wrote, "If any literary work is too long to be read at one sitting, we must be content to dispense with the immensely important effect derivable from unity of impression—for, if two sittings be required, the affairs of the world interfere, and everything like totality is at once destroyed." In other words, novels don't need to worry so much about achieving a coherent effect. The reader begins a novel, puts it down, goes to sleep, walks away, watches a film or TV show, gets inspired or angered over some news story, experiences the major and minor joys and tragedies of life, and then comes back to the novel to resume reading. As a result, novels are inherently episodic in how they are experienced by readers. The great writers understand this. I remember recommending *One Hundred Years of Solitude* to my brother, and when we talked later, he told me, "It's crazy. Every chapter, some new insane thing happens."

In novels, if you want, you can introduce something new in the middle of the book. If it's interesting, the reader will likely stick with you as long as you develop the thing you've introduced.

Emily St. John Mandel does exactly this in her novel *Station Eleven*. It's set in a post-apocalyptic world in which most of the human population has been wiped out by a strain of swine flu. Twenty years after the pandemic, the survivors and their descendants live in small communities, in fear of strangers. The novel moves back and forth between the years immediately preceding the pandemic and the years afterward, especially year 20, when a caravan of actors and musicians travel from city to city in the upper Midwest of the former United States of America, performing Shakespearean plays. It takes roughly fifty pages to set up this premise, and then something new is introduced: a man called the Prophet, who rules a small town visited by the caravan. The caravan leaves the town in a hurry, worried that they'll be followed and harassed. Then, some of the caravan's members vanish. As a reader, this is where you check the clock on your nightstand and decide to keep reading. It's great, tense writing. But there's a problem with such a plotline: something needs to happen next. Story lines must continue to a conclusion (at least they usually do), but when you've dropped a new story line into a novel, the risk you take is thinking, "Ooh, cool," and then not knowing how to keep it going. In road trip novels, the characters simply move on down the road (which is what Odysseus does after he escapes the Cyclops). But in novels with a confined world, characters can't just leave. They must continue to deal with the plot point you've introduced, and so you must reconcile the new plot with the novel and world you've already created.

On this page, Mandel does precisely that. We're given some rules (the separation protocol, or what to do if members of the caravan get split up), and these rules suggest that the characters we've been following from the beginning of the book have thought about this possibility. They've planned for it. This automatically gives the novel a way forward; they'll simply follow their plan. It also gives them somewhere to go: the Museum of Civilization in the Severn City Airport. As a result, the characters aren't heading into an unknown void, which is almost always a bad move for a writer, because that void can contain anything, and endless possibilities mean countless wrong paths for a writer to follow. In *Station Eleven*, the exact nature of the museum is unknown, but it is, at least, a defined space. What Mandel does very soon is fill that space, writing chapters from the viewpoint of characters in the airport so that when the caravan arrives, we have some sense for what they'll find. We can make predictions about what will happen once they get there, and those predictions create suspense.

So, *Station Eleven* introduces a new plot element a decent way into the book and then introduces a place for that plot element to go. Then, it spends time fleshing out that place before the plot arrives. In a way, Mandel begins to work backwards, which is what Poe suggested: "Every plot, worth the name, must be elaborated to its denouement before anything be attempted with the pen." In other words, writers must know where their plots are going before they begin to write. I'm not sure that is completely true. Mandel may have discovered her novel as she wrote it. But the final effect is one of clear direction and, to use Poe's word, *intention*.

If you're going to introduce new things to your novel, which is probably a good idea, you had better also create a direction for them to move and a destination for them to reach.

THE EXERCISE

Let's add new plot elements, using *Station Eleven* by Emily St. John Mandel as a model:

1. DEFINE THE WORLD THAT THE NEW PLOT ELEMENT WILL ENTER. This is the general *aboutness* of the story, often the first thing we learn about a novel in the book jacket. Films trailers are especially good at introducing this: *In a world where. . .* The novel *Station Eleven* is set in a world where a virus has wiped out most of humanity and the survivors live in isolated camps. But what about stories set in a world like the readers'? The same basic idea is still at work but on a personal level. If someone is receiving treatment for cancer, you'd better believe that their world is dominated by the disease and treatment. If someone is married and in love with someone else, that affair fills every empty crevice in their mind and life. There is the world we physically inhabit (Texas, the United States, Earth, whatever) but also the world we live in: gated suburban community, small town in the Rio Grande Valley where Spanish is as predominant as English, cancer diagnosis, marital affair. The question is this: What feature of the characters' world dominates their lives?

2. ADD THE ELEMENT. It's usually a complicating element. One of the oldest tricks in a writer's arsenal is to break a routine, to say, "Everything was going along as usual until. . . " If you're working on a novel, you'll know that ideas for new, complicating elements pop into your head all the time. I can imagine Mandel working on a post-apocalyptic novel and thinking, "You know what'd be cool? A cult leader!" She probably had other ideas as well. Keep a list. Pick one thing from the list.

3. CREATE CAUSATION. By causation, I simply mean that the new element causes problems for characters. Think of it as an equation: because of this new element, X happens, and so Y responds, which causes Z to happen. In *Station Eleven*, as soon as the Prophet arrives in the novel, the caravan troupe must respond. They leave town quickly, trying to get away. They encounter someone else trying to get away and who wants to join them; a decision must be made. The trouble continues and worsens. Once this chain of actions and reactions begins, follow it as far as you can. Eventually you'll reach a moment of panic: the characters' ability to respond to a problem seems dwarfed by the size of the problem. This is great for suspense but can be deadly to the novel if the writer doesn't know how to handle it.

4. ANSWER THE "NOW WHAT" QUESTION. If you've driven your characters into a very difficult place, it's tempting to rescue them with some outside force (deus ex machina)—and sometimes that's necessary and works. After Frodo and Sam throw the ring of power into the volcano, they're stranded in the worst place in Middle Earth—until an eagle arrives to rescue them. As a rule, if Tolkien does it, so can you. That said, you should first fall back on the wisdom of your characters. Once you've put them in the awful place, ask what their plan is for such situations. Do they have a premeditated protocol to follow? This is what Mandel does. Her characters supply the solution to their problem: follow the protocol and meet at the destination.

5. GIVE THE CHARACTERS AND PLOT A DESTINATION. Don't be subtle. Let one of your characters announce, "We're going to ____." Or "Here's Plan B." This happens constantly in all stories. In novels about affairs, people meet in hotel rooms. When they're found out, they plan to meet somewhere else: the woods, a museum. When they're found out again, they decide to run away, with a destination in mind. Or they decide to take some sort of action, with an intended result. Make that result or that destination as clear as possible.

6. FLESH OUT THAT DESTINATION. Make it fully realized before your characters arrive. This might mean leaving the basic frame of this part of the novel and moving into a new frame, with new characters—in effect, jumping away from a place and set of characters into the destination (a new place, possibly new set of characters). Or, it might mean

finding a device (a stranger who has seen the destination) to reveal its nature. It could also mean letting characters imagine what the destination will be like. For example, two people having an affair might plan to kill their spouses so that they can be together; before they do, they might imagine how their lives would be with their spouses gone.

The goal is create a sense of direction for your story by putting your characters into a difficult position and letting the develop a plan for what to do next. That plan (and the result or destination it suggests) gives your story a place to go, and you can heighten suspense by showing the readers that place before the characters arrive. When you think of a novel's plot in this way, it allows you to add new elements at any time—as long as you can develop them. This is how writers like Victor Hugo wrote such long books, and it's related to the strategy used by Alexander Chee in his long, epic, wonderful novel *The Queen of the Night*, which we'll look at next.

THE QUEEN OF THE NIGHT

Alexander Chee

Delsarte will tell anyone he lost his voice to the Conservatoire's methods, she said. It may even be true.

She let this stay in the air a moment before continuing.

There are two voices for an opera singer, Pauline said. Your speaking voice, which can be as ordinary as a wren's. And then the singing voice, which can sound as strange as something the wren found and holds in its beak, as if it comes from some other place entirely. For most singers, that voice is something made from the first, carefully, with both passion and patience. A patience born of that passion. For a few, their voice is a gift and can improve with training, but it has qualities that cannot be taught. And because the singer did not make this voice herself with careful training, she does not know what those qualities are except that she finds them by singing.

She paused and then said, She also does not know when the gift will break.

She smiled at me as she said that. Be careful of your roles, she said. I sang everything out of youthful pride in my three-octave voice, and I should not have. Yours is much like my own. It will not last forever, this voice. I know this seems very cruel, as you must give everything to become a singer and then it may be taken from you all at once. The voice can go quite suddenly or slowly, but even with slow departure, once it is underway, it will sound as if the original voice has already left you.

I said nothing, alternately warm from her compliment—she believed my voice was like hers!—and chilled entirely by this warning, which was, of course, meant to chill me.

She then began to play a slow scale and then went faster, the movement between high C to high E flat and back down again.

There, she said. Did you hear it? That's one place you may fall.

She played it again, the notes sounding this time almost like a trap.

Don't be afraid, she said. It's not just the melodies we should know. We must know also where we could fail.

Alexander Chee, excerpt from *The Queen of the Night*. Copyright © 2016 by Alexander Chee. Reprinted by permission of Houghton Mifflin Harcourt Publishing Company. All rights reserved.

PREDICT THE FUTURE

THE STRATEGY

In one of the most famous scenes in *The Empire Strikes Back*, Luke Sky-walker has crash-landed on the swamp planet Dagobah, hoping to train with Yoda. But the Jedi Master doesn't want to train him, believing that Luke is too old. Luke disagrees:

> Luke: I won't fail you! I'm not afraid.
> Yoda: Oh! You will be. You *will* be.

As we all know, Luke *will* become afraid, and in those moments of fear, he'll make pivotal decisions. This scene, then, tells the audience what's coming, that Yoda will train Luke and that Luke will encounter something terrifying. As the film continues, we eagerly await that terrifying thing.

It's a common strategy in all sorts of narrative: predict what will happen in the future so that the audience has something to look forward to. Alexander Chee does it repeatedly in his novel *The Queen of the Night*, and this page offers an example of how the strategy can work.

The scene is quite similar to the scene from *The Empire Strikes Back*. In it, a young woman is training with an accomplished opera singer named Pauline, just as young Luke was training with Yoda. Pauline explains the special power contained within the woman's voice (like the Force) and warns that this power leads inevitably to danger:

It will not last forever, this voice. . . . The voice can go quite suddenly or slowly, but even with a slow departure, once it is underway, it will sound as if the original voice has already left you.

But it's not enough to declare that danger awaits. We must glimpse the danger. In *The Empire Strikes Back*, Yoda brings Luke to a place where the dark side of the force is strong. Luke enters this place and encounters a phantom version of Darth Vader, the bad guy he must eventually defeat. Luke freaks out. In the same way, Pauline leads the young woman through scales, focusing on a few notes in particular: "Did you hear it? That's one place you may fall."

Now, the danger to the woman's voice is no longer hypothetical. It's real, and she and we have seen it. The page ends with Pauline giving some advice:

It's not just the melodies we should know. We must know also where we could fail. Learn them and you will never fall, not, at least, before your time.

The future has been laid bare. So have the tools for dealing with the traps it has in store. Pauline tells the young woman that a singer has two voices, the speaking voice and the singing voice:

"For most singers, that voice is something made from the first, carefully, with both passion and patience. A patience born of that passion. For a few, their voice is a gift and can improve with training, but it has qualities that cannot be taught."

Chee has given the young woman the singing equivalent of the Force, a natural ability that can be trained but which the holder cannot fully control or master. The last bit (not fully control or master) is crucial to a good story. If the young woman could fully master her voice—and if Luke could fully master the Force—all tension in the story would be killed. The result would be like one of those sporting contests where one team is so superior to the other that there is no doubt about the outcome.

When I was a kid, the Catholic school across the state line in Nebraska—Sacred Heart—won 87 games in a row. They played eight-man football, which includes a mercy rule: if a team was ahead by 45 points, the officials calls the game. In most games, Sacred Heart didn't play much of the second half. It's an astounding record that made for boring games to watch. It's the equivalent of *Star Wars: A New Hope* if the Death Star didn't have an architectural flaw that could lead to its destruction. So, give your character the ability to meet challenges, the opportunity to train that ability, but don't let the character become unstoppable. It's why Homer gave the otherwise unbeatable Achilles a flaw: when his mother dipped him in the River Styx to make him immortal, she managed to protect every part of him except the place where she held onto him. Even though he was one the greatest badasses in fiction, he's most remembered for his vulnerable heel, which tells us something about the important of making characters great, but not invincible.

THE EXERCISE

Let's predict the future, using *The Queen of the Night* by Alexander Chee as a guide.

1. GIVE THE CHARACTER A SPECIAL GIFT. In most stories—including true ones like the sinking of the *Titanic*—the danger that lies ahead is directly connected to some particular power, skill, or trait possessed by the character it affects. So, start by giving your character something special.

2. SELL US ON THE GIFT. Much of the opening sequence in *The Empire Strikes Back* involves reminding the viewer how awesome the Force is, epitomized by Luke destroying a giant machine with just his light saber and the voice of his dead mentor Obi-Wan telling him to go find Yoda. This is what Pauline does in *The Queen of the Night* when she says the young woman's voice "has qualities that cannot be taught" and uses that great image of the wren holding something precious and foreign in its beak. We're being told that the special thing is truly remarkable. How can you demonstrate or describe the gift so that it sparkles?

3. INTRODUCE THE DANGER. The danger stems directly from the gift, a setup that writers have turned to again and again. For Chee, the same traits that make the woman's voice beautiful will lead to its demise.

In *Star Wars*, Luke risks giving in to hate and the dark side of the Force he currently uses for good. Adrienne Rich wrote about Marie Curie and all women that "her wounds came from the same source as her power." The critic Daniel Mendelsohn titled a collection of essays, *How Beautiful It is and How Easily It Can Be Broken*. Even life seems to work this way sometimes: The *Titanic*, thought to be unsinkable, rams into an iceberg. So, what danger or risk is implicit in the power or gift your character has been given?

4. GIVE THE READER AND CHARACTER A TASTE OF THAT DANGER. Once you've identified the danger, it might be tempting to rush head-long into it. But then you've wasted the structural power of the prediction, which is that it allows you to write other stuff and make the reader sweat. So, show the reader and character a mild version of the danger.

5. LET THE CHARACTER PREPARE FOR THIS DANGER. That preparation might be practical and detailed. Or it might involve mental readiness. Whatever it is, let the preparation be convincing. We need to believe the character is ready for the challenge—but not *too* ready. Remember the Death Star and Achilles' heel.

The goal is to create suspense (and structure) by predicting something bad that will happen and pointing the character down a path that leads inevitably to that future. The greater the danger, the more powerful the character must be. But be creative about that power. Frodo in *The Lord of the Rings* has no magic talents or skills, which is what saves him in Mordor. Sauron is looking for a warrior, not a curly-headed wee person. So, his lack of power becomes a power—and that lack almost becomes his fatal flaw, when he refuses to throw the ring into the magma at Mount Doom, seduced by the power it would grant him. So, think of these elements in concert with one another: special power, fatal flaw, and how that flaw will rear its head in the future.

ARISTOTLE AND DANTE DISCOVER THE SECRETS OF THE UNIVERSE *Benjamin Alire Sáenz*

Over Christmas break, I was wrapping some Christmas gifts for my nephews. I went looking for a pair of scissors. I knew my mom kept a junk drawer in the dresser in the spare bedroom. So that's where I went looking for them. And there they were, the scissors, right on top of an extra large brown envelope with my brother's name written over the top, BERNARDO.

I knew that the envelope contained everything about my brother's life.

A whole life in one envelope.

And I knew that there were photographs of him in there too.

I wanted to rip it open but that's not what I did. I left the scissors there and pretended I hadn't seen the envelope. "Mom," I asked, "Where are the scissors?" She got them for me.

That night I wrote an entry in my journal. I wrote his name again and again:

Bernardo

Bernardo

Bernardo

Bernardo

Bernardo

Bernardo

Reprinted from Benjamin Alire Sáenz, *Aristotle and Dante Discover the Secrets of the Universe* (New York: Simon and Schuster, 2012), 209.

TURN A CHARACTER'S DESIRE INTO KNUCKLE-BITING SUSPENSE

THE STRATEGY

If you've watched many action movies or war movies, you've almost certainly seen a scene like this: two characters are fighting, and Character A sees a gun just out of reach. He wants it—*needs* it—badly, but it's just a couple of inches too far away. Yet he's not doomed. After all, this is a made-up story we're talking about. Anything is possible. Even though the gun is out of reach, if the character wants it badly enough, he might somehow be able to pull himself closer to it. This is one way to build suspense. Will he get to it in time? We hold our breath until he grabs the gun and, just before it's too late, fires a bullet into his enemy. This wrestling for the gun is not just well-choreographed action. It's also an example of creating tension with a character's desire.

Desire and *obstacle to fulfilling desire* are the foundation of many stories, not just action sequences. It's such a simple formula that it tends to show up in a handful of usual ways (for instance, nerdy boy loves girl, but she's dating a jock). The challenge and thrill is not in inventing a new formula but in adapting this basic one in surprising ways. Benjamin Alire Sáenz does exactly that in his YA novel *Aristotle and Dante Discover the Secrets of the Universe*.

The novel is about two teenage boys, loners who become friends. It's full of longing and desire of many different kinds, but on this page, the desire is pretty specific. The narrator (Aristotle) has an older brother who is in prison. His parents never talk about him, to the extent that Aristotle struggles to remember even basic things about him. Now, in this scene, Ari discovers a hidden envelope. It's got the brother's name written on it, but notice how Sáenz uses three sentences—each one given its own paragraph—to drive home how much this object is desired:

> I knew that the envelope contained everything about my brother's life.
> A whole life in one envelope.
> And I knew there were photographs of him in there too.

Literary writers tend to value subtlety, and, sure, subtlety is important. For example, characters—if they are to at all resemble real people—should be complicated, with nuanced virtues and vices. Setting, too, often affects a story in ways that aren't at first clear. In those cases, subtlety is a strength. But when it comes to plot, my feeling is that you should hit your reader over the head.

If you're skeptical, think of the plots of your favorite stories. How does the writer introduce major plot points? It may be in more direct ways than you think. For example, when it comes to literary fiction, George Saunders has more credibility than probably any other writer alive. When his story collection *Tenth of December* was released, the *New York Times Magazine* put a fortune cookie on its cover, along with the fortune "George Saunders Has Written the Best Book You'll Read this Year." A bold statement, yes? Especially when you realize it was the January 3 issue.

That collection contains the story, "The Semplica-Girl Diaries," which was published in the *New Yorker* and included in anthology *The Best American Short Stories*. (So, you know, it was pretty highly esteemed—and it's discussed later in this unit.) In the story, the main character scratches off a lottery ticket and realizes that he has won. His response is this actual line from that story: "Wow wow wow is all I can say!" It's not subtle—but what follows this moment is incredibly complex. He buys his daughter a birthday present, something that the neighbors own and that she has longed for, but also something that his other daughter believes is immoral. When she acts on this conviction, it presents a clear obstacle to the desire that was fulfilled and that led to "wow wow wow."

The same is true of Sáenz's novel: It's direct with plot. The envelope has a forbidden name written right on top of it. The contents of that envelope are deeply desired, and if you're not sure about that desire, Sáenz lets his narrator write the forbidden name in his journal six times.

And yet Ari doesn't open the envelope. He doesn't even let on that he's discovered it: "I wanted to rip it open but that's not what I did."

Why not? That's the question the novel spends its time answering. The obstacle to Ari's desire is himself. Understanding why requires understanding the complexities of the narrator, his family, and the place where he lives. In other words, the readers must read for the subtle clues about why the narrator has behaved in this way—and it's those clues that make the novel so fascinating. The plot is simply a mechanism that gives readers a reason to pay attention.

THE EXERCISE

Let's play with the basic formula of *desire* and *obstacle to fulfilling desire*, using *Aristotle and Dante Discover the Secrets of the Universe* by Benjamin Alire Sáenz as a guide.

1. IDENTIFY THE OBJECT OF DESIRE. Often, this will be simple. What does Cookie Monster want? Cookies. What does Scrooge want? Money. Frodo? To destroy the ring of power. In love stories, the object is a person. In quests, it's some version of the Holy Grail. Other times, though, the object will be harder to pin down. In most coming-of-age stories, a character wants to feel more certain about how to be in the world, but that's not easy to dramatize. Instead, that desire is translated into a more dramatic language: the character wants a car, a date, a different body, success in the classroom or athletic field or stage. When possible, make the object of desire something tangible or something that can be easily dramatized.

2. FIGURE OUT *WHY* IT IS DESIRED. Some desires need little explana-tion, like sexual desire. We don't often ask why people want to have sex. They just do. Even when a desire seems unusual or unexpected, it's hard to explain why it exists. For example, try explaining some-one who can't stand the taste of coffee why you deeply desire a good

cup of it. Or, explain a love of rhubarb to someone who immediately spits it out. What do you say? *Uh, I just like it.* So, here's another approach: What does the desired object represent? For instance, Ari desires the envelope, but it's pretty clear that what he really wants is to better know and understand his brother. Try using this sentence as a guide: He couldn't wait to get his hands on ____, but what he really wanted was _____.

3. **CREATE AN OBSTACLE TO FULFILLING THAT DESIRE.** In love stories, the obstacle is often money or class (think *Romeo and Juliet*). In heist movies, the obstacle is the guards, walls, alarms, and everything else that stands in the way of the jewels or gold. War stories use soldiers, armies, terrain, and the strain of combat as obstacles. In the film *Sharknado*, the obstacle is a tornado full of sharks (which, honestly, ought to be the obstacle in every story). Coming-of-age obstacles are almost always the character's own awkwardness and immaturity. In Sáenz's novel, the obstacle is Ari's feelings about his brother and family. In short, the obstacle ought to fit the story. You don't want a secret league of ninjas to be the obstacle in a quiet coming-of-age story, but you don't want inner conflict to be the obstacle in *Sharknado*. So, consider this: what does your character worry most about? How can you make that worry the obstacle to the desire?

4. **ASK WHEN YOUR CHARACTER WILL BE READY TO FULFILL THAT DESIRE.** This is a big part of most stories. In love stories, for example, to overcome the other suitor, the main character usually undergoes some sort of transformation. In sports films, to take on the reigning champ, the main character must train harder than ever before. So, ask yourself, how must my character prepare to face the obstacle? In what way does the character need to grow, mature, or develop? Or, what does the character need to obtain?

The goal is to create suspense (and, therefore, plot) by putting an object of desire just out of a character's grasp along with an obstacle to overcome in order to reach it. As with all great story elements, there is no limit to the number of ways this one can be adapted and personalized. So, play around with it. You may come up with a secret envelope or a Sharknado, you never know.

AN UNTAMED STATE   *Roxane Gay*

I drove out of the neighborhood and followed the familiar route to my office, the steering wheel slick against my sweaty hands. Nothing seemed familiar. It was quiet in the parking garage as I pulled into my space. I took a deep breath and studied the distance between my car and the elevator entrance. I calculated everything that might happen to me over that short distance. I opened my car door and planted one foot, then the other on the ground. I stood and closed the door softly behind me. A car slowly drove by and headed for the exit. I straightened my spine and tried to keep moving toward the elevator. I began sweating everywhere, my blouse clinging to my body. When I reached the elevator, it slowly hissed open but I couldn't bring myself to step inside, to put myself in a cage from which there was no escape. I slowly backed away, then turned on my heel and ran back to my car.

I didn't stop shaking until I was safely locked inside. I refused to look at myself in the rearview mirror. I couldn't go to work. I couldn't go home. I could drive, though. I drove to I-75 and I drove out of Miami. I kept on driving until I stopped seeing palm trees.

Reprinted from Roxane Gay, *An Untamed State* (New York: Grove, 2014): 266.

USE THE POSSIBILITY OF ESCAPE
TO RAISE THE STAKES

THE STRATEGY

There's a noxious remark sometimes made in discussions of politics. "If you don't like it here," they'll say, "why don't you leave?" As a piece of conversational rhetoric, it's not very effective because it shuts down debate. After all, how should someone respond other than with, "Why don't *you* leave?" However, the question is an excellent one to pose to your characters. The answer can reveal not just a character's motivation and rationale but also holes that might eventually kill tension.

Horror writers have known the importance of this question for a long time. After all, how does any horror film begin? With a dead car battery, a storm that makes travel impossible, or some other device designed to leave characters stranded. Why do horror stories take place in the woods? Because it's hard to run away when you're running through miles of dark wilderness. The *Nightmare on Elm Street* series invented a particularly chilling way to trap its characters. The monster, Freddie Kruger, would appear in their dreams, and the only way to escape him was to wake up—a scenario that depends on the near impossibility of waking yourself from a dream. Imagine if you could simply snap your fingers and wake up: oh no, it's that guy with the knives on his fingers, *snap*. The movie never would have gotten made.

In her novel *An Untamed State*, Roxane Gay poses this question to her character, Mireille Duval Jameson, in two ways. The novel begins with

Jameson visiting her parents' home in Haiti, where she is kidnapped for ransom. In a variety of specific ways, the impossibility of her escape is made clear. At one point, she's set free by someone sympathetic to her plight, only to learn that it was all a ruse to reveal her utter helplessness. Why can't she leave? Because the forces that have trapped her are too powerful to overcome.

Given this story premise, it would be safe to assume that once Jameson is freed from her captors, the novel will end. But that's not what happens, and this is where the genius of the novel lies. A ransom is paid, and Jameson is returned to her family and, eventually, to her home in Miami—but beatings, rape, and torture have left her mentally and physically exhausted, almost to the point of death. Everyone she sees, especially her husband, reminds her of her captivity. She can't function: not at home, not with family or friends, and not at work. In the scene on this page, we see this inability to play the roles of her life, and so she asks herself, "Why don't I just leave?" The question isn't stated directly, but it's present in these lines: "I couldn't go to work. I couldn't go home. I could drive, though." And so she drives, away from Miami and into America, leaving everyone and everything behind.

This escape is crucial to the novel's tension. If she'd stayed in Miami and slowly recovered, the reader might have become skeptical of such an easy resolution. But once she drives away, a new dimension of suspense is added. The plot becomes not just about whether she'll be okay but whether she *can be convinced* to receive the medical and psychological care that she needs. The novel replaces a physical captivity with a mental one. You can't escape a prison of the mind with guns or cash. The power of escape lies not with others but with the character who is trapped. It is that internal conflict that raises the stakes in the story.

THE EXERCISE

Let's ask a character, "Why don't you just leave?" using *An Untamed State* by Roxane Gay as a guide.

1. SUMMARIZE THE NATURE OF THE CAPTIVITY. What is it that prevents your character from pursuing and fulfilling her desires? In sto-

ries about love affairs, the answer is usually the character's marriage (and the children, finances, home, and social standing that accompany that marriage). In sports films, the characters tend to be trapped by lack of ability (*Rocky*, *Rudy*, *Hoosiers*, *The Bad News Bears*), geography (*Cool Runnings*), or the institutional limitations imposed by racism or religion (*42*, *Remember the Titans*, *Chariots of Fire*). To rephrase Nike's motto, the question to ask is "Why don't you just do it?" The more clearly you define the answer, the easier it will be to write scenes that push against and reveal the captivity.

2. MAKE THE ESCAPE ROUTE CLEAR. In *An Untamed State*, we're repeatedly told that once the ransom is paid, Jameson will be freed. The problem is that her father won't pay it. But the novel also anticipates escape plans that the reader—sitting at home, thinking, "Well, if *I* was in that situation, here's what I'd do"—might wonder about. So, Jameson fights back. She tries psychological tactics. When given the opportunity, she runs away. But nothing works. There is only one way to escape. So, make a list of the possible ways that your character *might* escape or overcome her captors. Then, write down the reasons why each one won't work.

3. ASK YOUR CHARACTER, "WHY DON'T YOU JUST WALK AWAY?" This is precisely the question that Jameson asks herself in *An Untamed State*. Her answer is a mix of "There's no reason not to" and "I can't possibly stay here," and so she leaves. In each of the sports films mentioned earlier, some version of this question gets asked. The answers tend to center on the character's determination and self-respect. The ultimate version of this is the moment in *Rocky* when Rocky realizes he can't win, that his goal is to simply stay on his feet until the final bell: "If I can go that distance, ya see, and that bell rings, ya know, and I'm still standin', I'm gonna know for the first time in my life, ya see, that I weren't just another bum from the neighborhood." Without this moment, the movie falls apart under its own impossible premise. But by asking, "Why don't you just walk away," the film reveals something important about its character. What matters isn't whether the character decides to stay or leave but *the rationale* for the choice. Ask your character this question and see how he responds.

4. IDENTIFY THE CONSEQUENCES OF THIS RATIONALE. The decision to stay or leave should matter. When Jameson leaves her home, she

puts herself in grave danger. She's so mentally and physically weak that the small obstacle becomes potentially fatal. In *Rocky*, the consequence of staying in the ring with Apollo Creed is the toll the fight will take on Rocky's body. He states this himself: "It really don't matter if this guy opens my head, either." But it does matter because if Rocky's trainers can't stop the bleeding, the fight's over. In both cases, the decision to leave (*An Untamed State*) and stay (*Rocky*) introduces dangerous possibilities. Suspense is created by the reader's desire to avoid those possibilities and the knowledge that they are unavoidable. We know what will happen and hope for the best but fear the result. So, what specific things might occur to the character after making the choice to stay or leave?

The goal is to clearly define the nature of your character's captivity and then probe the captivity for possible weak spots to reveal how they aren't so weak after all. Once the physical captivity is defined, you can begin to explore the character's mental captivity, that is, why she won't simply walk away. The answer is likely key to understanding the character, raising the story's stakes, and ratcheting up the tension.

DEVELOP

YOUR PROSE

STYLE

"THE SEMPLICA-GIRL DIARIES"

George Saunders

(September 5)

Oops. Missed a day. Things hectic. Will summarize yesterday. Yesterday a bit rough. While picking kids up at school, bumper fell off Park Avenue. Note to future generations: "Park Avenue" = type of car. Ours not new. Ours oldish. Bit rusty. Eva got in, asked what was meaning of "junkorama." At that moment, bumper fell off. Mr. Renn, history teacher, quite helpful, retrieved bumper (note: write letter of commendation to principal), saying he too once had car whose bumper fell off, when poor, in college. Eva assured me it was all right bumper had fallen off. I replied of course it was all right, why wouldn't it be all right, it was just something that had happened, I certainly hadn't caused. Image that stays in mind is of three sweet kids in backseat, sad chastened expressions on little faces, timidly holding bumper across laps. One end of bumper had to hang out Eva's window and today she has sniffles, plus small cut on hand from place where bumper was sharp. Mr. Renn attached hankie to end of bumper hanging out window. When Eva worried aloud about us forgetting to return hankie ("Well, Daddy, we are the careless kind"), I said I hardly saw us as careless kind. Then of course, on way home, hankie blew off.

Lilly, as always, put all in perspective, by saying who cares about stupid bumper, we're going to get a new car soon anyway, when rich, right? Upon arriving home, put bumper in garage. In garage, found dead large mouse or small squirrel crawling with maggots. Used shovel to transfer majority of squirrel/mouse to Hefty bag.

Reprinted from George Saunders, "The Semplica-Girl Diaries," *Tenth of December* (New York: Random House, 2014), 111.

RIFF OFF A SINGLE DETAIL

THE STRATEGY

When I was a kid, I didn't know how to talk to kids my own age. With adults, all I had to do was listen until I was curious what they were talking about. Then, I'd ask, "What do you mean . . . ?" a question that had two possible outcomes. Either they would explain the details of their conversation or they'd tell me to be quiet, at which point I'd ask over and over until someone shouted, "I am *trying* to *talk* here." But that didn't work with my peers at school. Starting in third grade, I lost the unthinking, un-self-conscious ability to make small talk that little kids have. I became aware of myself and, thus, paralyzed by the possibility that I might say something stupid. Once, I attended a basketball game, saw a bunch of my classmates sitting in the bleachers, and wouldn't go sit with them, instead sticking beside my parents, no matter how strongly they encouraged me to go say hi.

One day we went into an ice cream shop downtown, and one of my classmates stood at the counter. I froze. My dad said, "So, how about those Jayhawks?" and proceeded to talk about KU basketball with a kid he'd probably never spoken to before and knew only by name. On the ride home, he said, "Did you see what I did back there? He was wearing a KU hat, so I asked him about a question about it. That's what you do. Just ask them something." Inherent in that advice was a next step: don't think too hard. Just riff off whatever gets said. To this day, I use this strategy.

Most people would never guess that I'm still, at times, so socially anxious that it's hard to look people in the eye. I've learned the fine art of *visiting*, as people back home call the practice of open-ended conversation.

This same skill is essential to writing interesting prose.

While plot is crucial, the most pleasurable moments in most books—even plot-driven books—often aren't about plot. Instead, the lines and passages that make us laugh or cry, the ones we remember and read to our partners in bed, are short, open-ended riffs on a topic. This is exactly what George Saunders does on this page.

Let's distill the big paragraph on that page to a string of details:

- Park Avenue. Not new. Oldish. Rusty. Junkorama. Bumper fell off.
- Teacher retrieved bumper, was once poor, too—in college.
- Daughter says it's okay, dad gets mad. Kids holding bumper across laps. Bumper hangs out window, daughter cut by bumper.
- Teacher attaches hankie, daughter worries, hankie blows off.

What Saunders has done is choose a single detail (old Park Avenue) and riff on its condition. The pleasure—and the reason I have just snorted my water out of my nose—comes from all the new ways he invents to show how junky the car is.

The riff starts with the detail (Park Avenue) and adds a description (not new, oldish). Then it becomes a version of the joke, "How old is it? It's so old that _____." So, we get "junkorama" and the bumper falling off.

The riff continues by adding an element: the teacher. Now Saunders is taking a thing and shoving it in a character's face so that the character has no choice but to acknowledge it—with action (picks up the bumper) and words ("he too once had car whose bumper fell off").

Next, Saunders adds another character: his daughter, Eva. She responds to both the condition of the car and her teacher's response, which prompts the narrator to respond as well. Knowing a good thing when he sees it, Saunders shoves the bumper in this new character's face, almost literally, by making her and the other two kids hold it.

Finally, all the elements are brought together: teacher, hankie, daughter's worry, father's response, lost hankie.

It's tempting, when reading a writer as funny and talented as Saunders, to despair, to think, "I'll never be able to write something like that."

But even brilliant writers like Saunders start with a blank page. His genius is revealed in the way he riffs on the junky car, but any writer can start from the same place: a detail, description, the question of "How ___ is it?" and pushing the detail into the faces and hands of other characters.

THE EXERCISE

Let's riff on a single detail, using "Semplica-Girl Diaries" by George Saunders as a model:

1. START WITH A DISCLAIMER. Saunders begins this passage with the line, "Yesterday a bit rough." The statement gives everything that follows a particular charge—in this case, a negative one. It's the difference between telling someone, "You'll never guess what happened today" and "Stuff happened today." The first implies story. The second is what your kids say when you ask them about school. So, start by giving your passage a charge: negative or positive, hopeful or despairing, whatever.

2. MAKE AN UNREMARKABLE STATEMENT. When you're riffing on a detail, give yourself room to elaborate and amplify. Starting with something too outrageous can make everything that follows seem like a letdown. Saunders starts as basic and factual as possible: "'Park Avenue' = type of car." You don't need to start so basic. Think about what he states next: "Ours not new. Ours oldish." All he's done is tell us that the car is old. Of course, the *way* that he tell us this matters. Already we can tell that he's not eager to tell us the exact condition of the car. So, state something irrefutable about your character and/or the world the character inhabits. If possible, convey that information in a way (forthrightly, reluctantly, etc.) that suggests how the character feels about the fact.

3. ADD TO THE INITIAL DESCRIPTION BY ANSWERING THE QUESTION, "HOW ___ IS IT?" Saunders gives us "rusty" and "junkorama." The first one is important and descriptive. The second one isn't strictly necessary but gives the passage a vitality that makes it memorable. Saunders is having fun in describing the car, going beyond the basic requirements of setting up a scene. So, fill in the blank

of the question, "How _____ is it?" Imagine a crowd chanting the question, putting you on the spot, expecting a performance. How can you perform the description beyond what is strictly required? To answer the question, Saunders embodies the junkiness of the car in a single detail: the bumper. What detail can you use to embody some larger thing or essence?

4. ADD A CHARACTER AND FORCE HIM/HER TO DEAL WITH THE DETAIL. My wife and I once spent a month in Guanajuato, Mexico, where we spent most afternoons eating cake downtown, near the Teatro Juárez. On the steps of that theater, people often gathered to watch a clown, and his shtick was always the same: act goofy, tell jokes, and then force someone from the audience to interact with him, a move that turned his routine into story. Would the person kiss him? Would he pretend to fart on them? Saunders does the same thing. He clowns around with the car's condition (How junky is it?) and then forces a character (the teacher) to interact with it. Which character can you force to interact with the detail in your story? How do they respond? How does the main character respond to their response?

5. ADD ANOTHER CHARACTER. One of the funniest passages in the paragraph is the description of the kids holding the bumper. Again, Saunders thrusts his detail (the junkiness of the car, the bumper) onto a character, this time his daughter. How can you do the same thing: bring a character uncomfortably close to the detail you're riffing on?

6. BRING ALL THE ELEMENTS TOGETHER. The hankie doesn't get forgotten, nor does the bumper nor anything else Saunders has added to the scene. Each addition makes the passage more ridiculous and uncomfortable until something happens to relieve the tension.

The goal is to write a dynamic piece of prose by introducing a single detail and introducing characters to it in a way that they cannot avoid it. Each new character offers you the opportunity to consider the detail in a new way, and those perspectives will eventually become incompatible. As is often the case, everything in fiction leads to conflict.

"SUMMER BOYS"   *Ethan Rutherford*

and, standing next to his friend, in his friend's house, he feels a deformity calmed. Their chests are concave; their feet are growing. Their arms are marbled with the musculature of tiny woodland creatures. One has an innie, the other an outie. No one is home.

One of them, the taller one, holds a hair clipper that belongs to his father, a clipper that has been rescued from the dank recesses of an upstairs closet in the Laurelhurst house, a closet that smells like soap and shoes and motor oil and is as dark as dark gets, and he is saying to the other that now is the time to do this; now, while his father's at work in the motorcycle garage where he's employed on Saturdays; now, while his mother is at the market getting groceries that will include, per the boys' special request, Fruity Pebbles, Gushers, Dr Pepper, and frozen pizza (which is the reason they are always at this house; the other house is nothing but wheat germ and raisins, wooden cars and make-your-own-fun, early bedtime and no TV, ever); *now* is the time, he says, now is the *time*. It is 1987, and Brian Bosworth, the terror from Oklahoma, has arrived in Seattle to play for the Seahawks; it's time to make the magic happen. They love Walter Payton, they love Jim McMahon, they love the Bears (mostly because one of the boys' fathers, the father they idolize, loves the Bears), but it's more accurate to say they loved, because now the Boz is here, a hometown hero, an eleven-million-dollar man who will unify the city and bring a form of gilded greatness to the Northwest, and his arrival has obliterated everything else in their orbit of likes and dislikes.

Reprinted from Ethan Rutherford, "Summer Boys," *The Peripatetic Coffin* (New York: Ecco, 2013), 28.

USE LANGUAGE AND STYLE
TO SURPRISE THE READER

THE STRATEGY

One of the most difficult questions to answer, in any context, is "Why do you love that?" No matter how long the list of attributes that you compile, the sum will never add up to a complete answer. Perhaps you've dated someone your friends or family didn't care for, and they asked, "Why do you love him/her?" Nothing you say will make them see that person the way you do. The same is true for art. Few things are so aggravating as to reveal your love of a painting, sculpture, film, or book and be told, "I hated that. Why do you love it? Explain it to me."

My advice: don't explain it. You can't, and you're not obligated to. The point of aesthetics and appreciation of any kind of art is how it makes *you* feel. Forget everyone who doesn't agree. Instead, spend your time trying to tease out the craft of what took your breath away. In films, that moment is often a particular shot—the way it's framed and composed or the colors used (like the red that Jonathan Demme used in that great scene in *Philadelphia* when Tom Hanks' character describes an opera's aria to Denzel Washington's character). When we talk about beauty in books, we often quote a description or line that has stunned us so much that we had to stop reading and blink tears. If we're reading in bed, we shake our partner's shoulder and read it aloud to them. Moments like this can seem like magic. As writers, it's easy to think, "I'll never manage to write anything half as good as that." You might be right. There's no accounting for talent. I'll never drain threes like Steph Curry or race the length of the court to block a can't-miss lay-up like Lebron James, and I'll probably never write anything as beautiful as some of the passages in "Summer Boys" by Ethan Rutherford. Even now, as I sit at my kitchen table typing this, my wife walks by for a drink of water, sees the story I have opened beside me, and sighs. This story is that good.

The sentences dazzle. They introduce surprising images ("Their arms are marbled with the musculature of tiny woodland creatures"), switch vernaculars (from "musculature of tiny woodland creatures" to "innie" and "outie"), and jump free of the gravitational pull of the previous sentence's logic (from "innie" and "outie" to "No one is home"). They also run on to unexpected lengths, use rhythm and repetition (closet, now, love). They convey, with remarkable brevity, intimate human feelings that we've all felt but, when you read them, experience them anew all over again ("standing next to his friend, in his friend's house, he feels a deformity calmed").

What makes this passage even more wonderful is that so much of it is about the meaningless ephemera of life: "Fruity Pebbles, Gushers, Dr Pepper and frozen pizza." The object of the boys' attention, and the glue that temporarily holds them together, is a football player who is almost entirely unknown today except by those who were around to watch him. The kids these days know Walter Payton, but Brian Bosworth? He wishes. In other words, Rutherford isn't working like some czarist craftsman, making beautiful eggs out of precious gemstones. His materials are more humble, which makes the end result even more astonishing.

This book is built around the idea of imitating what you admire. In many of these exercises, I've tried to reveal the hidden mechanics at work, with the assumption that once you know they exist, you, too, can use them to great effect. But when it comes to style, to beauty (however you define it), there's a magic that lingers even when the mechanics that create it are unveiled. You can still imitate passages of immense beauty, but it's a bit like imitating Steph Curry's shot or the way Lebron uses his body to shield the ball as he drives down the middle of the lane. Just because you know what they're doing doesn't mean that you can do it, too. But you can try. Over and over. And the more you try, he more you notice about their game, their moves, their style—small things, how they place their feet, how they start sentences, the words they repeat, when they slow things down and when they jump ahead. At first, the writing—like any beautiful thing—is just beautiful. Then it becomes more comprehensible in its craft. The more you recognize, the more easily you can take your own shot.

THE EXERCISE

Let's write beautiful sentences, using "Summer Boys" by Ethan Rutherford as a model. Rather than working cumulatively to build to a single effect, these exercises will try out the different approaches he takes on the page:

1. INTRODUCE A SURPRISING IMAGE. In the sentence that begins, "Their arms are marbled with," Rutherford's setup is as clear as a quarterback dropping back to pass. We know what is coming—a pass, or, in this case, an image. He doesn't use the words *like* or *as*, but he could have. The sentence works because the image lives up to the time and space spent setting it up. So, set yourself up for an image. Start with *like* or *as*: The ___ is like ____. Then, write a new sentence without *like* and *as*. Instead, try using an unexpected but perfectly logical word. *Marbled* is a word often found in descriptions of muscle. So, try this setup: The ___ is (good verb-ed/ing) . . . Next, add a good noun. Simplicity is great, but *musculature* is a cooler word than *muscles*. So this: The ___ is (good verb-ed/ing) with (good noun). Finally add the image: *tiny woodland creatures*. Put it together: The ___ is (good verb-ed/ing) with (good noun) of (unexpected image). What has happened is that the setup for the image comes in bits and pieces, not all at once as it does with *like* and *as*.

2. SWITCH VERNACULARS. This is a strategy used so often by the great Junot Diaz that it ought to be named after him. In the opening pages of his novel *The Brief Wondrous Life of Oscar Wao*, Diaz starts with a beautiful passage about a transatlantic curse and then drops in words like *shit* and *hypeman*, Spanish slang like *jabao*, the phrase "had it good," and a reference to *The Lord of the Rings'* Sauron. All lexicons are fair game to Diaz. Rutherford does the same thing when he moves from "woodland creatures" to slang terms for bellybuttons. When this

switch works, it's because the different vernaculars feel natural to the character. Almost all of us switch up how we talk in ways subtle or dramatic, depending on the situation. What lexicons are available to your character/narrator? If you put the character/narrator next to different sorts of people (backgrounds, professions, personalities), how does the language change? How can you make that change happen as fast as possible?

3. LEAP AWAY FROM THE PATH BLAZED BY THE PREVIOUS SEN-TENCE. I'm cheating a bit by calling "No one is home" a leap. The boys are together in a house, after all. Pointing out that no one else is around makes sense. But the sentence does make a logical leap. The previous ones were describing the boys' physical appearance. "No one is home" shifts to the situation in which they find themselves. It's able to do this because the paragraph has two things happening at once: there is the house they're in and the bodies they're in. The paragraph introduces one, moves to the other, sits with the other for a while, and then quickly shifts back to the first one. You can try it: Give your passages two subjects. Start with one, transition smoothly to the other, drill down into this new one, and then shift, without warning to the first subject.

4. AT WHATEVER POINT YOU'RE TEMPTED TO PUT A PERIOD, KEEP THE SENTENCE GOING. Rutherford could have stopped after "an upstairs closet in the Laurelhurst house," but instead he repeats the word *closet* so that he can describe it. He could have stopped after the description ("as dark as dark gets"), but instead he tells us what one of the boys is saying in this place. And he keeps going. Try this: at a natural stopping point, use a comma instead of a period and repeat one of those words that you just wrote; then, describe it. Or, peer around the sentence and find something else in it besides the thing you were just writing about. Again, use a comma and the word *and* and then tell the reader about whatever you spotted while peering around.

5. USE REPETITION. Certain words lend themselves to repetition, words like *now*—but also any word that indicates causality or temporal logic, like *before, after,* and *while.* What happens if you start every phrase or sentence with the same one of those words? But you can also choose any word (*love* or *closet*) and see what happens if you use it as rapidly as possible. You'll be forced to explore the possibilities of the word. At

first, you'll find the most obvious way to use it. Then, you'll need to get creative. You may surprise yourself.

6. PINPOINT AN EMOTION THAT CAN'T BE NAMED AND DESCRIBE IT. The names that we give to emotions are mostly useless in identifying the actual way that we're feeling. So, instead of naming what your character feels, describe the sensation of the feeling or the observation or action that causes it to be felt or the action that results from it being felt. Or, as Rutherford does, give the emotion a shape—in his case, it's "a deformity." Make something happen to that shape: "a deformity calmed." Some things are easier to see in the midst of change than they are standing still and unaffected.

The goal is to write beautiful sentences by trying out strategies used by many writers, not just Rutherford. Try them over and over until you're able to begin adding your own flavor and style—*that's* when the beauty will emerge.

MR. SPLITFOOT   *Samantha Hunt*

Indemnity is a sum paid from A to B by way of compensation (for?) a particular loss suffered by B. From eight-thirty until nine in the morning, I
skim through claims. Three house fires. Seven no-fault car accidents. A
flood. One act of vandalism. Who is responsible? That depends. I gulp
cooling coffee. I don't handle business claims or life insurance. I make
phone calls. After lunch I have an inspection in the field. I check the
battery on my camera. By nine-thirty I need a break. I fire up my com-
puter and run a search on Lord's wife, Janine. Nothing new. No obituary or anything. A couple of old records she broke in high school track
and a picture from when she worked in real estate. Two eyes, a nose, and
a mouth. Hair on her head. There's nothing special about Lord's wife.

I click a link to a house in Budapest where the carpeting cost four
hundred seven dollars a square foot. My coworker Monique comes by.
I show her the carpeting. "What's the big deal?" she asks, squeezing the
bridge of her nose. Monique settles into her cubicle, sniffling mucus
down her throat. "I'm oozing like a slug." From a blister pack, Monique
pops a capsule brewed with such lovely stuff as guaifenesin, hydroxy-
propyl methylcellulose, sodium carboxymethyl, and magnesium stea-
rate. A little something to get the chemical day started.

I compare prices on a couple pair of shoes, break off the corner of
a nut-'n'-strawberry-flavored fruit breakfast bar. Overhead a fluorescent
flickers. I order the more expensive pair and experience a feeling of euphoria. Having made the correct shoe choice, I now understand the nature of mystery in the universe. I now belong to a tribe of shod people.
Waves of enthusiasm and moral righteousness inflate me straight up to
heaven.

Samantha Hunt, excerpt from *Mr. Splitfoot*. Copyright © 2016 by Samantha Hunt.
Reprinted by permission of Houghton Mifflin Harcourt Publishing Company. All
rights reserved.

LEAP BETWEEN LINGUISTIC FRAMES

THE STRATEGY

As a kid, I did not have access to bookstores since there wasn't one in my town or in any town nearby. The only time that I ever bought books was when the librarian at my school distributed the Scholastic catalogue sheets, with books offered at steep discounts. Back then, the comic strip *Calvin and Hobbes* was still running in newspapers, and old strips were collected in anthologies that I coveted and begged my parents to buy. Because they (primarily my father) loved them, too, I won out. Without *Calvin and Hobbes*, I might not be a writer today. It was one of the few books where I discovered recognizable emotions and experiences—things that, when I read them, I felt the stunned amazement of seeing something intensely personal made universal. As other *Calvin and Hobbes* fans know, the strip had some recurring storylines that were particularly popular: the transmogrifier and the monsters under the bed. And, of course, the game of Calvinball, with its total lack of rules except those Calvin and his tiger made up on the spot: invisible vectors and spots where they had to spin around until they fell down. Anything could happen, and that is what made the game so fun for the characters and so enjoyable to read.

I had a similar reaction in graduate school when I first read *Lolita*. The prose was popping and jumping with electricity. From sentence to sentence, I couldn't predict where Nabokov might go. When I read Samantha Hunt's *Mr. Splitfoot* just a few years ago, I felt the same way. The prose makes astounding, unexpected leaps, sometimes between clauses or phrases within the same sentence. Anything seems possible. As a writer, this is the best of all effects: for the reader to read every single word in anticipation of what might come next. As in Calvinball, this unpredictability isn't an accident. It's the point. It's planned. The trick is laying the groundwork so that anything truly is possible.

So, how does Hunt do it?

This page offers a case in point. It begins with the jargon of the insurance industry: indemnity, compensation, and loss. The syntax is formal, dry, and logical. The details that follow fit within this linguistic frame: claims, fires, accidents, floods, inspections. Even the description of Lord's wife (Lord is the name of the man the narrator has been sleeping with) hews to the language of insurance: obituary, records, an accounting of body parts.

Then, in the next paragraph, something strange happens. Suddenly we're in Budapest. It's still discussed in terms of measurement ("the carpeting cost four hundred seven dollars a square foot"), which is dry and concrete, like the language of insurance, but there's no way you can read the first paragraph and expect Budapest. The rest of the paragraph continues into unforeseen territory: "oozing like a slug," "blister pack, "pops a capsule," "brewed," "the chemical day." These terms are not thrown out randomly. The slug line is part of a string of terms that included "nose" and "mucus." And the "blister pack" is, of course, a real piece of packaging, but the word "blister" also leads to "pop," and now the language has run far afield of the original sentences on the page.

The next paragraph continues expanding the linguistic frame that began with "indemnity" and grew to include "Budapest" and "blister." Now we get "euphoria" and "the nature of mystery in the universe," ending with a sentence, "Waves of enthusiasm and moral righteousness inflate me straight up to heaven," whose language is utterly and completely separate from the accounting language of insurance.

Why does this matter? Later in the novel, when plot begins to get interesting, the novel must abide by the rules it introduced in its beginning. If the frame is narrow, then only there is a narrow set of possibilities, linguistically speaking—and language contributes to plot since you can't have something happen if the words for it don't fit within the novel you're writing. (If you don't believe that novels have linguistic frames, try lifting a line out of books by Tom Robbins or Larry McMurtry and dropping it into a Don DeLillo novel. It won't work.)

Language is possibility. What Hunt has done is expand the possibilities of her novel—while adhering to a basic tone set in the very first sentence. The tone in this section belongs to an insurance company where, also, euphoria is present.

I've mentioned Nietzsche earlier in the book and his theory that we structure language as an edifice: *poop* on one end and *face* on the other, *insurance* on one end and *euphoria* on the other. The trick is to start with one part of the edifice and then find ways to leap to other parts. If that seems daunting or impossible, don't worry. I doubt Hunt sat down and thought, "Well, *blister pack* leads to *pop*, which leads to. . ." What is more likely is that *mucus* led to *blister pack*, and that term is so wonderful and weird that it inspired her, consciously or not, to leap out of the language of accounting and into some other linguistic place. In other words, the leaps require listening to your own words and running with any that catch your fancy.

THE EXERCISE

Let's leap from one linguistic frame to another, using *Mr. Splitfoot* by Samantha Hunt as a model:

1. WRITE A SENTENCE USING A DEFINITE TONE. Try starting with an undisputable statement: for instance, a character declaring something that we all know to be true. (This is what George Saunders did as well, and the difference between his passage and this one shows how much your imagination can do with the simplest of details.) The first sentence on Hunt's page is just this sort of statement, a definition. It's not an "I believe" or opinion statement. In a way, this is a less direct way of revealing a character's interior self. Hunt's narrator is simply describing the world around her, and her personality comes through in her word choices. So, take a look around your character or narrator. Find something concrete and let the character or narrator describe it. What words will get used? How the character is feeling at that moment will influence his or her diction, as will general tempera-

ment or personality. You can also think about situational language: the way people tend to talk in their workplace or community.

2. NAME THE TONE. After you've written a sentence, try to define its tone. If you can't come up with a perfect name, don't worry. No one will ever see the term. Instead, you're simply trying to create a linguistic frame: insurance, for instance, or corporate or professional or dugout or NPR or arts administration. You're defining which bucket you'll be pulling language out of.

3. WRITE ANOTHER SENTENCE IN THAT TONE. In short, keep going. Keep the narrator or character talking. Stick with factual statements. Hunt's narrator describes her morning at work. She's telling us her routine, which is a great strategy. What is your character's routine? Tell it to us in the tone you created in the first sentence.

4. SHIFT THE ACTION OF THE PASSAGE. Halfway through Hunt's first paragraph, the narrator says, "By nine-thirty I need a break." Then, the action changes from work to screwing around on the Internet. If you're writing about routine, you can use a similar strategy: when does the narrator/character need a break? Or, how would the narrator/character change the subject from whatever fact statement began the paragraph? What else would the character/narrator naturally want to talk about? Write a few sentences on this new subject.

5. INTRODUCE A TERM THAT FITS THE ACTION BUT NOT THE ORIGINAL TONE. Hunt introduces Budapest. She could have chosen any city: Duluth or Baltimore. But she instead chose a city she's not likely to visit and certainly not likely to buy a house. It's an unexpected move for someone who has, until this moment, seemed dry and factual, as we might expect someone working in insurance to be. So, think about this: What weird detail could you throw into the paragraph? Don't worry if it's a good detail. Focus on the new action and give yourself this goal: write something weird or unexpected about that action. This may mean digging into your character's head. What naughty or secret thing would the character think while engaged in this new action? You're searching for a detail (word/term) that doesn't fit the linguistic frame you created in the first sentence. Listen for words that sound funny or surprising. There's a reason that George Ezra chose Budapest for his hit song about what he'd give up for his loved one and not Paris.

6. RUN WITH IT. Once you've got the weird or unexpected detail, keep going. Riff on it. If you've tapped into something in the character's head, leap from it to something else, like this: If the character had a weird thought, what would she notice after having it? The answer might be something not related to the linguistic frame you set earlier. It might be some odd detail that wouldn't be noticed unless her mind was already someplace else.

The goal is to create a frame for the language of your novel or story, to say, "This is the sort of language or tone that will provide the foundation of the story." Then, you're leaping out of that frame to other frames. Once you've leaped to them once, you can return to them later—consciously or not. It's safe to say that the most interesting parts of *Mr. Splitfoot* can't be told with the language of an insurance office, and so Hunt needs to give herself room early on to move out of that language and into the terms and possibilities of other frames.

THE RADIANT ROAD   *Katherine Catmull*

Clare passed through patches of Strange often, much more than just at Halloween. She passed through them the way you swim through patches of surprising cold in a summer lake: with a shiver, but swimming on. It was her mother who had taught her that word, when Clare was small, that word for it among others. "The Strange has been here—do you feel it?" she would say.

Or "The Other Crowd is passing through."

Or "Throw a pebble in that whirlwind for the fairies."

Fairies. Obviously, the world and time had ruined that word for Clare, to the point where she felt herself flush to hear it. But even at almost-fifteen—when she no longer believe in fairies (in the Strange, the Other Crowd: *whatever*)—even now, when she caught sight of something extraordinary, and Strange, she would hear her mother's words: *Ah, look— a fairy-making.*

It was the only name she knew, for what no one seemed to notice, but her.

For example, one day, not long before this story begins, as Clare sat alone in the living room, a book fell from a shelf all on its own. Its pages fluttered for a moment, like a butterfly balancing on a flower. Then the book settled open.

From a vase on a shelf above the book, one pink rose petal drifted down and landed on the open page.

Clare bent to look. The petal had fallen on a line of poetry: "Eternity is in love with the productions of time," it read.

Reprinted from Katherine Catmull, *The Radiant Road* (New York: Dutton, 2016), 2.

REFRESH OLD STORIES WITH NEW PROSE

THE STRATEGY

As a kid, I had no concept of genre, only the general belief that exciting books were better than dull ones. My town was small and rural, so there was no bookstore, only the public library and my school libraries and librarians who pointed me in the right direction—first to obvious titles like *The Hardy Boys* and *Hank the Cowdog* and then, after I'd exhausted those, to authors like Gordon Korman, Lloyd Alexander, John Bellairs, and Madeline L'Engle, whose novel *A Wrinkle in Time* contains a scene, kids walking out of their suburban houses all at once and bounce a red ball at the same time, is etched onto my brain.

But if I had any favorite genre, it was the Sensitive-Kid-with-Special-Powers genre, particularly if those powers involved a connection or trip back into myth. So, more than two decades later, I can still remember the thrill I got out of Nancy Bond's novel *A String in the Harp*. In it, three American kids move to Wales against their will and find a harp-tuning key that transports them back to the sixth century.

Imagine my pleasure, then, when I started reading Katherine Catmull's *The Radiant Road*. An American girl moves from Texas to Ireland, her birthplace that she's mostly forgotten. As in *A String in the Harp*, there's a dead mother. There are visions and talismans, and it's the kids—not the adults—who become emotionally mature and save the day. I have read so many versions of this story that I knew exactly how this novel would proceed, which is part of the appeal of genre novels but also a challenge in writing them. *The Radiant Road* is also written for teenagers. It's not a crossover book like *The Hunger Games* but, instead, a book firmly rooted in telling a story for—I'm guessing—twelve- to- fifteen-year-olds, probably mostly girls. It wasn't written for grown men. And yet I loved the book. Why?

Because the language refreshes the story. This page is a great example. It's explicit in taking an old story and putting a new twist on it, down to the terminology:

> Fairies. Obviously, the world and time had ruined that word for Clare, to the point where she felt herself flush to hear it. But even at almost-fifteen—when she no longer believed in fairies (in the Strange, the Other Crowd: *whatever*)—even now, when she caught sight of something extraordinary, and Strange, she would hear her mother's words: *Ah, look—a fairy-making.*
>
> It was the only name she knew, for what no one seemed to notice, but her.

In this passage, we get all the hits of the genre: a child on the verge of some emotional landmark (almost-fifteen), dead mother, and a magical connection to some extraordinary power that singles her out. Without this premise, the book doesn't exist. But the book must also find a way to put its own stamp on that premise. (At this point I'm obligated to trot out Ezra Pound's deathless quote, "Make it new.") You can see the beginnings of that stamp even in this passage: "in the Strange, the Other Crowd; *whatever*." Catmull is offering new names for a well-worn term: fairies.

She does something similar with style. In the first paragraph, we're given a description of the Strange, how it feels to encounter it. Again, this is beaten-down territory, familiar to anyone who loves the genre. So it's interesting to see Catmull's approach:

> Clare passed through patches of Strange often, much more than just at Halloween. She passed through them the way you swim through patches of surprising cold in a summer lake: with a shiver, but swimming on.

The passage starts with a familiar fairy story, with the reference to Halloween. But then it pushes past it. First, the Strange is not omnipresent but, instead, located in patches—that's interesting. So is the feeling of passing through the patches: the cold water in a warm lake. It's a quick, lovely, visceral description of the requisite premise. But what really makes the passage truly new is the final three words: "but swimming on." The shiver we get—and we're not surprised, but the fact that the character has the agency to keep moving, to leave the Strange, and that she does so casually and without great effort, is new. She is not a captive to the premise, which means that the premise is simply another part of her world. Of course, the novel becomes a quest narrative that most readers will recognize, but it's this promise at the beginning—that the character is not simply a tool of the premise—that draws us in. At least, it drew in this savvy adult.

The book will return to this kind of image again when describing the girl's grief at losing her mother: like sunlight shining through tree branches. And when the time comes to introduce the actual fairies—the Good People—it's done with a play on words that scrambles our expectations for the word *good*. The goal is to use language, the basic material of any written narrative, to refresh the story and make it appear slightly different than we expect.

A quick point: I haven't used the word *reinvent*, which is often used when literary writers talk about genre works. Some writers really do reinvent genres. Manuel Gonzales, for example, throws together elements from *Die Hard*, *Alias*, and comic books to create what is basically an office drama. But that's not what Catmull is doing—nor is it what any pure genre writer does. The trick is to make the story seem *just different enough* to draw us in, once again, to a story that we love.

THE EXERCISE

Let's refresh the language of a story, using *The Radiant Road* by Katherine Catmull as a model:

1. IDENTIFY THE PARTS OF YOUR STORY THAT READERS HAVE SEEN BEFORE. Think of your premise and the characters it requires. Catmull's book requires fairies (in a fairy world, with spells). A zombie

book requires zombies, a pirate book needs pirates, a marital affair needs a seducer, a love story needs a looker, a revenge story needs a villain, and a crime story needs a detective. You can also think about setting and what the reader will expect: apocalyptic wasteland, pirate ship, bedroom, seedy bar, police station. Finally, think about an expected action: foraging for necessities, sword fights, sex, interrogations.

2. IF POSSIBLE, RENAME THEM. Catmull renames the fairy-makings as the Strange. In part, it's because her character doesn't believe in fairies anymore, but it's also a way to remove a label that comes with a lot of preconceptions. Books and films do this all the time. How many names are there for zombies? The undead, the walking dead, the living dead, biters, cannibal corpses, and roamers—just to name a few. In part, each of these names is an addition or clarification to zombie lore (the wealth of knowledge about a subject that a genre creates). But they're also attempts to refresh a haggard monster.

These names often imply slight differences, which is especially crucial in detective fiction. A lot of the detectives are called something else—gumshoes, private eyes, and dicks, of course, but also priest and monk and serial killer and mystery writer (*Castle* and *Murder, She Wrote*). This may seem like cheating (after all, Jessica Fletcher was, basically, a detective *and* a writer), but it's not. By calling an anticipated element something else, it opens up possibilities for it even as it operates exactly as we expect it to (solving crimes). So, invent another name for your character, setting, or action (Shady Vale instead of Shire) or substitute some other word entirely (*priest* for *detective*). If the change in name requires changes to the character, make them. Experiment. Find ways to refresh the premise.

3. DESCRIBE THESE EXPECTED ELEMENTS IN A FRESH, VISCERAL WAY. A new name can take you only so far. Readers need to viscerally experience the renamed element. A good way to accomplish this is to move beyond the sense of sight. Try the other senses: smell, sound, touch, and taste. But even using all five senses might seem insufficient. Certain objects or characters might seem impossible to describe in a new way. Instead of waiting for inspiration that won't strike, try looking away from the thing you're trying to describe. For example, instead of describing the fairies, Catmull shows readers the world around them and how it is shaped by their actions. It's a strategy used

in some of the most famous scenes in film. Think about what Steven Spielberg does in *Jurassic Park*. When the T-Rex approaches, we know because the water in a plastic cup begins to ripple. The world is shaking under the dinosaur's feet. Something similar happens in Ridley Scott's film *Alien*; when the alien draws near, we can't actually see it. Instead, we hear the beeping of a motion sensor device tracking it— each *beep* is terrifying and visceral.

You can also think in terms of metaphor and simile. Catmull doesn't say that the patches of Strange are literal patches in a lake. The image is figurative. In the absence of a direct description, she's borrowing a description of a sharp, recognizable sensation (cold water in a warm lake). This is a great strategy. Take her sentence, "She passed through them the way you . . ." and play around with a stripped-down version of it: "The smell/taste/touch/sound of it was like _____." Fill in the blanks until you find an image that you like. Then, make it active, replacing "The smell/taste/touch/sound" with the character actually smelling/tasting/touching/hearing.

4. IDENTIFY A CHARACTER'S EXPECTED REACTION TO THE ELEMENT. How does the character respond to the smell/taste/touch/sound from the last step? Again, look beyond the most obvious response. Catmull's character doesn't freeze in place, chilled—which might be what the reader would expect after a reference to cold water. Once you know the most obvious response, you can work against expectation.

5. TWEAK THAT REACTION. Instead of freezing in place, Catmull's character shivers (a nod to the obvious reaction) and then swims on. Try it: nod to the obvious reaction but then keep writing. What does the character do after the initial response has passed?

The goal is to make the story you're writing your own, whether it's one that's never been told before or one that is as well-worn as an encounter with fairies. This can mean literally giving a common story element a new name. Or it can mean finding a new way to show readers that story element, a problem many great writers and filmmakers have solved by focusing on the things around the element instead of the element itself. These strategies become story once your character begins to interact with them. Sometimes all it takes is one good sentence to throw open the door to an entirely new experience for the reader, even if the subject matter is, on the surface, quite familiar.

PUTTING IT

TOGETHER

ON PAGE ONE

ONE DAY, YOU'LL FINISH A STORY OR NOVEL. When you do, you'll send it to your writer friends for them to critique. You'll take their advice, revise, and then you'll send it out to literary journals or literary agents. As soon as you click *send*, you'll feel sick to your stomach, and for the next few days, weeks, or months, you'll obsessively check your email for a response, wondering the entire time what the editor or agent is thinking as he or she reads your work. I've heard that question a hundred times, literally: "What are editors and agents looking for?" Of course, each person's tastes are different, so there's no way to generalize except this: They're looking for great first pages. Keep in mind, editors and agents read thousands of submissions, so many that they become a blur. If you don't grab them quickly, you won't grab them at all. Of course, this doesn't mean that you need to put a killer zombie ninja assassin in your first paragraph. Shock value isn't the only way to catch a reader's eye. In fact, it's not even a good one. Instead, the way to hook readers is to do all the things we've been working on in this book. Make setting and characters interesting, write great dialogue, create suspense and tension, and introduce plot. In other words, first pages are like the rest of your story or book. The only difference is that they're first. So, whatever you do, make it good. In these examples, you'll see how many ways first pages can use the strategies you have already tried out—and a few more than you haven't seen yet.

One practical note: rather than developing a single exercise for each one-page example, I will highlight several examples because each of these opening pages is doing multiple awesome things at once. (That's another version of the simultaneity that we discussed in the chapter on Jesmyn Ward's novel.) It's important to do one great thing on a first page, but it's even better to do several great things. No pressure. (Just kidding. You'll be fine.)

MIGRATORY ANIMALS   *Mary Helen Specht*

What Flannery first noticed when she arrived in Nigeria were the towering palm trees. It was like walking off the airplane into a land of giants. The next morning, Flannery, barefoot, crossed her new front yard and stood beneath one of the sturdy palms, her shoulder blades pressing into the grooved trunk. She tilted her chin to look up at the canopy when, suddenly, the tree shook its head at her. A flock of birds swept from the branches, crackling the leaves.

Flannery was on the lam. Ever since her mother's death when she was in college, she'd let graduate school and then various research grants in climate science take her farther and farther from Texas: Wisconsin, Juneau, the Klondike, West Africa. Sometimes she imagined herself as a spider spinning an enormous web, swinging from one corner of the globe to the other, and like the spider, Flannery didn't know exactly what she wanted—until she caught it.

She met Kunle at an outdoor canteen near the Nigerian university where she had been posted on what was supposed to be a brief data-collecting trip. Sitting at an adjacent table with a soda and a worn textbook, he leaned over to her and said, "You should try the palm wine." Kunle wore slacks and a blue button-down oxford, both ironed within an inch of their lives. Trim and preppy, he looked like one of those idealized husbands in films, the kind of man who kissed a beautiful wife before leaving for the office, the kind usually too straitlaced to be Flannery's type.

Reprinted from Mary Helen Specht, *Migratory Animals* (New York: Harper Perennial, 2015), 1–2.

MIGRATORY ANIMALS
BY MARY HELEN SPECHT

INTRODUCE SETTING WITH A FEW STRONG DETAILS—OR ONE DETAIL VIEWED MANY WAYS.

Stories contain setting, right? It's kind of a big deal. A story can't take place in a vacuum. Even Samuel Beckett's stripped-down *Waiting for Godot* is set somewhere: a country road, by a tree. But you know this already. The problem isn't where to set the story but how to introduce that place to the readers. The world contains too much for any story, and even limited views of that world are too complex to be exhaustively described. For example, if I look out my front window, I see houses, trees, green lawns, dead lawns, sidewalks, mailboxes, the street. But that's only one view. I could describe my neighbor's house in detail, with the garage doors always left slightly open. Or I could zoom out and describe my entire neighborhood or the city of Austin or even Texas. All of it is important. Not all of it can make the cut.

Mary Helen Specht faced a similar problem in *Migratory Animals*. The novel's first page is set in Nigeria, a huge country with many different types of geography and communities. Notice how she introduces us to the country: "What Flannery first noticed when she arrived in Nigeria were the towering palm trees."

Every sentence in the first paragraphs shows us a palm tree from a different view:

- Land of giants
- Grooved trunk
- Canopy
- A flock of birds swept from the branches

Stories are not textbooks. As a writer, you aren't responsible for getting every detail down on paper, and you can quote me when you go on book tour and someone says, "Hey, what about ____?" Tell them it's fiction and move on.

THE EXERCISE

Let's introduce setting, using *Migratory Animals* by Mary Helen Specht as a model:

1. IDENTIFY YOUR SETTING. This probably sounds obvious, but think about the view outside my window. Is my setting my street? My neighborhood? My city? My state? My country? My planet or galaxy (I'm looking at you, sci-fi writers)? Decide what frame you're using to view setting: a close-up of a small place or a panorama shot.
2. PICK ONE DETAIL FROM THAT SETTING. Specht could have chosen anything in Nigeria, and she picked palm trees. Was it the very best thing she could have picked? Who knows? Who cares? Answering that question would have required a search so exhaustive that she'd never have written the novel. So, pick a detail: a tree, a knickknack on a shelf, a lake or mountain or other geographic feature, a color, a sound. Just pick something. If it's not the right thing, you'll get stuck, which means you get to pick something else and try again!
3. SHOW THE DETAIL IN THE PLAINEST WAY POSSIBLE. Specht's sentence basically says this: she saw big trees. Her version sounds nicer, but the point of both sentences is the same: big trees. So, write a sentence that introduces the detail that you want us to see.
4. SHOW US THE DETAIL AGAIN. As a rule (and you can put this in your writing rulebook that you study each night in bed; what, you don't have one?), stories should return to their details. Show things

more than once. Specht's first paragraph has five sentences, and each one talks about big trees. She's dropping us into the world of her story, letting us look around a bit and get our bearings. Yet the details are not static. Flannery moves, the trees move, and birds move. So, show your detail from different angles. Allow us (or your character/narrator) to look up at the detail, down at it, around it, and behind it. Show us the detail in the morning and at night. If it's a place, show it to us crowded and empty. Show it straight (towering palm trees) and through metaphor (land of giants).

5. END ON A GOOD LINE. Specht takes us up the tree, into the branches, and when the birds fly away, the passage ends. What is the progression of your passage about setting? Does it move from morning to night? From inhabited to empty? From happy to sad? Thinking about progression will give you an idea of where to stop so that you can start the next passage, the next active piece of writing that your reader won't want to put down.

The goal is to move beyond the easiest introduction of setting to make it come alive in the reader's mind. In first pages, you can't do anything passively—whether it's introducing setting, characters, or conflict. Grabbing readers requires active, forward-charging writing, which is what Specht has done with a simple description of trees.

GET THE READER'S ATTENTION WITH A STATEMENT THAT NEEDS EXPLAINING— THEN, EXPLAIN IT IN AN INTRIGUING WAY.

Fiction may be a mansion with many windows, but all the views into it share one thing in common: they're interesting. Who wants a boring story? You never hear anyone say, "Oh yeah, it was so dull that I had to force myself to keep reading. I loved it." Regardless of what genre you're working in or how straight or experimental your prose, your story needs to make the reader want to keep reading. Literature isn't like cod liver oil; nobody reads because it's good for you. We read because we don't want to stop. The easiest way to do this is make a statement that causes readers to lean in. It's like if someone tells you they have a really weird tattoo. You don't say, "Oh, huh," and move on. You want to know what kind of weird. What's it look like? Where is it? Why'd you get it? A good, intriguing statement naturally turns into a story.

Specht does this in the second paragraph of her novel: "Flannery was on the lam." The sentence implies that she's on the run *from something*. What is it? We don't know, but I, for one, would like to find out. It's like the weird tattoo. You don't find out about it and walk away without knowing. The word *lam* suggests a story.

It's almost a purely literary word. Nobody uses *lam* in real life except actors on set for films about 1920s bank robbers. We're more likely to say *on the run* or *in hiding*. The fact that Specht would choose such a word is intriguing. It's unusual, and if grocery tabloids like *Weekly World News* has taught us anything, it's that we like oddity.

We're interested: now what? Specht explains the statement with details that continue to be unusual. It starts with a dead mother, which is emotional but also a common occurrence in fiction, but then the explanation moves into the unexpected: "various research grants in climate science take her farther and farther from Texas: Wisconsin, Juneau, the Klondike, West Africa." If you've ever seen a sentence that contained both *Klondike* and *West Africa*, you're much better read than I am. The list of places begs for more explanation. What was it like to move about so much and to such places? There's a story there, and we want to hear it.

THE EXERCISE

Let's make an intriguing statement that begs for explanation, using *Migratory Animals* by Mary Helen Specht as a model.

1. DECIDE WHAT TO STATE. Sometimes the sentence writes itself: "I was once eaten by a bear." I'm pretty sure you'd keep reading. But what if your character hasn't had the good fortune to get mauled? The content depends on the type of story you're writing, which means that it's important to know what kind of story you're telling. (There's an exercise on just that in a couple of pages: "Show readers the kind

of story they're reading.") Good writers know how to *craft* intriguing sentences. For example, imagine how Specht *could* have described Flannery's moves: "She had done climate research in many places." Now it's a snoozefest. How you write the sentence matters. But, first, figure out what you're working with. Is it pirates or research? Write a sentence that states what's going on at the beginning of your story in the plainest language possible.

2. JAZZ IT UP. Hemingway wrote that we should try to write one true sentence, and he was a serious fellow and I don't want to argue with him, but let's keep it light. Write one interesting sentence. Choose a good, unusual word like *lam*. Or create an unusual pairing of words: *eaten* and *bear* is a more unlikely pairing than *attacked* and *bear*. We've seen one more often than the other. Describe what is happening in the most colorful way possible.

3. KEEP IT SIMPLE. Don't look like you're trying too hard. I once read a story that began something like this, "I was walking along the highway with a paper bag full of feces and a heavy heart." Now, that's not a terrible sentence, and I am curious about how the narrator came to be in such a situation. But I also question where the story can go from here. Rappers drop the mic at the end, not the beginning, of their performance. Be interesting, but leave yourself room to build the story.

4. EXPLAIN THE STATEMENT. You've got us hooked. Now keep us hooked. Just as catching a fish requires more than hooking the fish, keeping readers engaged requires maintaining tension. Don't let the line go slack. For that reason, Specht gives us "farther from Texas: Wisconsin, Juneau, the Klondike, West Africa" instead of "many places." Kids will often tell stories that go like this: One time I was eaten by a bear, then I died. A good writer won't kill the character yet. Instead, the writer will add more intriguing details, like this one: "The tongue was warmer than I imagined, and the breath was sweeter." So, offer an explanation that doesn't completely close the door on the mystery you've created.

The goal is to tell readers enough to make them keep reading to find out more. The job of fiction on any page, but particularly the first page, is to keep readers reading. Keep them turning the page.

USE FIGURATIVE LANGUAGE, BUT BE QUICK ABOUT IT.

An adjective that you'll find in a lot of blurbs on the backs of novels or in reviews is *lush*, as in, "The lush language carries the reader along." Such praise can create a certain expectation for the prose: lyric description, rich and layered metaphors, and complex sentence structures. The surprising thing, however, is how fast even lush language can move.

Specht gives a great example for how a complex image can get on and off the page quickly:

> Sometimes she imagined herself as a spider spinning an enormous web, swinging from one corner of the globe to the other, and like the spider, Flannery didn't know exactly what she wanted—until she caught it.

The image is great, right? Can't you see the spider swinging across the globe? It's so clear—and so complex. Think about it: Specht has paired a spider with a globe. Have you ever seen that pairing before? I'll bet you don't even see it literally: I bet you see a spider and an image of Earth and blackness all around, not a house spider on an actual globe sitting on a table; at least that's what I see. So, it's lush and rich and complex—and fast, on and off the page in a single sentence.

The imagery also creates intrigue. What did she catch? This is important. It can be tempting to use metaphor to capture something: a place, an idea, a feeling. We want to really show readers what it's like, and when we find the right image, it's like the final puzzle piece fitting into place. The problem is that this can create closure, which is fine on the last page but not so great on the first page, when the entire point is to make the reader want to know what comes next.

THE EXERCISE

Let's create a quick, intriguing image using *Migratory Animals* by Mary Helen Specht as a model.

1. **INVITE THE IMAGE ONTO THE PAGE.** Remember, the first page is spent setting up basics: setting, character, plot. Any imagery, then,

should probably be connected to one of these things. In other words, it needs to enter the page in a logical way, not out of the blue. Notice how Specht introduces the spider image. The previous two sentences have had a clear focus on Flannery (as opposed to the previous paragraph, which focused on trees): she is *this*, and she's done *that*. So, the logical entry for an image is through Flannery, which is exactly what Specht does: "Sometimes she imagined herself as . . ." You can use this same construction if you're introducing an image through character: *Sometimes he/she imagined himself/herself as* _____. If you're introducing the image through setting, simply cut the imagining and get to the image itself: *It was like/as if* _____.

2. FINISH DESCRIBING THE IMAGE QUICKLY. As with everything in a story, you may need to write a lot to create one good sentence, but that should probably be your goal: close the image out in a single sentence. There are many exceptions to this, of course, and if you can pull off a multi-sentence metaphor or image, then, by all means, do it. But if you can't, be efficient. So, whatever image you're playing with, once you're happy with it, try to condense it to one sentence.

3. USE THE IMAGE TO SET UP THE NEXT THING. Flannery caught something. What is it? We find out in the next paragraph: a man named Kunle. The key is to connect the image to a character's desire or dilemma, which is usually what kicks off the story in the first place. If an image is beautiful but not attached to the driving force of the story's beginning (the mystery or question that makes readers want to turn the page), then it might not be the right time for that image. Save it to use later. Then, invent another image that raises the readers' eyebrows.

The goal is to give your writing style purpose and help it stand out by making an image appear and vanish as quickly as possible. Since we're talking about style, we're inevitably talking about aesthetics, which means there is no one statement that can hold true for all works of fiction. There are writers I admire tremendously—Jeffrey Renard Allen, for example—whose style can feel overwhelming at first, until you become accustomed to it. As a writer, you should follow your gut. Write what feels right to you and trust that it will find an audience. That said, it's often a good idea to dole out heavy style in small doses. Then, if you find that those doses need to be increased or enlarged, do so.

SHOW READERS THE KIND OF
STORY THEY'RE READING.

My tenth-grade English teacher liked to say that no one had written a fresh plot in four hundred years: we've all been simply ripping off Shakespeare. While I'd quibble a bit with that claim, it seems fair to claim that stories tend to fall into categories: love, death, revenge, coming-of-age, road trip, detective, war. It's not an exhaustive list, but you get the point. Our stories reflect the major turning points of our particular and universal human existence. What this means for writers is that it's a good idea to make it clear, as soon as possible, what kind of story your readers have picked up. As readers, we want to know. For example, is it a love story? The answer matters. Some readers won't read it no matter what (their loss) while others stole their local video store's VHS copy of *Love Story*, and the proprietors will see them in hell before they give it back. Also, book reviewers and booksellers also like to know what kind of story you've written. It makes it easier to shelve it and say to shoppers, "If you like *this book*, then maybe you'll like *this one, too*"

Your book is a work of art, yes, but it's also a commodity. Such is life and literature.

Still, you might be thinking, Hey, my book is literary fiction. It can't be categorized into genre. My response is this: Read Specht's first page. This novel is as literary as they come (beautiful language, complex characters), but it announces a major plot element by the end of the first page. Well-dressed Kunle says, "You should try the palm wine," and then we're told that he looks like "one of those idealized husbands in films." It's clear that we've entered *love story* territory. Is that all there is to the novel? No. But it's a significant plotline.

THE EXERCISE

Let's show readers what kind of story you've written, using *Migratory Animals* by Mary Helen Specht as a model.

1. IDENTIFY YOUR STORY. For genre writers, this may appear easy: it's a space opera, so it's got spaceships—duh. Be careful, though, about

confusing genre with conflict. Spaceships aren't a conflict. This is: a spaceship racing for home with a killer alien hiding in the stomach of a crewmember. This distinction can sometimes be difficult to grasp early in the writing process, when you're building the story's world and marveling at the cool stuff it contains. But eventually something has to *happen* in the midst of that cool stuff. That *something* is story. To find your yours, go back to the list of common examples from earlier: love, death, revenge, coming-of-age, road trip, detective, war. Which one seems most applicable to what you're writing?

2. TURN THAT STORY INTO CONFLICT. Here's a good definition of conflict: one character or group of characters wants something, and another character or group is in the way. Here's how it works: the conflict in a love story usually means that someone doesn't want the relationship to flourish. In a death story, someone often would do anything to forestall that death. In a revenge story, the vengeance is best served cold, which means one character doesn't see it coming. In a coming-of-age story, maturity is usually accompanied by something unpleasant that the character would rather not have. In a road trip story, the road and its inhabitants usually try to stop the characters from passing through. In a detective story, the bad guys don't want to get caught, and in a war story, the other side wants your character dead. Find the kernel of opposition in your story, the character or obstacle (like the deserted island in the Tom Hanks film *Castaway*) that will try to prevent your protagonist from getting what he or she wants.

3. TRY SUMMARIZING YOUR PLOT IN A SENTENCE OR TWO. A great place to find examples of this is on book jackets, which quickly distill a book to its conflict. Here is part of the jacket copy for *Migratory Animals*: "When Flannery, a young scientist, is forced to return to Austin after five years of research in Nigeria, she becomes torn between her two homes. Having left behind her loving fiancé without knowing when she will return, Flannery learns that her sister, Molly, has begun to show signs of the genetic disease that slowly killed their mother." Specht has combined two of the story types: love and death. Try your own two-sentence summary. Start with "When . . ." and then put your character into a situation that is untenable. Something must give. What are the two possibilities for what it might be? For Specht, it's Flannery or her fiancé.

4. WRITE A SHORT SCENE THAT SETS UP SOME ELEMENT OF YOUR
   JACKET COPY. Specht uses the scene where Flannery meets the man
   who will become her fiancé. We don't yet know that he's her fiancé,
   but the word *husband* pops up, and we can guess where this encounter
   is going. We're also told that he's not her type, which of course means
   they'll end up together—at least for a time. Imagine how else Specht
   could have written that scene: Kunle could have been simply a random
   guy. Maybe Flannery could have been focused on something else, like
   her research. Maybe there were multiple good-looking guys there. But
   because the novel is a love story—and Specht knows it—she introduces Kunle with statements and words (like *husband*) that clue us in
   to the kind of story this will become. What are the words and phrases
   that might clue your readers in to where your short scene is going?

The goal is to quickly orient the reader, creating expectations so that you
can play with them. Treat your readers as if they're well-read. Fiction is
often like a good joke: there's the setup and the punchline. You're setting expectations with the first and meeting them or cutting across them
with the second. Either way, you've got to provide that firm ground at
the beginning.

LONG DIVISION   *Kiese Laymon*

LaVander Peeler cares too much what white folks think about him. Last quarter, instead of voting for me for ninth-grade CF (Class Favorite), he wrote on the back of his ballot, "All things considered, I shall withhold my CF vote rather than support Toni Whitaker, Jerome Wallace, or the White Homeless Fat Homosexual." He actually capitalized all five words when he wrote that sentence, too. You would expect more from the only boy at Fannie Lou Hamer Magnet School with blue-black patent leather Adidas and an ellipsis tattoo on the inside of his wrist, wouldn't you? The tattoo and the shoes are the only reason he gets away with using sentences with "all things considered" and the word "shall" an average of fourteen times a day. LaVander Peeler hates me. Therefore (I know Principal Reeves said that we should never write the "n-word" if white folks might be reading, but . . .), I hate that wack nigga, too.

My name is City. I'm not white, homeless, or homosexual, but if I'm going to keep it one hundred, I guess you should also know that LaVander Peeler smells so good that sometimes you can't help but wonder if a small beast farted in your mouth when you're too close to him. It's not just me, either. I've watched Toni Whitaker, Octavia Whittington, and Jerome Wallace sneak and sniff their own breath around LaVander Peeler, too.

If you actually watched the 2013 Can You Use That Word in a Sentence finals on good cable last night, or if you've seen the clip on YouTube, you already know I hate LaVander Peeler and you're probably wondering about my feelings for that short Mexican girl from Arizona who kicked me in my knee.

Kiese Laymon, excerpt from "One Sentence" from *Long Division*. Copyright © 2013 by Kiese Laymon. Reprinted with the permission of Agate Publishing, Inc.

LONG DIVISION BY KIESE LAYMON

GIVE THE VOICE SOMETHING TO COMMENT ON THAT ISN'T ITSELF.

In job interviews, one of the first questions often asked is "Tell us about yourself." In the age of social media, you'd think this would be a softball question, but it remains one of the most difficult. Most people don't walk around thinking, "This is me doing the laundry. This is me driving my car. This is me hanging out with my kids." I say this in full understanding of the prevalence of selfies, which, yes, seem to be photo answers to the unasked question, "Tell us about yourself," but this is not actually how they function most of the time. We post selfies so that other people will comment on them. The point is not to talk about ourselves but, rather, to get other people to say nice things about us. It's the equivalent of walking into an interview and saying, "Tell me about me."

This distinction matters when we begin to create the voices for our characters and narrators. If we ask these voices, "Tell us about yourself," they might not have much to say. But if we say, "Tell us about the people and world around you," get ready. What they say might make you fall in love with them.

That's exactly what happens on the first page of Kiese Laymon's novel *Long Division*. The narrator is Citoyen Coldson (City for short), and so that's who's speaking in this excerpt. But he's talking about his classmate LaVander Peeler, and the first thing we learn about LaVander is

City's opinion of him: "LaVander Peeler cares too much what white folks think about him." What follows is an anecdote about something that La-Vander said about City, which provides the foundation of City's introduction of himself:

> My name is City. I'm not white, homeless, or homosexual, but if I'm going to keep it one hundred, I guess you should also know that La-Vander Peeler . . .

And then we're back to the object of City's fascination. It's an amazing illustration of how to build voice and character.

- Talking about someone/something that *isn't* the narrator/character gives the voice a chance to show attitude. It's like asking someone, "What do you think about ____?" Neutral answers are boring. Charged answers lead to stories.
- That attitude, and the stories that stem from it, create the opportunity for a narrator/character to define himself *against* someone/something else. All we know about City is that he *isn't* what La-Vander says he is, but what an interesting place to begin.
- The attitude can lead to fascination or obsession. When City says, "LaVander Peeler smells so good that sometimes you can't help but wonder if a small beast farted in your mouth when you're too close to him," he reveals more than he could with any statement focused on himself. To some extent, people (or their personas) are defined by their obsessions and their attitudes toward them.

THE EXERCISE

Let's give a narrative or character voice something to comment on, using *Long Division* by Kiese Laymon as a model:

1. **START WITH SOMETHING THE VOICE THINKS ABOUT A LOT.** I've used the word *obsession*, but don't let its negative connotations get in the way. The mind goes where it will—for people and characters alike—and where it goes is often the manifestation of some internal conflict. We think about certain people, things, events, or places be-

cause we haven't completely worked out what we feel about them. So, let your character answer the question, "What do you think about ____?"

2. FOLLOW THE ANSWER TO AN ANECDOTE. City follows up his assessment of LaVander with the story about the ninth-grade Class Favorite contest. This should feel like a natural progression. Once a voice gets charged up about someone or something, it's easy to say, "Like, this one time. . ."

3. LET THE VOICE DEFINE ITSELF AGAINST THAT STORY. We do this in real life all the time, telling stories about other people just so we can say, "Of course, *I* would never do such a thing" or "That's not the sort of person *I* am." Let your character or narrator hold him/herself up against the object of fascination and comment on the differences between them.

4. GET BACK TO THE OBJECT OF FASCINATION. Let the voice find the other person/thing more interesting than itself. The more the voice talks about the object of fascination, the more the voice reveals about its proclivities, preferences, personality, and internal conflict.

The goal is to create a mini-rant that will carry the voice and reader into the story. Voice is so much more important than, for example, what a character looks like. It's a clear distinction between films and novels/stories. Even famous figures like Sherlock Holmes are, in their written versions anyway, more mind than image. We've been influenced by the many television shows and movies that had been inspired by the stories, but the stories themselves drop us into rational thinking and problem solving—a mind obsessed with something other than itself.

INTRODUCE SOMETHING INTERESTING THAT WILL HAPPEN, BUT DON'T TELL US YET HOW IT HAPPENED.

One of the oldest tricks available to a writer or storyteller must surely be saying, "This crazy thing happened," and then delaying the reveal of exactly what happened. It happens on social media constantly. Someone will write, "Big news! But can't share it yet." Or "Really rough day. Don't want to say too much, but need your support." The first comments are almost certainly some version of "What happened?" You can probably get away with this on Facebook or in fiction once. Do it again, and readers will get frustrated—just tell us what happened, they'll think.

The key, then, is using the strategy without ticking off your reader.

Laymon finds that balance by assuming that the reader already knows what happened:

> If you actually watched the 2013 Can You Use That Word in a Sentence finals on good cable last night, or if you've seen the clip on YouTube, you already know I hate LaVander Peeler and you're probably wondering about my feelings for that short Mexican girl from Arizona who kicked me in my knee.

Of course, we didn't watch the show on cable or see the clip online because we just now learned about both. But we don't care. Laymon has let us in on the act. I'm hardly the first person to state this, but it bears repeating: fiction is a performance. Readers know it isn't real. Yes, the writer hopes to lure the reader into the fictive dream—the illusion that they are immersed in the story as in a dream. But the writer isn't *fooling* the reader. People enter into stories willingly, of their own accord, and so it can be helpful to help them in by letting them in on the performance.

Imagine if Laymon had instead written this: "I was on a major television event last night, and it was crazy. A girl kicked me in the knee, and now I hate a guy, but I'm not going to tell you why just yet." This version is the equivalent of the narrator saying, "This is my story, and I'm in control. You just sit back and enjoy." Perhaps it would still create suspense and cause the reader to turn the page. But the reader might also respond the way that many of us respond to being told that someone else is in charge: We say, "Screw you, I'm out of here."

The sentence that Laymon actually wrote creates suspense *and* invites the readers to be part of the act by suggesting that they already know what happened.

THE EXERCISE

Let's hint at a plot point without fully revealing it, using *Long Division* by Kiese Laymon as a model:

1. **IDENTIFY THE PLOT POINT YOU WANT TO PARTIALLY REVEAL.** It can be anything: something that has already happened or something

that will happen in the future. It can even be a detail that, once we learn it, changes our understanding of the character and story (like the fact that Bruce Willis is dead in *The Sixth Sense*). Ideally, it's something key to the story but not the most important part of it. Remember, the goal is to keep the reader reading, not to give away the story.

2. ASSUME THAT THE READER KNOWS AS MUCH AS THE NARRATOR OR CHARACTER. There are two ways to do this. Laymon does it by assuming that the reader has been present in the story before it began. Mark Twain did something similar in *The Adventures of Huckleberry Finn* when he began with Huck saying, "You don't know about me without you have read a book by the name of *The Adventures of Tom Sawyer*; but that ain't no matter." Both examples assume that the reader contains prior knowledge of the story. In the case of Twain, the readers actually had seen Huckleberry before. In *Long Division*, Laymon is just pretending that the readers know things. Either way, the effect is the same. Another approach is the one often used by thrillers. A dead body shows up in the prologue or first chapter, and the novel is spent figuring out what happened to it. In this case, neither the detective characters nor the reader know what they'll find out. They're both starting from the same place of ignorance.

3. PLAY TO WHAT THE READERS "KNOW." Decide what your character or narrator knows about the plot point you've hinted at. Introduce that plot point as if the readers know exactly the same information as the character or narrator. You don't need to reveal the actual information, only say some version of "You and I both know that. . ." or "What's going on? We'd better find out."

The goal is to play with the idea of "in medias res"—the strategy of dropping readers into the middle of a narrative, not the beginning. You don't need to drop them into the true middle. Instead, you can create the impression that they've walked into the show a couple of minutes late. They'll catch on to whatever they've missed, but in the meantime, they should sit down, be quiet, and pay attention.

INTRODUCE AND THEN BREAK A RULE.

When I was a kid, Burger King ran an advertising campaign with the slogan "Sometimes you gotta break the rules." For fiction, this is absolutely true, to the extent that *sometimes* can be replaced with *almost always*. If a character is told, "Do this or don't do that," readers automatically assume that the character will do the exact opposite. That assumption is how archetypal images and storylines develop. Sensible rules like "Don't go into the deep, dark forest" get broken again and again, and pretty soon *the forest* becomes synonymous with *bad place* and going into it becomes a necessary rite of passage for certain types of characters. In your story, then, it's important to find the right rule for your character to break.

Laymon introduces a rule as explicitly as the old fairy tales introduced the ban on walking alone in the woods: "I know Principal Reeves said that we should never write the "n-word" if white folks might be reading, but. . ." His narrator, City, breaks that rule immediately, which tells us a lot about him. If he'd followed the rule, he would become a very different character. The question for a writer becomes this: What rule will the story introduce and when will the character break it? In *Long Division*, as rules go, this isn't a very big one—or, at least, it's not treated as significant by the narrator. As a result, he's able to break it right away. A bigger, more dangerous rule might not be broken so casually. A version of this has appeared in a thousand action movies. Someone says at the beginning, "Whatever you do, don't hit the red button." The rule gets followed until, suddenly, things are so dire that the character has no choice but to hit it. So, it's useful to ask yourself, "Is this rule a *self-destruct button*?" If so, you can create a lot of suspense by making the reader wonder when it will get pushed.

THE EXERCISE

Let's introduce a break a rule, using *Long Division* by Kiese Laymon as a model:

1. START WITH CHARACTER. In the place your character lives and in the situations where he often finds himself, what rules must he follow? Think about place in large geographic and cultural terms (the South, the city, the country) and specific terms (home, church, school, work). What rules are inherent to The Way Things Work in those places?
2. FIGURE OUT *why* THE RULE EXISTS. Often this is understood but unstated, as with the rule "never write the "n-word" if white folks

might be reading." In that case, the *why* is an extension of the contentious idea of the New Negro, the belief that if black people could impress white people, then they wouldn't suffer from racism so much. Even though City breaks the rule as soon as it's stated, the *why* behind the rule doesn't go away in the novel and becomes part of its *aboutness*. For your rule, the *why* might be cultural, as with Laymon's rule, or it might be practical, like the rule about travel in certain cold temperatures that's introduced at the beginning of Jack London's story "To Build a Fire" (Don't do it, or you'll freeze to death). The point is to make clear there's a reason the rule exists—or, if the rule has been made at someone's whim, then that should be clear as well.

3. **UNDERSTAND HOW AND WHEN THE CHARACTER WILL BREAK IT.** This is another part of the fictive quality of fiction. Readers know that rules are made to be broken. The question is when and why. To answers those questions, consider these points: What does the character sacrifice by breaking the rule? The bigger the sacrifice, the more difficult the rule probably is to break. Who is enforcing the rule? With Laymon's rule, we get the sense that it's likely only enforced if broken right in front of the principal; otherwise, there are no consequences. Does the rule carry implications for the plot? If someone enters the deep, dark woods, something bad is going to happen. As a result, more is riding on it. Laymon's rule doesn't affect plot so much as build character. So, less is riding on it.

The goal is to find the right rule for the story and the best way to break it. Both the rule and how it's broken are connected to the setting and characters you've created and reveal the kind of conflict that's just ahead.

THE FRIENDSHIP OF CRIMINALS
Robert Glinski

Corral a hundred little kids and announce Santa Claus, Easter Bunny, and the Tooth Fairy do not exist. Not head, not gone. Just not real.

Of the hundred, fifteen never believed. They're above the gray, like birds watching a car crash from some distant tree. Three dozen go Code Red, their bodies overwhelmed by the desire to fight, run, or both. Twenty obsess over missed clues. Another twenty-five reject the new reality. They cry.

The remaining four are the cynics. Their zombie eyes hold fast as the conspiracy confirms what they suspected all along—lies trump truth when people want to believe. Bow-tied rabbits hiding chocolate? Fairies trading cash for human teeth? What a bunch of suckers, ripe for the picking and deserving, too. A cold-blooded takeaway, sure, but it's how these future grifters and televangelists filter the world.

Now take these same one hundred kids and gift them a gun. Pistol, rifle, or shotgun—doesn't matter as long as it's designed to stop a human heart. Unlike in the Santa/Bunny/Fairy experiment, the shorties cluster. Is that a real gun? Yeah, I'll hold it. No crossroads here.

Little Bernie Jaracz of Port Richmond wasn't any different. Since watching a teenager hypnotize a pubescent ____ with a chrome revolver, he'd wanted a gun. Not to hurt a rival or pursue revenge—he wasn't that kind of kid.

Reprinted from Robert Glinski, *The Friendship of Criminals* (New York: Minotaur, 2015), 1–2.

THE FRIENDSHIP OF CRIMINALS
BY ROBERT GLINSKI

START WITH A SHARED EXPERIENCE
AND MAKE IT UNFAMILIAR.

Readers and (sometimes) critics will claim that they're able to identify (or not) with a character—that it is important and perhaps necessary for readers to be able to do this. But I think that's a bit of a dead end for writers and not true of so many of our most beloved characters. We might identify with Walter White at the beginning of *Breaking Bad*, but we certainly don't for long, or at least not all of the time, not unless you're a ruthless egomaniac. Even that claim might be suspect. At the beginning of the series, he's a sad sack: unhappy in his job and life in a dopey, pushover kind of way. Some viewers might identify with that sort of character, but most probably don't. What they *did* identify with was his situation: diagnosed with lung cancer but without the money to pay for treatment. Cancer is so prevalent that most of us know someone who's had it; it's so prevalent that it exists in our minds like a bogeyman, the worst possible of all bad news. Most of us also can identify with the stress of the medical payments required to treat cancer.

In short, it's not the character we identify with but the situation—the experience of being in the midst of it. Robert Glinski begins his novel *The Friendship of Criminals* with a similar experience, one shared by many of his readers.

If you grew up Christian in America, then you've almost certainly had the experience that begins this novel: discovering that Santa Claus isn't real. I bet that you remember the moment it occurred, and the fact that you *do* remember helps explain why so many of our most-loved films (*Miracle on 34th Street, Elf, Ernest Saves Christmas*) offer alternate scenarios for that moment: what if Santa Claus really did exist?

There is practically no end to these types of experiences. Here is an example: losing a sock in the laundry. I'm willing to bet that every single person who wears socks and does their own laundry has had this experience. It's not as dramatic as learning that Santa isn't real or being diagnosed with cancer, but it's almost universal nonetheless. As a writer, what do you do with that experience?

Glinski pushes his Santa scenario into unexpected territory, moving from the ranges of reactions (which most of us will recognize) and then adds a surprising element: "Now take those same one hundred kids and give them a gun." It's a twist that probably no one saw coming, and so we're naturally drawn into the story—*wait, what? A gun?* The same thing can be done to any experience. Here's the missing sock again:

> You're looking for your clean pair of socks, but you find only one in the dryer. You search between the washer and dryer, on the floor, in the laundry basket, and then realize, oh, it's still in your backpack full of explosives.

The strategy draws the readers close with the shared experience and then hooks them with the twist.

THE EXERCISE

Let's throw a twist into a shared experience, using *The Friendship of Criminals* by Robert Glinski as a model:

1. IDENTIFY THE SHARED EXPERIENCE. The possibilities are vast. Shakespeare used weddings in almost all his comedies because a wedding was a recognized symbol of a happy ending—because his audience knew how to feel at a wedding. It was an experience they all shared. So, you can choose from any of the rituals that most of us will experience: weddings, funerals, graduations, moving day, the first day

of school, tours of colleges, tours of nursing homes, job interviews. You can also choose from the many shared experiences contained within major holidays: religious holidays but also national ones like (in the United States) Independence Day, Halloween, Thanksgiving, the Super Bowl, Valentine's Day, March Madness, and Spring Break. Or, you can choose from the myriad of everyday moments: losing socks, locking your keys inside your car, making coffee, making lunch, walking the dog.

2. PERSONALIZE THE EXPERIENCE. Glinski does this by describing the range of reactions to the news that Santa isn't real. He's digging into the experience and not relying entirely on the reader's own feelings about it. He does this without having introduced his characters yet; in other words, the shared experience is still pretty general, but he personalizes it by giving the reader more nuances to identify with. With your experience, slow down the moment: what are some common reactions to the experience? Reactions are a good way to proceed because they focus on how the moment *feels*.

3. THROW IN A TWIST. It can be something totally random, like a gun or a backpack full of explosives. Or it can be something drawn from the world around the experience, like (to stick with the laundry theme) finding lipstick on a shirt collar. As you know from being a living, breathing person, the biggest moments of our lives often reveal themselves to us while we're doing the laundry or some other mundane task. How can you use that shared experience to set up the twist that will propel your story forward?

The goal is to draw the reader in, to make the reader identify with a character, by portraying a near-universal experience. The character may not be likable or easy to identify with, but his or her situation might be. As a rule, if it works for *Breaking Bad*, then it's probably a good idea to try in your own work.

MAKE ONE TYPE OF CHARACTER SEEM LIKE ANOTHER TYPE OF CHARACTER.

In the third paragraph, Glinski writes, "The remaining four are the cynics. Their zombie eyes hold fast as the conspiracy confirms what they've suspected all along." A couple of sentences later, those cynical, zombie-eyed kids think, "*What a bunch of suckers, ripe for the picking and deserving, too.*" It's a nifty piece of writing. Glinski has transformed kids stunned at the news of Santa's nonexistence into "coldblooded . . . grifters and televangelists." It's a necessary move to get us where the novel requires we go: kids doing bad things with guns. It's a move that's accomplished with two words: *cynics* and *zombie*.

Neither word would normally be used when referring to children, at least not with these connotations. As the parent of two young boys, I've seen the zombie eyes that they get after watching too much television or spending too much time on a tablet. But that *zombie* means *zoned out*. Glinski means *zombie* in a more sinister way. When paired with *cynic* (a word that we usually associate with world-weary knowledge), the stage is set to make these children into something new and unexpected. Sure enough, they begin to think adult thoughts about "suckers, ripe for the picking."

This transition happens so quickly because Glinski takes advantage of words we know well, substituting them for a word we've already been introduced to: *little kids*.

THE EXERCISE

Let's transform the possibilities for a character by describing it as if it's some other type of character, using *The Friendship of Criminals* by Robert Glinski as a model:

1. IDENTIFY THE CHARACTER YOU WANT TO TRANSFORM. Think in terms of specifics: this person named ___, who looks like ___. But think about category as well: gender, age, race/ethnicity, sexuality, masculinity and femininity, size, role (parent, child, teacher, professional). Explore every characteristic possible: country, city, streetwise, naïve, nerd, jock. While you don't want to reduce your character to any category, the categories are useful for setting and breaking readers' expectations.

2. DESCRIBE THE CHARACTER IN TERMS OF CATEGORY. Glinski starts with children responding to a recognizable element of child-

hood: Santa. The entire second paragraph describes their reactions in utterly familiar terms. In short, Glinski is establishing that these children are, in fact, children. They behave exactly the way we'd expect them to behave. How can you describe your character as meeting the expectations of a particular category?

3. SUBSTITUTE A NEW CATEGORY FOR THE PREVIOUS ONE. Glinski does this twice, first with *cynics* and then with *zombies*, each one serving as a kind of stepping-stone to the place he wants to take us—a place where the character appears to us not as a child but as someone dangerous. The key is that he makes the move in stages. Readers might become suspicious of sudden reversals and changes. So, think about the new categories in two ways. First, where do you want to end up? What category or image or type of character embodies that feeling? Second, what is a place in between? Try choosing an emotion that feels like it's sliding toward your ending point. What embodies it? Try describing your characters in that way.

The goal is to twist the reader's expectations about a character or group of characters. The Greek myths and stories did something similar with the Sirens: beautiful women singing beautiful songs and then. . . you're shipwrecked and drowning. Many great monsters (as in the movie *Gremlins*) start out one way and transform into something much scarier.

ADD AN ELEMENT OF DANGER.

I've said this before, but when you read enough, you begin to realize how quickly good novels and stories introduce conflict, and one of the best ways to get conflict on the page is with an element of danger. Chekhov wrote about putting a gun on the wall in the first act, and this is almost literally what Glinski does by the end of this page: "Since watching a teenager hypnotize a pubescent cabal with a chrome revolver, he'd wanted a gun." Instead of an actual gun, Glinski has given a character the deep, burning *desire* for a gun. In a way, this version is better than an actual gun.

If you take anything from this book, let it be this: desire is crucial to narrative. That's not exactly news. You'll learn that in any writing class.

But here's *why* it's crucial. A gun is full of potential danger, but once a gun is introduced, the range of possibilities narrows. We know it will go off, and when it does, someone will be in the path of the bullet. The question is who. But when the desire for a gun is introduced before the gun, the range of possibilities is much wider. We know that a gun will show up, but we don't know when or under what circumstances. More questions to answer leads to more narrative—in a novel, especially at the beginning, *creating narrative* is the name of the game. Even when the gun shows up (spoiler alert: it happens on the next page), the question of desire is still front and center, more important than the gun itself.

THE EXERCISE

Let's create the desire for an object of danger, using *The Friendship of Criminals* by Robert Glinski as a model:

1. FIND A DANGEROUS OBJECT FOR YOUR CHARACTER TO DESIRE. Some objects, like guns, are inherently dangerous. But not all novels are crime novels, and so not every dangerous object can be a gun. The point is to find an object that poses a risk to your character or the characters nearby. A gun gives its holder extra power. So, you can ask, what object can become an extension (and amplifier) of the power that a character already has. Of course, power and desire can be quite similar. So, you can also ask, what desire does your character have (to get even, to find love) and what object can help fulfill that desire to an unexpectedly strong degree? For another approach, consider what object can negate something important to the character; how can you make your character want that object, even with its danger in plain sight?

2. MAKE THE DESIRE CLEAR. Glinski does this by giving his character a moment of inspiration: the character saw a gun and wanted one. Countless films have done this: character sees a home run, rocket ship, or car—and a moment later the character is older and in a baseball uniform, flying a rocket, or driving a racecar. Romantic comedies and love stories do something similar, sometimes in such familiar ways that they get spoofed: the slow-motion moment when the man or woman looks up or walks by. These moments are not subtle in film,

books, or in life. In high school, I played in the pit orchestra for our school musicals, and after one rehearsal, one of the actresses came up and told me that she knew I liked her. I was dumbfounded. How had she known? "Because," she said. "You keep looking at me." With desire, be clear and quick. Don't be afraid of the thunderclap of inspiration. What moment of inspiration can you give to your character? What did your character see or hear or experience that made him/her think, "Yes, that is what I want"?

The goal is to introduce a desire for some dangerous object—and a moment of inspiration for that desire—to make the reader dread what will happen once the character acquires that object.

EVERYTHING I NEVER TOLD YOU

Celeste Ng

Lydia is dead. But they don't know this yet. 1977, May 3, six thirty in the morning, no one knows anything but this innocuous fact: Lydia is late for breakfast. As always, next to her cereal bowl, her mother has placed a sharpened pencil and Lydia's physics homework, six problems flagged with small ticks. Driving to work, Lydia's father nudges the dial toward WXKP, Northwest Ohio's Best News Source, vexed by the crackles of static. On the stairs, Lydia's brother yawns, still twined in the tail end of his dream. And in her chair in the corner of the kitchen, Lydia's sister hunches moon-eyed over her cornflakes, sucking them to pieces one by one, waiting for Lydia to appear. It's she who says, at last, "Lydia's taking a long time today."

Upstairs, Marilyn opens her daughter's door and sees the bed unslept in: neat hospital corners still pleated beneath the comforter, pillow still fluffed and convex.

Reprinted from Celeste Ng, *Everything I Never Told You* (New York: Penguin, 2014): 1–2.

EVERYTHING I NEVER TOLD YOU BY CELESTE NG

BEGIN WITH INCOMPATIBLE IDEAS.

This is one of those pieces of writing that is so great that no introduction is needed. I've taught it in classes, and as people read it, you can hear them saying, "Ooh," to themselves and, when they finish, looking around as if hoping someone will catch their eye and say, "Right? How freaking awesome was that?"

Most obviously, it begins with a dead body, once again confirming that the only thing more interesting in a story than sex is death. It's human nature to want to see the body and know what happened to it. But a dead body also isn't very novel. Most detective shows on network TV start the same way. What distinguishes this body is the context that's built around it. That context begins with situation: "Lydia is late for breakfast." In a single line, Ng personalizes the body. It's not just some random person named Lydia but a young woman whose death creates an absence in a world of other people, objects, and expectations. The line is another example of the great teacher Ron Carlson's advice: *There's the story and the world that the story enters.* By the third sentence of this novel, Ng has established both parts.

What follows, then, is a passage that fleshes out that world—a world that is, on its face, a highly unlikely setting for a dead body. That incompatibility is a big part of the hook. If the novel began in a morgue, emergency room, or battlefield, there would be much less surprise because death is an expected element of those places. Keep in mind: any novel that contains a dead body is likely to, at some point, involve a scene in a morgue, hospital, or cemetery, but that doesn't mean it needs to start there.

THE EXERCISE

Let's create the story and the world it enters as quickly as possible, using *Everything I Never Told You* by Celeste Ng as a model:

1. TEASE THE STORY IN A SINGLE LINE. You can't get more succinct than "Lydia is dead." The sentence, in large part because of its brevity, packs a big punch. It also immediately orients the reader to the direction of the plot in the same way that traffic signs orient drivers. There's a reason why those signs never contain more than two or three words. Of course, if you read the entire novel, you'll soon learn that Lydia's death is just the tip of the iceberg (to finally give Hemingway his obligatory hat tip), but it doesn't matter if that first line doesn't convey the enormity of the novel that follows it. The line simply needs to draw the reader in. So, how can you distill the most immediate or pressing aspect of your plot into a short, quick sentence? It might seem a daunting task, but try not to overthink it. Look at Ng's verb: is. She's simply stating a fact, one that suggests a certain incompatibility. If it's noteworthy that she's dead, then she probably ought to be alive, right? If the sentence was "Ulysses S. Grant is dead," the reader would be like, *yeah, and I know where he's buried, too.* So, try stating something that *is* that *shouldn't be* or that *is desired* but *should not be desired.*

2. INTRODUCE THE WORLD THROUGH SITUATION OR ACTION. Ng eventually shows us the kitchen table where the novel begins, but that's not our introduction to the place. Instead, we learn that she's late for breakfast; then, we're shown the kitchen table where she *isn't.* It's another example of how we're naturally drawn toward action, not descriptions of things standing still. None of the characters is passively waiting for Lydia. They're actively engaged in their lives. So, write a sentence that drives the story *into* a particular bit of setting. This strategy is the reason so many movies begin with a character running late; it makes us wonder where they're going and what the place will be like once they arrive. Of course, you can't use lateness exclu-

sively. Try any sort of arrival or departure. Or start with action, big or small (biting her tongue, checking his pockets, drawing a weapon) and then finish the sentence by placing that action in a place or situation (breakfast). Keep in mind: the more unexpected the place/situation, the more interesting the sentence probably becomes. (Though there is a limit to this, as my kids know: "There's a party . . ." they might say, "in my butt." So, you know, be more creative than a little kid.)

The goal is to introduce basic elements of any story (what's going on, where it's happening) in a way that will quickly hook the reader. In great fiction, nothing is static. There are no placeholders. Get that story moving right away.

INTRODUCE CHARACTER PERSONALITIES IN A SINGLE LINE.

In Anton Chekhov's story, "The Lady with the Dog," a married Russian man meets a married Russian woman while on vacation and falls in love. At the time the story is set, there's not much either of them can do about this unexpected romance—at least not without utterly wrecking their lives. So, the guy, Dmitri, spends much of the story walking around in a desperate, half-stunned state. It's in that state that he walks out of a gentleman's club after playing cards. He boldly says to an acquaintance, "If only you knew what a fascinating woman I made the acquaintance of in Yalta!" The other man ignores him but, before leaving, says, "You were quite right, you know—the sturgeon was just a *leetle* off." That's the only line the guy gets and the only time we see him, and yet in that short space, he is revealed to us so clearly.

Ng does the same thing over and over, seemingly at ease, in the opening paragraph of her novel:

Here's Lydia's mother:

"As always, next to her cereal bowl, her mother has placed a sharpened pencil and Lydia's physics homework, six problems flagged with small ticks."

Here is her father:

"Driving to work, Lydia's father nudges the dial toward WXKP, Northwest Ohio's Best News Source, vexed by the crackles of static."

Her brother:

"On the stairs, Lydia's brother yawns, still twined in the tail end of his dream."

And, finally, her sister:

"And in her chair in the corner of the kitchen, Lydia's sister hunches moon-eyed over her cornflakes, sucking them to pieces one by one, waiting for Lydia to appear."

Each of these character descriptions is one sentence long and captures each character *in an action that conveys attitude and personality*—exactly what Chekhov does in his great sentence. We don't yet know what any of these characters looks like (height, body type, etc.), but we can "see" them nonetheless.

THE EXERCISE

Let's introduce characters through action and attitude, using *Everything I Never Told You* by Celeste Ng as a model:

1. FOCUS ON AN OBJECT THAT REVEALS THE CHARACTER'S TOUCH. In the sentence about Lydia' s mother, we see the sharpened pencil and the homework marked with "small ticks." We know who sharpened the pencil and made those ticks, and we automatically draw inferences about the person who made them. In a way, this exercise is a version of the one you know already: look around the room and see what's in it and what objects matter to the character. Now, you're adding the small ways that the character tends to those objects. Every house contains mostly the same objects, but the way they're kept reveals a great deal.

2. SHOW THE CHARACTER MANIPULATING AN OBJECT. Don't feel the need to find some grand, important object. Lydia's father nudges

a radio dial. More important than the action is the impulse behind it: he's annoyed by static and so will spend time making small adjustments to correct the thing that has annoyed him. I've stated this elsewhere, but it bears repeating: emotion is a great place to begin. Try it: Because so-and-so was _____ (emotion), he/she ___ (action) to _____ (object).

3. CONNECT AN ACTION TO CONTEXT. If the sentence about Lydia's brother followed the yawn with "hungover from the night before" or "exhausted from his night shift at the Sac-N-Pac," our understanding of that yawn would be changed drastically. Context matters. So, choose any action, large or small, and add a few words that state the context (the *because*) behind it.

4. SLOW AN ACTION DOWN. I'm not sure exactly what we learn from the cornflakes eating done by Lydia's sister except that she acts just like a kid. The descriptions taps our own knowledge, gained from all the kids we've watched eat. Ng does this by expanding "eats her cereal" with a physical description (moon-eyed), a particular detail (the brand of cereal), the precise way that she eats that cereal, and what she's doing while she eats (waiting for her sister). Try adding any of those elements to some piece of action that you might normally write (or is currently written) in the plainest, most general terms.

The goal is to capture a character's personality through his or her relationship to the things in his or her world. As in the exercise on action scenes using Rachel Kushner's *The Flamethrowers*, sometimes the best way to see something is to look to the side, not directly at it. It's hard to learn much from watching a character just stand there (though great portrait photographers would disagree). In fiction, it's often better to watch them interact with the things around them.

USE SHORT SENTENCES.

I love long sentences, and there are plenty of writers who use them beautifully. But there also seems to be a belief, especially among some beginning writers, that *stylists* write exclusively with long sentences and ornate language. Some teachers inadvertently promote this idea with lessons on opaque and clear style. *Opaque* style draws attention to itself, as with prose by writers like James Joyce or Pulitzer winners Toni Morrison and Paul Harding. *Clear* style, the idea goes, leaves no mark. You see through it to the action and story as you do through a window. These terms are well and good, but they can lead us into the belief that short, clear sentences are not stylish. This just is not true, as Ng demonstrates on this page.

There is, for lack of a better word, a snap to the language. Read close, and you'll find all sorts of literary devices: alliteration ("crackles of static"), consonance ("twined in the tail"), and figurative language ("moon-eyed"). She even uses parallel constructions, beginning each sentence that describes a family member with a place-setting clause: "next to her cereal bowl," "Driving to work," "On the stairs," "in her chair." Ng also employs a slick bit of grammatical delay at the end of that paragraph, adding "at last" as a way to make us wait just a moment longer for the snippet of dialogue that will kick the scene and plot into gear.

Just because the sentences are short (and when they're not short, they contain short, compact phrases) doesn't mean they lack style.

Ng also does a wonderful job of stating basic details outright. When is this novel set? "1977, May 3, six thirty in the morning." Where is it? Northwest Ohio. Too often, we're tempted to get cute with certain information. But style doesn't need to be applied to every sentence, a fact that Ng understands. The third sentence begins with a literal date, and it works. We note it and keep reading, which is the beauty of a truly *clear* prose style. Why slow down the reader when it's not necessary? That said, Ng also finds creative ways to convey that basic info, like when she uses the radio announcer to tell us where the novel is set.

Long sentences are great. Short sentences are great. Both can be stylish. Both can be opaque and clear. If you naturally write long sentences— awesome. If you don't, that's fine, too. Your sentence length reveals nothing about your skill as a writer.

THE EXERCISE

Let's write some sentences with a *clear* style, using *Everything I Never Told You* by Celeste Ng as a model:

1. JUST TELL US WHAT WE NEED TO KNOW. Ng does this with the date, just as she did with the first sentence: "Lydia is dead." Be blunt.

Ng even dispenses with the usual grammar of a complete sentence; she could have written "It's 1977 . . ." but didn't. So, consider what information the reader must know. Where appropriate, state it as clearly as possible. The point is to deliver the information as quickly and seamlessly as possible so that you can get to the next cool thing. While it can be good to sneak such information into the fabric of the story, that sneaking can also lead to confusion. Readers often miss details unless they're stated outright.

2. EMBED ESSENTIAL INFORMATION INTO THE ACTION. Ng puts Lydia's father in the car, listening to the radio. I'm sure you've all heard radio announcers give their station name and ID; it's an easy thing to drop into the natural flow of the moment. Where can you do this in your own story? Use an object that you'd mention anyway as an opportunity to indicate something essential about setting, character, or situation. This can often be done with a simple descriptive phrase. For example, every small town where I'm from has its name on a water tower and a sign on the city limits announcing which team won a championship in which year. In Austin, billboards often name-drop the city or famous landmarks within it. In certain places, you're likely to see flags for local sports teams. Put yourself (physically or mentally) into the place and time you're describing. What do you see or hear that identifies the place? You can also just add this construction: comma-identifying tag-comma, as Ng does when she names the radio station: "WXKP, Northwest Ohio's Best News Source,". She could have just named the station, but the rest both makes us hear the station along with the father and know where we are.

The goal is to write as stylish as you want *when it's called for* and as clearly as possible when necessary. As I wrote in the chapters on style, this is no doubt a matter of taste. Some readers want clear writing (a pared-back or plainspoken style) all of the time. Others want heavy style in every sentence. There's no accounting for any taste but your own, and so it's important to be aware of what you're trying to achieve in a given sentence or passage. Is a heavier style a better tool for achieving it? Is clarity? There's no way to find out except to tinker with the sentences, which is the reason we're writers. Warm up those fingers and get to work, playing around with words.

CONCLUSION: NOW WHAT?

If you've read this entire book, then the answer to the question "Now what?" is easy: now you're a writer. Go write your book, hit the best-seller list, make readers laugh and cry, and take your millions to England to buy a castle next door to wherever J. K. Rowling lives.

You mean she doesn't live in a castle? And most writers need to keep their day jobs? And hitting the best-seller list once doesn't mean you'll ever hit it again? And your books might sit on the bookstore shelf, un-purchased, until they're sent back to the publisher to be boxed up in a warehouse somewhere, not seeing daylight or fluorescent light again until they show up next to the coloring books at Dollar Tree—or until some executive decides for them to be pulped and turned into someone else's book? And you mean that most books don't even get published in the first place?

Bob Dylan once said that when he was young, he didn't tell anyone about the songs that were half-written in his head or about his dreams for what those songs might become because, as soon as he did, those dreams and songs might die. And another great artist said, "Life is too short to have anything but delusional notions about yourself." That was Gene Simmons from KISS, so take that for what you will. The point is this: writers are artists who pursue their craft and translate their dreams into their chosen medium, with no guarantee that anyone will ever experience their work. It takes a healthy dose of egotism (or, to be kinder, of significant self-regard) to say to yourself at 4:30 in the morning before the kids wake up or late at night after you've finished your paying work for the day, "People need to read this." Most likely, objectively speaking, they don't. But you can't tell yourself that. If you do, you'll quit writing. Delusion is a necessary trait for a writer. Of course, Charles Manson said, "Sanity is a small box. Insanity is everything." You've got to find that fine line between ignoring reality enough to keep writing, but not so much that you become an insufferable jerk or psychopath. Not all writers have succeeded. I hope you will.

I developed these exercises and many others like them in the midst of writing and teaching. As a teacher, it's tempting to pontificate, to spout off after the writing is over and done with about The Craft or The Process or The Art. If I've done so in these pages, I apologize. As my father and brothers might point out, someone who isn't excessively intelligent has no business spouting a bunch of nonsense.

My father still farms. He has fewer hogs than he used to, more cattle, and he sells much of his grain instead of feeding it to animals. But he's still doing basically the same work that he did when I was a kid, when he was first starting out. Back then, he raised sorghum (or *milo* as we called it), the plant that that produces the grain in your birdseed. It's a plant like corn but shorter and with a single, shaggy head of grain on the top. In June and July, he'd drag us kids out of bed at six in the morning to walk through fields of it, cutting out weeds like buttonweed and cocklebur and mutant, taller-than-normal milo stalks that weren't causing any trouble but looked funny. It was terrible, awful, miserable work. Dew clung to the sorghum leaves and covered the soil between the rows, so by midday your feet were muddy, your pants were wet and drying stiff, and the sharp leaves had left long red cuts on your forearms. And the pollen: no one walks out of a sorghum field without a runny nose, snot on their shirtsleeves, and red eyes. You cut down the weeds with bean hooks: broom handles with sharp, curved blades at the bottom. You'd hook the blade around the bottom of a weed stalk and pull quickly. It was a mechanical skill that I learned when I was so young that my dad tied a red construction flag to my hat so that he could see it bobbing over the sorghum and wouldn't lose me in the field. In the midst of such work, it was often difficult to imagine why on earth we did it. There had to be easier jobs in the world.

But then my dad would drive past a field that we'd cleared, and he'd slow down to appreciate the sight of acres of milo, in near, even rows that stretched as far as you could see. In farming, beauty and work are inseparable. It's not always easy to tell where one ends and the other begins. This is also true of writing. It often feels mechanical, and you slog through sentence after sentence, no idea where you're going or when you'll be done. But then you'll catch a glimpse of something that you've written that's beautiful or captivating or wickedly suspenseful, and you'll feel elated. Then you'll go back to work.

So when I say get to work, what I mean is, create something wondrous. And, also, I mean get back to work.

Good luck.

APPENDIX:
FICTION BY NARRATIVE TROPE

Fiction is often categorized by familiar genres: science fiction/fantasy, crime, thriller, mystery, romance, women's fiction, and so on, with many subgenres within each one. Knowing which genre you're working in—and the conventions common to them—allows you to play toward and against readers' expectations. But there are other ways to classify stories that you should become familiar with as well: narrative tropes that crop up over and over again. Here are a few of those tropes and examples of them from *Field Guide*:

FAMILY AND GROUP DYNAMIC STORIES

- "Waiting for Takeoff" by Lydia Davis
- *The Friendship of Criminals* by Robert Glinski
- *The Regional Office Is Under Attack!* by Manuel Gonzales
- *The Flamethrowers* by Rachel Kushner
- *Everything I Never Told You* by Celeste Ng
- "It Will Be Awesome Before Spring" by Antonio Ruiz-Camacho
- "Proving Up" by Karen Russell
- "The Semplica-Girl Diaries" by George Saunders
- *Salvage the Bones* by Jesmyn Ward

FRIENDSHIP AND PARTNER STORIES

- *The Peripheral* by William Gibson
- "Lazarus Dying" by Owen Egerton
- *Honky Tonk Samurai* by Joe R. Lansdale
- *Long Division* by Kiese Laymon
- "Pomp and Circumstances" by Nina McConigley
- "Summer Boys" by Ethan Rutherford
- *Aristotle and Dante Discover the Secrets of the Universe* by Benjamin Alire Sáenz

HERO VS. VILLAIN/DEFEAT YOUR ENEMY STORIES

- *Percival Everett by Virgil Russell* by Percival Everett
- *A Brief History of Seven Killings* by Marlon James
- *NW* by Zadie Smith

LONE WOLF AND QUEST STORIES

- *Open City* by Teju Cole
- *An Untamed State* by Roxane Gay
- *Mr. Splitfoot* by Samantha Hunt
- *The Moor's Account* by Laila Lalami
- *Station Eleven* by Emily St. John Mandel
- "My Views on the Darkness" by Ben Marcus
- "The Lost & Found Department of Greater Boston" by Elizabeth McCracken
- *Half-Resurrection Blues* by Daniel José Older
- "Nobody You Know" by Elizabeth Tallent

LOVE AND BREAKUP STORIES

- "The Night of the Satellite" by T. C. Boyle
- *Cartwheel* by Jennifer duBois

- *Gone Girl* by Gillian Flynn
- "Encounters with Unexpected Animals" by Bret Anthony Johnston
- *Migratory Animals* by Mary Helen Specht

PARENT/CHILD AND TEACHER/STUDENT STORIES

- *Jam on the Vine* by LaShonda Katrice Barnett
- *The Radiant Road* by Katherine Catmull
- *The Queen of the Night* by Alexander Chee
- "The Heart" by Amelia Gray
- *Pull Me Under* by Kelly Luce
- "Boys Town" by Jim Shepard
- *Who Do You Love* by Jennifer Weiner

ACKNOWLEDGMENTS

No book can come into the world without a community of writers to support it, and this one is no exception. Thank you to Jill Meyers, my editor who not only made the book inestimably better with her feedback and notes but who has also supported me, my teaching, and my writing for a decade as a journal editor, writing class organizer, and friend. Without her, this book would not exist. Thank you as well to Callie Collins for helping create an amazing press, to Amber Morena for project management and superb design work, and to Zoë Faye-Stindt for copyediting notes. Thank you, too, to the many people who have taken my writing classes and participated in the writing exercises I created for them. To Neena Husid for encouragement and lunches, to Tom Hart for finding Read to Write Stories out of the blue and saying many kind things about it, to the writers who have allowed me to pick their brains about craft in interviews for the blog, and to everyone who has visited the blog and tweeted their support. In late nights at my kitchen table writing the exercises, this has meant so much. To an invaluable group of writer friends: Mark Barr, Angie Beshara, Justin Carroll, Owen Egerton, Becka Oliver, Ben Reed, Michael Rosenbaum, Stacey Swann, and Mike Yang. To the teachers at Texas State University who provided the foundation to my study of writing craft: Tom Grimes, Debra Monroe, and Tim O'Brien. To Tom, Bill Johnson, and Laila Knight for all they do to keep the Katherine Anne Porter House running and for allowing me to live there for a time. To my parents and siblings for giving me things to write about, even in a book about craft. To Xavier and Elias, whose imaginations fuel mine. And to Stephanie, my partner in everything.

ABOUT THE AUTHOR

Michael Noll is the editor of Read to Write Stories and program director at the Writers' League of Texas. His short stories have been published in *American Short Fiction, Chattahoochee Review, Ellery Queen Mystery Magazine, Indiana Review,* and the *New Territory,* and been nominated for *New Stories from the Midwest.* His story "The Tank Yard" was included in the *2016 Best American Mystery Stories* anthology. He lives in Austin, Texas, with his family.

ABOUT A STRANGE OBJECT

A Strange Object is an award-winning press founded in 2012 in Austin, Texas, that champions debuts, daring writing, and striking design across all platforms.